BROKEN LACES

EAGLES HOCKEY #1

ELISE FABER

BROKEN LACES
BY ELISE FABER

Newsletter sign-up
This is a work of fiction. Names, places, characters, and events are fictitious in every regard. Any similarities to actual events and persons, living or dead, are purely coincidental. Any trademarks, service marks, product names, or named features are assumed to be the property of their respective owners, and are used only for reference. There is no implied endorsement if any of these terms are used. Except for review purposes, the reproduction of this book in whole or part, electronically or mechanically, constitutes a copyright violation.

EAGLES HOCKEY SERIES

Eagles Hockey Series (all stand alone)
Broken Laces
Knotted Laces
Lace 'em Up

ONE

Chrissy, Ten Years Before

I WINCE as I slide up the window, hoping the soft scrape as it opens won't wake my dad.

It's nearly midnight and he's finally headed to bed.

But he'll be right back up again at five in the morning.

Because he's a workaholic.

Considering the hours he spends pursuing his various business ventures, I would swear he loves work more than anything.

Only I know he loves me more.

It's just that his love is a heavy, stifling blanket intended to keep me warm, but instead, it...

Suffocates.

I exhale and shake that thought out of my mind.

I have five hours.

I have plans to make them count. With Bobby Montgomery.

And...I can see him outside my window—or see the soft

flicker of the flashlight on his phone turning on and off, his signal that he's parked on the road leading into the vineyard and is waiting to meet me.

My heart leaps, thinking of the way he kissed me.

His body lean and hard, his grip tight as he pressed me against the cool metal of his truck. His lips soft and maybe a little too wet, but we were still learning each other and how to kiss and the extra wetness didn't really bother me anyway. The way he smelled. The rumble of my name in his chest.

Even now I feel the pulse in my belly, between my thighs.

My body knowing where tonight's going to lead, even if I haven't really let myself think that far ahead.

A romantic midnight picnic under the stars.

A blanket hidden amongst the grapevines.

Warm summer air flowing through my hair, lips and fingers trailing over my bare skin. Our bodies pressed together and—

I push the fantasy away and focus.

I'm never going to lose my virginity if I don't get out of this damned house first.

I can't go out one of the doors downstairs, not without triggering the motion detectors that my father surely activated when I announced I was heading up to bed, and I couldn't have snuck out before *he* called it a night because he would have caught me on the exterior cameras.

My only way out—discovered by trial and error—is to climb down from my gilded tower.

So, I shift carefully, pulling one leg up, slipping it over the sill, waiting until my toes are secure on the ledge before I sweep my other leg over. I've done this dozens, maybe a hundred times in the years since we moved to California, so I know to take my time, to adjust my grip so it'll support my weight, and then I heave myself up so that I can reach the tiny lip on the outside of the window were plastic meets glass.

My fingertips connect and I grunt softly as I clutch the pane, allow my body weight to draw it almost all the way down.

Just the barest bit of open space along the bottom so I can get back in.

Then I make my way down to the ground, hooking fingers and toes into the stone facade that makes up the exterior of my house, moving efficiently and confidently—exactly as my climbing instructor has taught me—until my feet are on the dirt and my second story window is just a faint glow above.

"Good job," I whisper to myself, brushing my hands on my jeans as I stick close to the wall, staying out of sight of the cameras until I can get lost in the rows and rows of grapevines that surround my father's estate.

"Go!" I hiss when I reach the safest spot to cross, darting through the shadows and reaching the thick covering of the vines.

Then I'm no longer careful as I run through the grape-laden plants, knowing they'll hide my movements, mentally keeping track of how many rows I've crossed so I know when to turn out to the main road.

And out to Bobby.

And his old pickup padded with blankets in the back.

And his strong body and insistent kisses and—

I turn, out of breath now but not caring.

Because I can see the shadow of Bobby's truck, can see the faint glimmer of his cell phone's flashlight, the outline of his body.

Nerves flutter in my belly and my pace slows.

This is going to change everything.

I know it will.

And...I can't wait.

"Breathe," I whisper, pressing my palms flat to my stomach, trying to settle the butterflies within. I exhale, hold my empty lungs for the count of three like I would before I'm about to attempt a tough assent. Then I inhale and move forward again.

Not running.

But walking steadily, heading toward my future, toward me finally getting out from beneath that uncomfortably heavy blanket of my father's overprotectiveness.

I'm almost an adult.

I can make my own decisions.

I near the end of the road, the night quiet except for the soft shush of the wind through the vines. "Bobby?" I call quietly.

Footsteps on the asphalt, that light shifting.

I frown but push it aside.

Probably, I'm too far away and he can't hear me over the rustling leaves.

Or he's playing a game on his phone and is distracted.

I grin and shake my head. Men. *Seriously.*

And then I keep walking forward, out of the empty space between two rows of vines and step up onto the road—

And freeze, heart suddenly in my throat.

Because it's not Bobby standing behind a beat-up truck that's more rust than metal.

It's a man dressed all in black who's positioned near a sleek, dark SUV.

And he's pointing a gun in my direction.

TWO

Chrissy

"MEOW!"

I smile down at the kitten who's so small she's struggling to poke her head out of the blanket I tucked around her while she slept earlier.

She's awake now though, awake and summoning the courage to start exploring like her siblings are.

"Come on out," I coax, waving the feather toy in her direction. "It's fun to mingle and be social."

She considers the toy, me, the chaos happening behind me...

And stays put.

I grin.

An introvert.

I know the feeling.

Sometimes, those social batteries take a good long while to recharge.

"Come on, baby," I say softly, jiggling the toy again,

sending the bell going, getting her interested enough that she starts to creep forward. First her head then her shoulders, her hips and tail...until finally her fluffy body slips free.

"Meow!" She looks at me with disdainful eyes, clearly not happy to be out from beneath the blanket.

"I know it's not exactly fun being social," I tell her as she extends a tentative paw toward the toy. "But it's good for us."

"Meow."

I grin. "I know," I say. "Tell me all about it."

"*Meow.*"

I laugh, but don't stop with the toy. Jingle, jingle goes the bell.

She stops complaining and crouches, readying herself to pounce.

"That's right," I tell her, "you can't let your siblings have *all* the fun."

She leaps, catching the edge of the feather, attacking it with a vengeance before she releases it and sprints off, running like a tiny fluffy maniac around the space, courage apparently found.

I watch her launch herself at her brother—a tabby that's already twice her size—before she rolls off and commences zooming around the room, little paws slipping this way and that on the tile floor.

She upends a rug, runs into a tower, nearly turns over a water bowl before she gets her legs under her and starts playing with one of her sisters—Petunia, if I caught the color of her coat correctly before all the details blurred in a flurry of running and jumping and rolling.

Ten kittens, all named after flowers. Six grayish brown girls—Petunia, Tulip, Lily, Rose, Iris, and Jasmine. Three tabby boys—Clover, Cassia, and Aster. And Petal—my brave girl now running around like she owns the place—who's almost completely pure white with the exception of two swathes of color across her face, one orange and one gray. An unusual sight in my feline rescue operation, so much so—and she was so filthy when we first brought her in—that I thought she was gray like her sisters.

But she's not.

The majority of her fur is as white as snow. Which means she should probably be named something like Crystal or Snowflake or Fluffy.

But flowers were the theme.

So...Petal.

The bell over the front door tinkles and I laugh under my breath as all the cats in the vicinity freeze, their heads cocking to the side.

Bells and feathers.

I would be screwed without them.

I turn my gaze from Petal and look toward the entrance, some part of me already knowing that it's going to be my dad.

He doesn't go long without checking in.

He hasn't since...

Well, he hasn't kept his distance since the night I sneaked out to meet Bobby Montgomery.

And met...other people.

Who didn't have my best interests in mind.

I get to my feet carefully, looking out for stray kittens and shuffling when the kitten brigade attacks my laces, halting when my dad closes the distance between us and presses a kiss to my cheek, seemingly unaware of the kittens crawling up the legs of his very expensive suit, leaving claw marks and copious amounts of hair.

Then again, I've been in cat rescue for long enough that claw marks and hair all over his clothes is old hat.

"How goes the opening?" he asks as he straightens,

turning his gaze toward the space, and I have no doubt he's taking in every detail—analyzing what could be done better and more efficiently.

"It's going," I say. "There's always hiccups on the first day, right?"

He smiles, his thumb brushing over my cheek before he winces and bends, scooping up a particularly determined kitten (Rose) and holding her close to his chest. "I like this idea of yours."

To open a storefront for adoptions. People come in and pay to play with the kittens (under carefully structured rules, including clean hands, booties on their shoes, limited numbers of visitors at one time, and not pushing the cats to interact), and the kittens, adult, and senior animals all get excellent socialization. We can place them better because we know how they'll react around kids and other cats, crowds and noises and unpredictable movements. It's a win-win-win all around.

"Meow."

I glance down, see that Petal has come back over to me. "Hi, baby," I say.

"Meow!"

My dad huffs out a laugh. "I think that one has picked her new owner."

I bend down and scoop her up, holding her securely against my chest. "You know that I can't bring any home, not with Joan being how she is."

Joan—a.k.a. Joan of *Freaking* Arc—is my cranky senior cat with epilepsy and diabetes. My oldest rescue, she must be about thirteen now and has absolutely zero fucks to give. Which basically means that she dislikes everyone and has no compunction about using her talons, er claws, if someone dares to mess with her.

And *messing with her* includes doing awful things such as walking by her cat tower, sitting on my favorite armchair, or trying to feed, water, or—God forbid—*pet* her.

Oddly, she only likes my dad.

Who the outside world thinks is an unfeeling robot.

"Right," he says, pivoting—probably because he can read with one look at my face how upset I'll be to let my little Petal go. "Well, that one is young and cute and I know you'll find her a good home quickly."

He's right.

But it'll be hard.

I'll miss her. But...that's the nature of rescue work. I either have to get used to letting these animals go to carefully selected homes, or I'll turn into a crazy cat lady.

And I can do a lot more good by *not* turning into that crazy cat lady.

"Yeah," I murmur, giving her one last cuddle before setting her back on her little paws, a part of my heart breaking off and going with her when she runs back to join the action.

"Are you going to stay at my house tonight?" he asks, drawing my eyes back to his.

Suspicion immediately grows in my belly. "Why?" I ask.

"I want you with me at the board meeting."

I still. Sigh. "Dad," I murmur, "I told you already. I'm done working with the Eagles."

The *Oakland* Eagles to be precise.

Because my dad, owner of several successful, world-renowned wineries bought a hockey team.

Wine and hockey might seem like an odd combination to the outside world—most of whom think he is that hard, stoic businessman.

They don't get the connection.

But those who know the real Jean-Michel Dubois understand.

He grew up in Montreal, was just a normal kid from normal parents and dreamed big of playing in the NHL. On the ice early in the morning, late at night, helping his dad make a rink in their back yard so he could get extra practice in.

For years, hockey was his blood.

Until his dreams were shattered with an injury.

But my father is nothing if not a fighter. He pivoted, worked hard, and sold a series of self-made, increasingly more successful businesses. Until his interest in wine was piqued and he moved us to France to dominate the wine industry there. Something he was so good at that, a few years later, he moved to California to take over a string of failing vineyards and wineries.

Wineries that are now some of the most profitable in the nation.

So, when the beleaguered Eagles came up for sale, the fit was natural from my father's perspective—he saved businesses and moved on with his bank account balance loving him, and I...well, I moved along with him.

But even I have my doubts about his prowess when it comes to the Eagles.

The roster is a mess. The players seem to hate each other —and their coaches. Their record...well, last season they were, by far, the worst in the league.

I played hockey for a bit growing up, and again not that long ago as an adult searching for some exercise and pushing myself out of my social comfort zone, but I don't *love* it.

Not like my dad.

Who seems willing to go to any length to make the Eagles successful.

Even if it means ruthlessly acquiring players (and then trading them away when they aren't living up to his expectations). I know that my father has had to be relentless and unrelenting in order to make his businesses successful, but... they're people to me.

And seeing them traded away, their lives uprooted because of his decisions...

It's like saying goodbye to another cat.

Only...it's a person.

I sigh, start to remind him that I've resigned from my full-time position as a physical therapist and only agreed to occasional contract work.

But, as usual, he's...relentless.

"You don't have to work for the Eagles," he says, but it's a lie because I know that *he* knows that he'll wear me down sooner or later and then my life will be less about adorable furballs and more about hockey pucks. "I just want you to sit in and tell me your opinion on the new members. You know I trust your instincts more than anyone's. You're the only person who's always honest and straightforward with me."

Flattery.

But also truth.

Ever since that night when I met a gun instead of Bobby in the vineyard—I've been completely honest with my father.

Always.

And now—because of that night and what we both almost lost—when I talk—at least about cats or business—my dad stops and listens.

And more often than not, he takes my opinion into account.

"Fine," I say on a sigh, saving myself an argument when we both know it will end with me giving in anyway. "I'll go to the meeting. But I'm staying at my house tonight," I add when his expression becomes far too triumphant.

"That makes no sense," he tells me. "That'll double your commute."

He's not wrong.

"Regardless, I'd rather stay at my place." My new house, one I've finally moved into after years and years of my dad pulling various shenanigans to keep me under his roof. It's beautiful and amazing and *mine,* and I like that it's a distance away from his downtown apartment. I like that it's nestled in a small wine-based community just outside of Oakland. It's peaceful and quiet and my dad can't just pop over.

Not easily, anyway.

Because he still shows up unannounced at least once per week.

And, of course, he has other ways of keeping me close.

One he employs right then.

"You know that you'll be driving out of your way."

"I know."

"But all of that driving means that you'll lose out on more time here with the cats," he says. "If you stay at my place, you can come here before the meeting."

Ugh.

I hate that he's right.

My shoulders slump, and I bite back a sigh.

"Fine," I mutter, "But I'm going home first to get my stuff."

THREE

"YOU'RE STILL one of us, you know that, right?"

I look down at the slender blonde with deep brown eyes and see the sincerity in those chocolate depths.

Brit isn't lying. She's made an effort to be a part of my family for a long time now. Not just talk, but taking my back, looking out for me, supporting me exactly as family should—exactly as my biological family does when we happen to find time in our busy schedules to talk.

It's just...

I'm not.

I'm not one of them any longer.

I'm not a member of the Gold, not part of the boisterous, nosy, good-hearted team who have banded together and become a family like no other.

I'm an Eagle.

I'm going from a team where we put everything on the line for each other to a team full of...

Assholes and grumpy bastards.

All-for-one to gotta-get-mine.

A winning record and strong playoff showing each and every season to last in the standings and a locker room in disarray.

They're looking for a leader.

A leader who's supposed to be...me.

Which makes no fucking sense.

It's people like Brit who are the leaders—setting an example, steadying us when we falter, pushing us to be better.

I'll work my ass off—I always do—but how the fuck am I supposed to inspire that same urgency and intensity in others?

I don't know what I'm doing. I fucking don't—

"Rome?" Brit asks, stepping a little closer, concern bleeding into her eyes. "You know that, right?"

Fuck.

Now I'm making it harder on my family, my friends.

Cool. Cool. That's what the newest captain of an NHL team is supposed to do, right?

Fuck up and make things harder?

Yup. Yup.

I grind my teeth together when my head starts to throb, and barely resist the urge to rub my temple. Instead, I force a smile. "I hear you, Banana," I say, using the Gold goalie's newest nickname to distract her before she can tip over into full-blown worry. "I know I'm stuck with you jokers," I tell her. "Once you're in, there's no out. It's like the freaking mafia."

She smiles at me, showing off that million-dollar grin that's garnered her more than a few endorsement deals and has graced billboards all throughout the Bay Area. "Damn right," she says, nudging her shoulder with my own. "And I'll also expect you to forget every single weak spot of mine when you're shooting on me, yeah?"

"You mean that high blocker?" I tease.

She narrows her eyes, giving me a glimpse of the intense goalie that has been the face of the Gold for years now. "I kill," she warns in a crappy evil villain voice.

"Lies." I drag her close, kiss the top of her head. "How are you doing really?" I ask softly. "With everything."

Her body tenses against mine, and I brace.

Because she's had a shit time of it, what with news of her and Stefan's divorce hitting the media. The NHL's power couple, who were together a decade and sickeningly happy, had...broken up. "It fucking sucks," she says and then drops her arms with a sigh. "But it's getting better."

I draw away, get a look at her face, and want to immediately pull her right back into my arms.

"Brit," I begin.

A sharp exhale before she retreats another step and juts her chin toward the road. "You need to get going before traffic makes you want to never come back across the bridge."

"There's more than one bridge," I point out.

"They're all bad this time of day," she says and she's not wrong. "Go on. I'll bother you again soon."

"How ominous," I quip, thankful when she smirks. I had turned down the offer of the Gold Moving Service (a.k.a. a bunch of Gold players schlepping furniture and boxes) and hired a real moving service, so it's just the two of us standing on the sidewalk. Partly because I didn't want to inconvenience my former teammates, partly because it would hurt like hell to have them helping, knowing that everything is different now, and partly because the league pays for movers.

So, my shit is already in my new home.

It's just me, a couple of final boxes, and my car.

And Brit.

Other goodbyes have been conducted, a farewell party thrown. My new reality is right in front of me.

Without everything I've ever known.

I'm lucky, I know that. Plenty of guys bounce between teams, never find a home base, never have stability.

I had it for four years.

Now, I need to make my own way.

Brit shifts, and I know she's going to try to say something else, try to make me feel better, but—God—she has enough on her shoulders without dealing with my shit.

I force another smile, sling my arm around her shoulders, then start drawing her toward her car. "Go get some rest," I say. "The first game of the season is coming up and the boys need you in top form."

"Alex will be in starter shape in no time."

Said in a chipper tone about the player brought in to replace her when she was injured and it seemed unlikely that she would return to professional hockey.

That was before the divorce.

Before Stefan started dating someone else.

"Alex is never going to be you," I tell her.

She goes still, her body so tense it could snap like a cold rubber band.

Then she thaws and glances up at me, that trademark smile in place. I hate that it feels more like a mask than a genuine grin. "You're all right, Rome Dawson."

I tug the end of her ponytail. "Say that again the first time I score on you in a game that counts."

Now her smile transforms, less mask and more real and...

"If you score," she says, "it's only because I've let you."

We both narrow our eyes at each other.

Then burst out laughing.

And I think that even though everything I've known in my life is changing, it can't be a bad sign that this new chapter is beginning with laughter.

It doesn't take long for me to realize I was wrong.

Very wrong.

Laughter wasn't a sign of this next chapter in my life beginning on a positive note.

It was fate laughing at me.

"She was fucking *mine*," Pat growls the next day, his big hand wrapping around Duncan's throat as he shoves him back against the wall. Duncan's skull narrowly misses a row of hooks that usually hold our gear (empty now, since the equipment guys have gathered all of the dirties), but even if he was impaled on one of those pegs, stabbed and bleeding out, I don't think Pat would have stopped.

He's ready to commit murder.

Over pussy.

Cool. Cool.

The rest of the room is tense, all of us guys in various states of undress, just wanting to shower, do our post-game cool downs, rehab, or—in my case—a light workout that I find helps with my recovery.

We don't want to be here.

I don't want to be here.

But I also can't sit on my ass and watch a teammate get choked out.

Over pussy.

Sighing, I stand up and cross to Pat. "Look, man," I say, settling my hand on his shoulder. "Let's just take a deep breath—"

Touching him—something I would have realized if I had been thinking clearly—is the wrong move. But I'm *not* thinking—or not thinking about anything other than preventing a murder and getting the hell back to my empty house.

And that not thinking means that I touch a testosterone-fueled idiot.

While he's thinking about committing murder.

The moment my hand makes contact with his shoulder, he rears back.

This is a good thing because the rearing back has him releasing Duncan, who was turning purple.

This is a *bad* thing because his rearing back means that Pat releases Duncan and whips around and—

His elbow collides with my eye.

"Fuck," I growl as pain explodes through my face. It has to be Pat, who's got a good six inches on me, leaving me right at prime elbowing height. It also has to be Pat, who's the biggest fucker on the roster and thus who can do damage without breaking a nail.

Just breaking my face.

Cool. Cool.

I glare up at him through my one remaining good eye. "What the fuck?"

He glares back, jaw tense, hands in fists at his sides. "You got in the way," he snaps. "You should know better than to intervene in a fight."

"You were choking out a teammate," I growl. "In our fucking locker room." I straighten, exhale, drop my hand from my face, ignoring my throbbing eye. "Where anyone might walk in—Coach, media, our owner who's fucking on site for a meeting today. You're fighting over sticking your dick in some probably sloppy pussy instead of focusing on what we should be focusing on this season. And that," I say, waving a hand around the space, encompassing my teammates who look a combination of disgusted (only two, Kingston and Cam), amused (the bulk), or completely enthralled (the remaining chunk), like they're ready to bust out a bucket of popcorn and start chowing down while they watch the show, "is hockey. We should all be focused on playing fucking hockey and scoring goals and maybe winning a goddamned game every once in a while."

But no one looks ready to concur.

No one except for Kingston, who lifts his brows and tilts his head to the side, and Cam, who starts to stand up.

I shake my head slightly at them, turn back to Duncan and Pat. "There's no shortage of ways to get your dick wet," I grind out. "Keep it out of the fucking locker room."

And then I spin around, stomp back to my stall and finish getting changed, swapping my sweaty practice underclothes for dry but soon-to-be sweaty workout clothes.

"Is that what you did with the Gold?" Pat asks. "Try to motivate the room with a rah-rah inspirational speech?"

I jerk my head up, taking my eyes off my laces I'm doing up in preparation of my post-game stair run (something that Brit inspired long ago), and look across the room.

Pat Walkins.

Great skater. Great shooter. Great play maker.

Fucking poison in the locker room.

Not typically the volatile shit that he's just sprayed around the space. Instead, it usually comes in the form of a slow, insidious creep. It takes a season or two before the effects are felt, and then it begins. Motivation dying off. Anger growing. Teamwork falling apart.

It's happened with every team he's played with—which

now number six in total—but he produces such big numbers that he still somehow finds his way onto rosters.

And he's been here with the Eagles for three seasons.

So that poison has been embedded deeply, has seeped into the surrounding tissue, causing it to blacken and decay.

He's the worst.

But he's not the only problem.

We've got manwhore Duncan, hotheaded Kane, Lazy Matt, Asshole Anthony, and many more.

And me.

Who's supposed to somehow bring these fuckers together.

My directive made clear by Coach, by the owner, Jean-Michel Dubois, by the board.

"I didn't need to do that with the Gold," I snap. "It was understood that everyone would pull their weight and work together as a team. The winning is just a positive by-product of that."

Silence.

Then Pat starts laughing, loud and long and so intensely that he clutches his stomach and bends over.

I smother a growl, do some more teeth grinding, and then I just...shake my head and look away, eyes catching on Kingston's as I reach down to finish doing up my laces.

He opens his mouth.

I give him another slight shake of my head before I stand up.

Before I walk out the door.

Before I go run some fucking stairs.

Later that night, I'm sitting on my deck, looking up at the clear sky, the stars glimmering gems overhead, and I hear noise from next door.

This is a surprise because, while I haven't been here long, I haven't so much as caught a glimpse of my neighbor.

Maybe they travel for work, or they were on vacation, or—

The thoughts freeze in my head, drop away one by one as I watch her—yes, *her*, a slender brunette with hair flowing down her spine, walk out from her house and lean on the railing, doing the same thing I am—staring into the canyon behind our houses, dropping her head back and looking up at the stars above.

There's something beautiful about her, beautifully lonely maybe, and it calls to me. *She* calls to me.

I want to hop the fence between our properties, want to move to her side, find out why sadness clings to her bones.

And I almost do, my feet dropping off the railing, my beer hitting the small round table next to me, my hands pushing at the arms of my chair.

But before I can lift myself up, she spins back for the house.

And disappears inside.

FOUR

Chrissy

I HAVE to give it to my dad—he has the best mattresses.

Which means I had a great night of sleep.

I want to say that I've tossed and turned, that I didn't get a minute's rest so I have a stronger excuse to put him off the next time he insists on me staying over, but some part of me doesn't *want* to resist.

Because my brain and body know that I'm safe when I'm here.

So, yeah, I slept like a baby.

"You need to grow up, Dubois," I mutter then sigh, snag my purse, and get out of my car. The fall air has that tinge of warm clinging to it, the weather this time of year unable to decide if it wants to be hot or cold. Today might top out at the mid-fifties and tomorrow I'll be sweating in my hoodie because we'll be cruising into the eighties. In a month's time, fall will fully set in, and I'll be able to enjoy the leaves changing color and the temperatures dropping.

But today, for now, Mother Nature will keep me guessing.

At least it's warm enough for a climb.

And I'm making plans for exactly that as I walk toward the Eagle's practice facility, my purse on my shoulder and my mind on this meeting. It's several hours after my dad arrived because I stopped to make sure the cats were happy at the facility, that the girls on shift this morning had fed and watered and socialized them, that the roof hadn't fallen in or whatever other cat-tastrophe (no pun intended) my mind could conjure hadn't happened, and that the kitties weren't overwhelmed with visitors.

And also...Petal.

I had to check in on that little fluff ball.

Who was running around, more confident every moment, more outgoing and adorable.

When she's old enough, she's going to be adopted in a second.

And I'm going to miss her.

Which is reality.

I have to let go. I have to move on.

My throat goes tight, my heart rebelling, but I push that down and pick up my pace. The extra Petal cuddles I sneaked mean that I'm running behind, so I hustle to the exterior door of the facility, swipe my key, and yank open the door, digging through my purse for my notebook and pen.

Notes help me think.

Also, this notebook has a kitty on it and was given to me by a little girl who's the best owner *ever* of one of my cats.

Can I be bought by cute cat stationary and pens that write so smoothly their ink feels like liquid silk?

Well, clearly.

Anyway...see? I'm fine.

So, my dad is pushy (bordering on overbearing), and I often feel like Rapunzel escaped from her tower as he tries to lock me back inside.

But I'm safe. I have a roof over my head (or two, if I include my dad's place). My fridge is full enough for one person. And I'm working, doing something important to help innocent critters when I wasn't sure I would ever be confident enough to leave the gilded prison of my father's estate again.

I'm out here.

Doing my thing.

Everything is good.

Everything is great.

I have no excuse not to do my part, especially after all my dad has done for me. I have no reason to text him and weasel out of what will undoubtedly be a long, boring, drawn-out meeting with a bunch of grumpy old men.

Including my dad.

Because...life is great.

So, why does it feel like I'm trying to convince myself of that fact?

I sigh, grit my teeth, pick up my pace, and promise myself that this meeting won't be all bad, that this gnawing feeling in my belly is just a normal part of life. Growing pains or the seasonal blues, not the increasingly intense feeling that I don't know what the hell I'm doing with my existence and—

"*Oof!*"

I run into a wall.

Literally, it feels like I've run into a wall.

My notebook goes flying. My pen drops from my hand and hits the concrete floor, rolling to the side. My purse slips down my arm, swinging around my wrist and whacking against that wall—

Or rather, whacking that hockey player who's apparently tried to check me, I realize as a deeply masculine voice reaches my ears.

"Oh, shit," he says, seemingly unbothered by my heavy purse slamming into his ribs again as his hands go to my shoulders to steady me. "I'm sorry."

But the contact, the movement...it's too fast, too jerky, too *much.*

Hands yanking at my hair, my body, my...clothes.

I flinch back, and promptly trip over my feet, and it only takes a heartbeat longer for me to know that I'm going down.

There's that moment of weightlessness, almost as if I'm hovering in the air for a second before I'm tumbling back, the unforgiving floor rising up and—

"*Oof!*" I grunt again, but this time it's because all of my momentum has come to a screeching halt and instead of colliding with that concrete floor, I'm jerked to a stop, floating in mid-air, and—

Then I'm on my feet again, and he's released me, and—

I'm looking up at the most beautiful man I've ever seen.

Deep brown eyes that are filled with concern, thick, dark bristles covering his jaw, a purplish bruise blooming on the top of one cheek.

It looks fresh.

And painful.

"Ouch," I murmur.

He winces. "Shit, I'm sorry." He rubs a hand over the top of his head, mussing the thick curls, sending one tumbling over his forehead, kissing the arch of one faintly scarred eyebrow. "What hurts?" he asks. "I can take you to our trainer to get you checked out if you want." His voice is warm and rumbly and slides down my spine like velvet.

And…I'm dumb.

Because instead of telling him that my shoulder hurts from the wrench of him catching me before the concrete floor and I had the chance to become intimately acquainted, or from the impact of his big, hockey body against mine before that, I…

God. I'm *so* dumb.

Because I reach up and gently brush my fingers over that still-darkening bruise at the top of his cheekbone. "That looks like it hurts," I murmur.

He freezes as my fingertips make contact.

So do I.

Sparks shoot up my arm, trailed rapidly by tingles that flow over my skin, gather in my belly. Lower. …

I shudder, my exhale shaky, and wonder if he feels it too.

Then I realize that's stupid.

I realize that I'm touching a strange man—no, a strange hockey player, who works for my dad. Who my dad will certainly find a quiet and isolated vineyard to dispose of his body in if he so much as catches a glimpse of us standing this closely.

I start to drop my hand. "I'm sorry," I whisper. "I shouldn't have—"

His hand moves fast, so fast that I flinch, those clawed, hidden memories slipping out one razor-tipped hand, threatening to slice me open, to expose me to the world. But then his hand is on mine and the door in my mind slams closed, aided by one large, slightly roughened palm. "Don't apologize," he says softly, and there's no doubt—based on the fury in his deep brown eyes—that he clocked the way I recoiled from him. But he doesn't comment on it. He just stands there, holding his big body still, and staring down at me. "It's my fault. I should have watched where I was going."

"I—"

But I clamp my lips together.

Because I hear a familiar voice coiling through the corridors, just faintly hitting the edges of my hearing.

My *father's* voice.

And if he sees this man this close, with his hands on me—

D.E.A.D. *Dead.*

"I need to go," I whisper, slipping my hand from beneath his, stepping back.

He doesn't touch me, but he follows, keeping our bodies just a couple of feet apart. "What's your name?"

Danger. Danger. I shake my head. "I *really* need to go."

That big, warm hand which felt so good on mine, presses to his chest. "I'm Rome."

Rome. Why does that fit?

Because he's giving me Roman gladiator vibes? Because if I was a betting woman, I'd say that body of his—currently covered by a skin-tight tee and jeans that cup his thighs so lovingly they should be illegal—could belong to the lead in a 300 remake?

Yes. And also, *yes.*

A laugh echoes down the corridor.

My father's laugh.

Shit.

"Bye, Rome," I murmur, spinning on my heel.

"Bye, Kitten," he rumbles softly behind me.

My pussy spasms, but I don't stop, just hustle around the corner, move toward my dad, who I know has come searching for me.

Because I'm late.

I also know that I'm going to remember Rome's husky *Kitten* for a long time.

Maybe it'll cling to my mind until I slip into my bed tonight.

Maybe it'll stick around for much, much longer.

FIVE

Rome

PRACTICE WENT...

Yup.

It went.

That's the single good thing I could say about it—that it's done.

And I didn't end up with a second black eye.

Of course, there was the side of nearly plowing over a woman half my size. A woman who flinched when I reached for her.

Twice.

I grind my teeth together, take a swig of my beer, and sink down into the chair on my back porch, sling my legs up onto the railing, and dig my phone out of my pocket.

Because it's been buzzing non-fucking-stop.

With messages on the Gold group text.

I shouldn't still be on this chain—not with them making post-practice plans, arranging team get-togethers, and giving each other shit about what happened on the ice. I'm not there to do anything *on* the ice with them, and I'm not going to drive an hour-plus there and at least two hours back (thanks, traffic) for a post-practice beer. I can't do that drive on the regular and remain sane and rested and without a fucking rocket launcher installed on top of my car.

I'll make it to the big team events because those fuckers are my family and I'm not willing to let them go.

But...I'm on the outside of the day-to-day stuff.

"And now *that's* my pity party for the day," I mutter, taking another swig of my beer and thinking back to practice.

Trying to find something good.

Kingston, I guess. And Cam.

They're both not assholes.

So, not one good thing, but two. Look at me, all Bob Ross-ing it, finding the joy in the happy little accidents, *er* hockey players.

I exhale, polish off my beer, and sit in the warm fall air, trying to get comfortable in the silence.

I haven't been alone much since I came to the big leagues —first living with Brit and Stef, then sharing an apartment with a couple of the young guys on the team, and even when I got my own place, it was often inundated with teammates or I was crashing someone's dinner, meeting up at the local ice cream joint, chilling with a beer and watching their kids run around until they finally passed out.

But the quiet isn't bad.

I don't mind silence or being alone.

The problem I have is being alone with my *thoughts.*

I need a fucking hobby. Or a dog. Or a—

"*MEOW!!*"

"Cat," I mutter, my head jerking to the side, searching for the source of the sound.

I don't find it.

And anyway, I'm not home enough for a pet. I'd have to board them half the time or get a pet sitter. That wouldn't be good for either of us. Sighing, I debate getting another beer, knowing that it's not really allowed in the diet plan I'm following, but—

"Fuck it."

I'll do some extra stairs tomorrow. Which isn't all that far away considering the sun's barely holding on.

It's dipped below the hills behind us, but its influence isn't completely gone, the sky a swathe of red and orange, pink and yellow.

Which is enough light, for the moment, for me to forget about the second beer...and take in the commotion happening next door.

My neighbor—my only neighbor since the canyon backs up to our little hillside on three sides—bursts out the door, yelling, "Joan!"

Shit.

My feet drop off the railing, stomach immediately sinking at the panic in that yell.

Is Joan a kid?

Because the canyon, the growing dark—

Fuck, that isn't a good combination.

I jump up, move to the edge of my deck. "Hey!" I call. "Are you okay?"

The woman freezes, clamping a hand over her heart, then spins to face me.

I can't see her expression from this distance and with the waning sunlight, but her voice is familiar. I frown, trying to place it, even as I know that I don't have time to waste—not if a kid is involved.

"Is Joan okay?" I ask, putting the blip of recognition aside to examine later.

"I—" Her hand drops. "Um, yeah," she says quietly, so quietly that I have to move closer to hear. "I mean, she's fine and I'm fine. It's just—"

I clomp down the steps, stride over to the metal fence. "It's just what?"

"Nothing," she says quickly, turning away from me. "Go on with your evening." She waves her hand. "I'm sorry I disturbed you."

I want to push the issue, but...I don't know this woman, and I'm just a strange man to her, and—

"You didn't disturb me," I blurt. Hell, I should be thanking her for getting me out of my own head and canceling my freaking pity party.

"Oh." She turns back. "Right."

And then we both just stand there, the fence between us, shadows clinging as the darkness descends.

Until she starts to turn away again. "I should get on with..." A thumb hitching over her shoulder.

"With Joan," I say.

A pause, her head bobbing, hair sliding in front of her face. "With Joan," she says softly.

I stand there for a moment, but I don't have an excuse, don't have a reason to linger.

So, I...go get another beer.

And I drink it, lingering inside in order to not be a creepy asshole, watching her as I hang on my deck.

But, eventually, curiosity brings me back outside and—

"What. The. Actual. Fuck?" I hiss, plunking my beer onto the railing and booking it down the stairs, heading for the fence, not stopping to think when I reach the stretch of rod iron—I just wrap my fingers around the top rail, push and leap, launching myself over. I barely clear the hedge lining my neighbor's side, and I'm pretty sure that I trample a few of the remaining summer flowers in the planter bed, but I don't have time to worry about crushed petals and...trespassing.

Because the woman—my neighbor, who said she had everything under control—is in the tree.

Up.

In the tree.

Swinging from a branch.

With one fucking hand.

"What the fuck are you doing?" I snap.

Which is the wrong thing to do—yelling at someone in a precarious position—because she slips and I sprint forward, preparing to catch her, certain that she's a heartbeat away from plummeting to her death.

Or...a good ten feet to the dirt surrounding the base of the tree at least.

But even before I get there, she's hauling herself up with a confidence that is just...*whoa*. The grip strength alone— holy shit. But also the way she recovers and draws herself up and over the branch without panicking, without hesitation, without plummeting to her death (okay, that ten feet into my arms) is fucking impressive.

The way she glares down at me is...less so.

Especially now that I'm close enough to see that the woman in the tree is the woman...I nearly body-checked at the rink earlier today.

Pretty as fuck with a pert nose and delicate features and irises the colors of blue topaz. Long, silky brown hair that hits the middle of her back and makes me want to say,

"Rapunzel, Rapunzel let down your hair."

That glare intensifies and I realize...

Fuck. I realize that I'm even more of an idiot than I previously thought.

Because I *did* voice that out loud.

And...Jesus...who even says something like that?

Idiots, that's who.

Christ.

I clear my throat, try to play it off like I didn't just completely misread a situation, sprint through my back yard, hop a fence, and nearly scare an innocent woman out of a tree, only to then quote fairy tales like a weird ass hero from a romantic film. "I...uh...I'm sorry." I cough into my hand, retreat a step. "I didn't realize you were climbing the tree for...fun." For fun? What in the actual fuck is wrong with me? "I'll—" Another cough. "Just let you get back to it."

I turn for the fence, realize that it's actually a fair amount higher than I recall from my panicked rush, and wonder if I should attempt to climb over (and risk trampling those flowers again), or if I should make my walk of shame through the side yard and skip the second round of fence scaling.

But I don't have to make the decision because her cold, tart voice stops me before I get that far.

"For the record, I'm not climbing this tree at night for *fun*."

I still, turn back, look up at my dark-haired Rapunzel. "Then why are you in the tree, Kitten?"

She stills again, then swings her leg over the branch she hefted herself up onto a few moments before, and looks down at me, sighing. "Joan."

SIX

Chrissy

ROME IS JUST as beautiful in the fading sunlight as he was beneath the bright fluorescents of the practice rink.

And the way he calls me *Kitten*.

I shiver, nearly lose my balance on the branch, but luckily my instincts aren't dickmatized. My fingers and thighs immediately tighten so that I don't topple over, so that I stay on top of the branch.

"Joan?" he asks, stepping closer, as though prepared to catch me if I *do* fall.

He can probably do it too. With those broad shoulders and solid arms and thick thighs.

I shiver, heat blooming between my legs.

But I shove that nonsense away, refocus, and look up. "Joan," I say, pointing up at the branch a good six feet still above my head. How my senior cat, who never freaking leaves her perch, managed to climb that high that fast, let alone sneak through the back door when she is either neither particularly mobile nor adept at hefting her considerable *heft*, I don't know.

Probably punishing me for staying at my dad's last night.

Probably punishing me for moving her out of my dad's and also for leaving her alone last night.

Probably...being typical surly Joan of Arc, who lives to make my life difficult.

"Joan of *freaking* Arc." I glance back down in time to see Rome slide closer, his brows pulling together, his gaze flicking to me and then over my shoulder.

A curl slips forward, draping itself over his forehead. "Joan is...a cat?" he asks.

Joan—right on cue—hisses as Rome moves into her field of vision—which means that he's obviously come too close (those twenty feet separating them are far too few).

That's the world according to Joan.

"Joan of *freaking* Arc," I correct, slowly standing on the branch and reaching for the one above me, testing if it'll hold my weight, "is indeed a cat."

"Joan of *freaking* Arc?"

I adjust my grip on the limb overhead. "Because she's strong and fierce, and she'll cut a bitch if you get too close."

He laughs softly, which earns him another hiss from Joan, though Rome seems completely nonplussed by my pussy's protests.

Heh.

Focus.

"Did you name her?" It's a quiet question as I prepare to ascend.

"Yeah," I say. "She was from one of my first rescue litters. I actually found her in my dad's back yard—her and her siblings were all left behind by Mom."

Either that, or something bad had happened to her, but...

I'd rather believe she was out there, living a happy kid- (or kitten-) free life, and not alone and suffering and hurt—

I exhale.

Like, potentially, *my* mom.

Who is...well, I don't know where she is.

I don't know *who* she is.

And neither does my dad.

I'm just a baby on a doorstep, left behind like a too-flat basketball, forgotten on the corner of a porch, undiscovered until the gardeners came and heard my soft cries and—

Found me.

I'm biologically my father's, that's all I know.

Whether I'll ever find out more...I'm not sure.

Because...she's never come back for me.

So, I hope she's out there, happy and whole, and not in a shallow, unmarked grave somewhere, same as I hope that Joan's mom lived a full and wonderful life without pain and with plenty of mice to catch.

"How did she get her name?" Rome asks, jerking me out of my thoughts.

A good thing, that. Because thinking about my mom is almost as bad as—

Bobby's truck not being there.

A gun pointed my direction. Days and days of darkness, the fear creeping into my bones and not leaving for years.

I drag myself up to the next branch, hold my breath as it creaks but holds. One more and I'll be close enough to snag Joan by the scruff of her very annoying neck and attempt to not die as I help us both descend.

"The litter she was found with was all girls." I shrug, carefully move up to that next branch. "Not one brother in sight and I was a bit of a history buff, so I named them all after important women throughout time. We had Elizabeth the first and Joan, Marie Curie and Rosa Parks, Frida Kahlo and Eleanor Roosevelt." I shrug, feel my cheeks heat. "Mouthfuls I know, but I've always loved a theme when we rescue a litter."

It lets me focus on the unimportant things when the real shit gets so damned heavy.

"You've said rescued twice," he murmurs.

"I have a rescue organization," I tell him. "We've hit our fifth year and saved and rehomed over two thousand cats."

There's pride in my voice.

Because I'm fucking proud of myself. I could have sat at home and hid. I could have used my dad's black AmEx and gone shopping every day.

Instead, I did something more.

And, truthfully, they help me more than I help them. I just have to look at their little, innocent faces to know that I'm doing a good thing, doing the *right* thing.

Not just thinking about myself.

Being better.

So, yeah, pride.

And climbing trees for a stubborn senior cat who isn't fit for another home.

"That's amazing."

"The need is there and I'm—"

I was about to tell him that I'm happy to do something that makes me feel good and useful and like a productive member of society, but I mistime.

Because I've reached Joan and I'm inching closer and—

I dart my hand out.

She hisses and bats at my arm, claws fully out and slicing right into my skin.

"*Shit*," I say, doing some hissing of my own.

"Kitten?"

"I'm fine." I readjust my grip, shake out my stinging arm, then creep closer. Watching and waiting, not about to mistime this go around and risk Joan's claws again.

"*Meow*," she growls, the sound vibrating through her expansive chest.

Total *Don't Fuck With Me* vibes.

But it's getting darker by the second and I want the hell out of this tree.

So, I step closer, keeping out of reach of those claws, sneak my arm over the branch, and—

"*Meow!*"

It's an ear-piercing protest, but I've had a hand in rescuing over two thousand cats. I know how to corral one, even hanging from a tree branch. I tighten my grip on her scruff, holding tight to her as I focus on rapidly descending before the limbs give way or her wriggling causes me to lose my grip.

"*MEOW!*"

"Yeah, yeah," I mutter, making it down to the next branch, then the next.

"Joan's war cry is impressive," Rome says, the words barely audible over her objections.

"Yup," I say dryly. "Her lungs rival a two-year-old's."

He laughs, loud and outright and...

This is where I make a mistake.

Because the sound—warm, rumbly, and wonderful—draws my focus down.

And away from on my descent. Away from the wriggling, pissed-off cat I'm carrying.

To Rome.

Beautiful, handsome Rome.

His smile is a flash of white in the waning light, but it steals my breath, especially paired with the amusement creeping into the edges of his expression. I watch it grow, listen to that laughter, and...

I slip.

My foot sliding right out from beneath me, sending me sailing through the air.

Unbidden, my hand opens, and Joan starts falling alongside me.

"Fuck!"

I'm still watching Rome, so I watch the smile get wiped from his face, his eyes going wide, panic taking over as he closes the remaining distance between us.

But I'm in the air and he's standing on the ground.

I bounce off a branch, the impact stealing my breath, some of my momentum.

But not *all* of it, even though I'm trying to grab on to any of the limbs as I fly through the tree, my clothes catching on sharp, little boughs, leaves pulling at my hair.

"*Oof!*"

I wrap my arms around the biggest branch at the bottom of the tree, the one that's still a good six feet off the ground.

Maybe more.

Because as I collide with it, a warm hand grips my ankle, pushing me into that limb, steadying me so that I stop falling.

The skin on my palms protest, my arms shake, my lungs are still struggling to pull in air.

But I've stopped falling.

"Shit, Kitten," Rome says, his words slightly breathless. "Are you okay?"

I know the feeling. It takes a solid ten seconds of me focusing before I'm able to make my lungs work enough to help me form words, and they're only, "I'm okay."

Then I remember that I'm using both of my hands to grip the branch. "Joan!"

That hand at my ankle shifts, becomes an arm wrapping around my thighs that lifts me, drawing me off the tree limb. It slides up—thighs, waist, stomach, chest—as I slide down a warm, strong body, my back to his front.

And this time my lungs aren't working for a completely different reason.

"I have Joan," he says quietly, lifting one arm to show me my cat in his hand. Not fighting him. Not making one sound of protest.

No claws. No hisses or growls.

Just a quiescent Joan of *freaking* Arc.

I narrow my eyes at her.

She narrows them back at me. Bares her teeth.

Fucking traitor.

SEVEN

Rome

I FORCE myself to release her, to drop my arm away from the breasts I'm pretending that I don't feel pressing into my forearm, and step back.

I don't release the devil cat, though.

I keep my grip secure, nod toward the house. "Should I carry her inside?"

She startles, like her mind was somewhere else—and I hope it's the same place mine was, the same place my brain keeps drifting off to.

Her lush body. That plump mouth. Her long hair trailing over my naked skin as she kisses her way down to my cock, parts her lips and takes my dick deep, tongue drawing up along the shaft, and—

"Yes."

Yes.

Fuck, I want it to be, *Yes, I'll blow you now, Rome.*

Alas, I have the wrong pussy in my hand.

Exhaling, I force my dick to behave, clear my throat so I don't sound like a creepy motherfucker who's turned on by her mere proximity (even if it's true), and say, "Lead the way."

Her head jerks, and I have the feeling I haven't masked my creepy-motherfucker-who's-turned-on-by-her-proximity well enough.

But she doesn't comment on it, just nods slightly, and takes off through the back yard, picking her way around the flowers and bushes until we're back on the concrete path that leads to the deck.

Do I watch her ass as she climbs the stairs in front of me?

Sure as fuck I do.

And it's as lush and tempting as the rest of her.

She stops at the back door, pulls it open, and holds it for me to precede her.

Joan has been totally cooperative up until this point—proving she's smart enough to understand that I saved her ass, though maybe not that she had nearly offed her owner—the owner that, presumably, feeds her.

So, smarts are questionable, I guess.

Especially when, as soon as I cross the threshold into the house, she starts squirming.

And hissing.

And releasing those ear-piercing yowls.

"Joan of *freaking* Arc," I mutter, holding tight, waiting until the door is secured behind us before I lower the cat to the floor and release her.

She jumps away from me as though I've committed the worst offense on the planet, yellow-green eyes narrowed, teeth bared, back up.

Then she turns, her tail stiff behind her, and it flicks angrily as she slowly strides away.

"Christ," I mutter, running a hand through my hair,

trying—and failing—to straighten the curls that are always on the wrong side of control.

A soft sigh has me rotating to the right, seeing my little Rapunzel shaking her head, sending *her* hair swooshing behind her. When a strand clings to her cheek, she lifts a hand, pointer finger shaped like a hook, capturing the piece and pulling it away from her face.

She repeats the movement on the other side, and my heart clenches.

I dart out a hand, wrap my fingers around her wrist, turning her palm upward. "This happen when you fell?"

She flinches and...I'm an asshole.

"Sorry," I whisper.

Still. She goes so damned still, brows dragging together, bright blue eyes darting up to meet mine. "It's okay," she whispers back.

I run my thumb lightly over her abused skin. "Did this happen when you fell, Kitten?" I try to moderate my tone, to keep it gentle, to lock down my protectiveness, since she's obviously standing in front of me, safe and whole and *okay*, but it doesn't work. I sound like I'm ready to go out back again and rip that tree apart, literally limb by limb by *fucking* limb.

Her head tilts to the side, hair sweeping behind her again. "I was in the radius of Joan's claws," she says and shrugs. "That's all. I'm fine."

Fucking cat.

"Don't worry," she says, properly interpreting my scowl. She stretches out a hand, gently resting it on my arm. "This is neither the first nor the last time Joan's claws and my skin have become intimately acquainted."

I can't lie.

Hearing *intimately acquainted* slip out from between those plump lips has my dick twitching.

Again.

But that this is the first time she's initiated contact, that she touched me first, doesn't fail to register...or cause more twitching in my pants.

It's barely a touch, but I like it—way too much, considering how messy my life is and how little I know her.

And that we live next door to each other.

And maybe also that she hasn't even given me her name.

She trembles—likely adrenaline letdown from her near miss with the ground—and I exhale silently, try to punch down the raging urge to protect her that showed up the moment I saw her up in that fucking tree.

But it doesn't *want* to stay down.

So, stupid or not, I end up keeping my fingers around her wrist, end up drawing her a little closer, near enough to scent her shampoo, near enough that the silken strands of her hair drift over my bare arm, raising goose bumps on my skin.

"Where's your first aid kit, Kitten?" I ask softly.

Brown brows pulling together to form a vee I want to kiss away. "I don't have a first aid kit."

Christ.

That protectiveness escapes, welling up in the back of my throat, making it hard to think, to breathe, to speak, which is why my next question comes out in a rasp. "Where is your bathroom?"

Bright white teeth in her plump pink bottom lip, worrying it.

I reach forward, press my thumb there, gently tug it free. "Bathroom, Kitten."

Her shoulders rise on a sharp inhalation, drop on the

exhalation. "Up the stairs," she murmurs. "It's the last door on the right."

"Got it."

Those brows start to drag together again, but they don't get all the way there before I'm bending and scooping her up, sending them flying apart in surprise.

"Rome!" she exclaims. "What are you doing?"

I can't answer her, not at first, not because she's heavy—she feels like she weighs nothing as I carry her toward the stairs and then up them—but because her in my arms...it feels right.

There's a part of me that feels as though it's come home.

And after the last few months of upheaval and stress and feeling like a boat that's lost its anchor and is floating adrift in the ocean, that is...unnerving, scary, and...*freaking amazing*.

Then I'm pushing through the last door on the right, skidding to a stop at the sight of a large bed with crisp white linens, a cerulean quilt that reminds me of the color of her eyes folded over the end of the mattress. The vision of crossing to it, of laying her down on the plush surface, stripping her naked, and fucking her senseless has my cock twitching, my mind hazing, but I manage to focus enough to tear my gaze from the bed.

I spot a pair of doors, both slightly ajar, and carry her over to them, poke my head through the first, see that it's an insanely organized closet—so much so, I figure if I turned the lights on, every item would have been color-coded.

But a closet isn't what I'm looking for, even if I *am* tempted to take a peek in her underwear drawer, so I move to the other door, pushing through into the bathroom.

I flick on the lights, blink against the brightness, and take a moment to get my bearings before I settle her on the counter and turn on the water, waiting for it to warm.

"What are you doing?" she whispers.

"Cuts from a cat's claws can get infected if you don't wash them properly," I say, sticking my hand under the water and testing the temperature.

Too hot.

I adjust it then reach over and grab the bottle of hand soap and a washcloth sitting on a folded stack of towels.

Not ideal, but it'll do in a pinch.

I go back to her, check the water temperature again, and find that it's warm, but not too hot.

"Here, Kitten," I order softly. "Put your arm under this."

More brow-pulling, that vee coming back.

But she sticks her hand under the water.

I guide it forward a bit more, making sure the scratches are getting washed out, and she winces. "Sorry, Kitten," I say, rotating her arm, sending water over the other abrasions that were the result of her tree climbing.

Or *falling* because I yelled, rather.

She exhales, but doesn't reply, just cooperates as I spread soap over her skin and gently wash it away.

I wrap the cloth around her forearm then repeat the process on her other side.

"You know, Kitten," I say as I retrieve a second washcloth and pat at her skin, "I still don't know your name."

She stills, eyes coming to mine, blue depths I want to dive into, want to sink to the bottom of and discover all the secrets hidden below.

"What?" I ask, gently peeling both washcloths free.

She shakes her head.

I set the sodden material to the side, study her closely. "Is it a secret?"

A breath. "No," she murmurs, "but it feels like it maybe should be." Half of her mouth hitches up. "Silly, huh?"

Heart squeezing, sense of home growing, I touch her cheek. "No, Kitten."

The other half of her mouth curves, and her eyes go wide in surprise. "No?"

I shrug, tug a lock of her long, brown hair. "My tree-climbing Rapunzel can do what she wants."

Laughter in the air. "You've clearly taken too many pucks to the head."

"Maybe," I tell her with a grin, not able to resist teasing her by adding, "but I'm also not the one who was locked up in her tower with her hair cascading down her back."

"I'll remind you it was a tree!" She shoves lightly at my chest. "*And* I was saving Joan of *freaking* Arc."

"Po-tay-toe," I say, capturing that hand, keeping it pressed to my body. "Po-tah-toe, Kitten."

Her breath slides out in a rush. "You don't know my name, so you're just going to make shit up?"

I nod. "Sometimes the only thing I'm good at is making shit up."

I was going for light, for a self-deprecating jibe at myself.

Instead...my tone is far too fucking dark for that, and it's too fucking bright in this bathroom, the incandescent lights overhead exposing everything.

Her head cocks to the side, seeming to see right through me, and I brace.

Preparing for the probe.

Preparing to give an easy explanation that will settle us right back into the light and easy and teasing.

But she doesn't give me a chance to unleash that, to turn the tone right back to superficial. Instead, she reaches for my hand, lacing our fingers together. "And pretending you're okay until you're not."

I inhale sharply, then something in me unlocks. "And

saying that embracing change is a great growing experience, but really, it's fucking shit."

"Change is the worst," she whispers.

"Unless it involves rescuing a Rapunzel trapped in a tree."

She sighs, rolls her eyes, and starts to push off the counter. "I have some Band-Aids in the linen closet."

"I'll get them."

"It's okay—"

I drop my hand onto her thigh, squeeze lightly. "I'll get them."

"It's fine. I'm—"

"*I'll get them.*"

She sighs again, rolls her eyes again. "Fine," she mutters. "Knock yourself out."

"I will, Kitten."

EIGHT

Chrissy

HE STRIDES across the room after going all caveman.

"Me get bandage," I mutter under my breath in a poor approximation of his voice. "You sit there and stay still like a pretty, pretty princess."

"Like a gorgeous goddess," he says, tossing the words over his shoulder as he opens the door to the linen closet then turns back to survey the contents within.

He snags the cardboard container in his big hand like he's never asked someone where the bottle of ketchup is—even though it's right there in front of his face—then crosses back over to me, pulling open the lid and lining up supplies on the counter like he's a surgeon about to take on a complicated case.

"It's just a couple of scratches," I feel obliged to remind him. "Not skin graft surgery."

His head shoots up, and our eyes connect again, the chocolate brown depths pinning me in place. It's as though I know him, but I don't recall meeting Rome except for today, a few hours ago at the rink. It's weird, though, the sensation of right that settles in my belly. As though my body knows I'm safe with him.

When I don't *know* him.

He can be an ax murderer—

Except, it would be really dumb for him to murder his next-door neighbor, especially when he and I are the only two who live up in this neighborhood, the rest of the houses in our development not yet built.

And it would be even more dumb for him to murder his next-door neighbor who is the daughter of his employer.

And Rome doesn't seem like a dumb man.

In fact, he seems very aware, very in tune, very much... someone I want to know better.

I exhale.

Probably, I feel safe for all of those reasons—my father's protective shield, the panic buttons I have installed in all rooms of my house, the security team ready to respond at any time—and who can get a full background check on anyone. And Rome is a part of my father's business, his public profile as a successful hockey player.

He wouldn't want the extra attention that comes with ax murdering.

Or kidnapping.

I shiver, and...he notices, stilling, our eyes connecting.

"Want to do it yourself?" he asks, lifting up a Band-Aid.

My throat goes tight, heart beating hard once. "I can do it myself."

Fingers on my cheek. "But do you want to?"

I inhale, hold it for long enough that my lungs are burning. Only then do I release it. "No," I whisper.

Those fingers brushing my cheek again.

Then he murmurs, "Okay then."

And it's that easy. I just have to hold still as he puts the bandages on my arms—far too many for the tiny scratches and minimal amount of damage Joan and my fall through the inside of the tree caused. I just have to hold still as he helps me down from the counter.

I just have to hold still when he lifts my arm, lightly presses his lips to my skin.

My heart squeezes, and suddenly, I find this is too much, find that I need to draw back. "Happy now?" I mutter, slipping from his hold.

He slants me a look that has my thighs clenching together—this man who is big and strong and...touches me with gentle hands.

My heart pulses and I exhale softly.

"What is it?" he asks. "What's eating at you?"

I draw in a breath, let it slide out in a thin stream of air. "Nothing."

His brows come up, and he studies me. "Bullshit," he mutters.

Stupid penetrating brown eyes.

I wrinkle my nose.

His mouth quirks up, his hand lifting, brushing a fingertip along the bridge, smoothing out my bunched-up skin with that soft touch. "What is it?" he asks again.

I scowl. "You're pushy, you know that, right?"

He just shrugs. "I am what I am."

"A person who makes shit up?"

He grins. "Nice try reintroducing that to the convo to push me away."

My scowl deepens.

"And yes," he says. "I've had to make up a lot of shit—sound bites for media, saying I'm glad that the conditioning coach is kicking my ass, pretending to be happy about the trade and the"—he does finger quotes—"opportunities it's going to afford me." He taps one of those fingers against my nose, leans back. "But the truth of the matter is that I don't like having to do it. I hate slapping on a smile and making up those sound bites about the Eagles. Which makes me a dick, I know. Because I'm lucky—" He sighs, rubs a hand over his face. "Ignore me."

"No." I reach for him, but he snags the box of Band-Aids and walks to the closet, puts it away on the shelf. "Don't do that," I say softly when he turns around. "You're allowed to resent the change. When I have to let a kitten go, especially one that I've bonded with—"

Like sweet, mischievous Petal.

"—it sucks. Like, a lot." I start to slap on a smile then stop because I don't want to reduce this conversation—perhaps the most honest one I've ever had—to superficial bullshit between two almost strangers.

This is...more.

Different.

And—

"I cry every time," I say. "I'm happy, of course, that they're getting their forever home, but a part of me is tucked away in those cats, especially the ones that are very good at weaving their way into your heart."

"Like Joan of *freaking* Arc," he murmurs, seeing way too fucking much, considering we don't know each other.

"Like Joan." I agree then ask softly, "What about the opportunity of the Eagles is hard to accept?"

He's quiet for a long moment then nods toward the door like he's ready to sprint out of it. "Should we take this out of the bathroom?"

Another squeeze of my heart. "It's okay if you don't want to talk about it."

His big chest expands, and then he exhales in a rush. "I know it sounds hokey and like something out of a sappy movie, but the Gold were the first pro team I played for. They drafted me. They put time and energy—and patience—into developing me. And I don't just mean that the coaches and back office and support staff helped me. My teammates did too. And Brit took me under her wing and—"

I wince.

Because the Bay Area might have a population of more than seven and a half million people, but it seems like everyone knows about the breakup of Brit Plantain and Stefan Barie.

Bay Area royalty.

Going their separate ways.

"Yeah," he says softly, correctly reading my grimace. "I can't imagine what Brit's going through because she worked so hard to make the team like a real family, and now her own has fractured."

"That really sucks."

He brushes back my hair. "Yeah, it does. And that's what makes my trade worse—I'm seeing my family's foundation shudder, and having to leave them behind in order to have a future in the league..." He sighs. "It's not like they don't get it. They're in it. Of course they understand."

I touch his arm. "Of course they do."

"And it's not that I don't want to be successful," he says. "I just...I don't know what the hell I'm supposed to be doing, trying to pull this team together. *How* the hell I'm supposed to be doing it." He shoves a hand through his hair, clenching at the curls then drops it, and I watch him try to put a spin on his emotions. "It'll work out. I know it will. I loved being with the Gold, but there's more to me than just a franchise. I can be successful here, and the team will rally."

But there's something about his tone that tells me he's not so sure about that.

And I don't have the right words to make those worries go away.

So...I nudge his shoulder, start walking toward the bedroom. "You know what I do when I'm not sure what the correct path forward is?"

"What?" he asks, trailing me.

"I go and pet kittens."

NINE

I'M STANDING TOO close to her as she unlocks the heavy glass and metal door, holds it for me, and then hurries over to the keypad to punch in a code.

There's a beep and then she's turning back to me, rocking to a halt, I presume, when she realizes that I'm only a couple of feet behind her. But then her bright blue eyes clear and when they come back to mine, they're sparkling with excitement. "Are you ready?"

I want to see more of that.

More of her.

I want to see the light inside her grow.

Which...has panic slicing through me. But luckily, I don't have time to worry about it because she takes my silence as an answer and pushes through another door and—

"Holy shit," I whisper.

"Close the door behind you, yeah?" she says, stepping further into the space, and doing it carefully.

Because she's surrounded by cats and kittens on all sides, coiling around her ankles, pawing at her leg, meows echoing all over.

"Rome?"

I jump.

"The door?"

"Shit," I mutter, swinging the panel shut, and doing it while having to nudge a couple of the cats back, the bravest ones having left her ankles to come have a sniff at mine. "You know," I say, bending and scratching one of them under the chin, "I still don't know your name."

A soft laugh as she sinks to the floor, kittens rolling and tumbling, jumping and clawing into her lap and up to her shoulders. They're chewing on the strings of her hoodie, batting at her hair, and she loves it.

"Meow?"

I feel tiny paws hit my knee and look down into the face of...fuck. The cutest kitten I've ever seen. Bright white fur. A splotch of orange and gray across its face, curious green eyes.

"Meow."

My mouth twitches. "What's up, kitty cat?"

"Meow!" she yowls and then—

"Whoa!" I say as I topple backward onto my ass, luckily not committing any kitten-cide in the process. The mini cat and her friend immediately pounce, assaulting me with little paws and needle-like claws and tiny bodies.

It's...well, it's pretty fucking cute.

It might be the cutest thing I've ever seen.

"That's Petal," Rapunzel says. "And her sister Rose is the gray tabby trying to gnaw off your knee." A beat. "And *my* name is Christina."

Christina.

I pause, consider that name. It's pretty, but it's...ordinary, and it doesn't seem to fit this interesting, perplexing goddess currently being assaulted by rescue cats.

"I know." She laughs and I jerk my stare up from the hole currently being formed in my sweats to see her smiling widely. "I don't like my name either," she says. "I've always gone by Chrissy. It's less stuffy and ordinary."

"Christina is a pretty name."

"The same pretty name that six girls from my graduating class had," she says with a grin. "Luckily, I've been Chrissy for as long as I remember instead of another Christina D."

"I don't know," I say lightly. "Christina D has a nice ring to it."

She rolls her eyes, cuddles a kitten close. "I prefer Chrissy."

I do too. But she doesn't need to know that. It's her name and she can be called whatever the fuck she wants. Plus, my parents named me Rome, so what room do I have to talk?

"So, do all the cats just stay in this room?" I ask, looking around the space that's open, but also filled with furniture and cat perches, shelves and baskets screwed into the walls. It's like part open-concept house, part office, part kitty heaven with all toys and goodies around.

"We have three rooms, actually," she says, not bothered by the cats' use of her body like a jungle gym. "This room is for socialization, for those cats and kittens who'll soon be adopted."

"Meow?"

She laughs. "Yes, like you, Petal, and your sisters," she says, scratching the kitten between her ears before carefully standing and moving over to me. She plucks Petal from my lap, offers me a hand up. "Want to see what else we do here?"

"THIS IS AMAZING," I murmur as I move through what Chrissy called the Medical Room, this space lined with cages and smaller pens that keep the special needs animals separated as they recover from various ailments and injuries.

"I think so too," Chrissy says, just as quietly, moving to the side when one of the overnight vet technicians moves through the space, running her checks on the animals that need extra help. "This was actually my dad's idea."

"Yeah?"

She nods. "We didn't have the capability to handle cases like this at first. We could get them to a vet, fund hospital care, but we never had enough foster homes to be the go-between between the high-level-care cats and the fosters. Now we have a space for them to recover in peace, and then two step-ups until they're ready to go to homes."

Meaning the other two rooms—the large open space I was first introduced to, and a smaller one for the super shy and scared cats to slowly desensitize to the noises and people they can hear in the front of the center, the workers coming through and doing checks here in the back.

"So," she murmurs, tilting her head toward the exit so we can make our way out of the Medical Room. "That's my entire rescue operation." A beat. "With the exception, of course, of the foster homes and our chain of volunteers who help identify situations where our help is needed."

"Like what?" I ask as we push through to the main room and the cats come running.

"Hoarders are a big operation. But also doing shelter interventions, catching ferals for a spay-and-release. That kind of stuff."

A lot more complicated than I could have imagined.

But I like hearing her talk about it. She's passionate and excited and the way the cats follow her around like she's some

Disney princess and they can understand what she's saying is fucking adorable.

"Anyway," she says, scooping Petal up again, cradling her against her chest, crooning down at her. "Enough talk about cats. It's getting late and I should get you home."

"She's one of the special ones, isn't she?"

Chrissy goes still, her face buried in the top of Petal's head. Then she sighs, cuddles the kitten for one more second, and sets her on the floor. "Yeah," she murmurs. "She is."

A shake of her head.

A soft smile that's laced with sadness.

"But that's the job," she says. "You soak in the happy moments while you can, and then when that time is up, you move forward and find some other way to make new ones."

I look down at the kitten then back up at Chrissy.

And I wonder how often she's shoved down her sadness in lieu of moving forward.

Her words from the bathroom echo through my mind.

Pretending you're okay until you're not.

And I know that this woman with the soft heart for animals and the big dreams for saving the world, one cat at a time, has done it far too fucking often.

TEN

Chrissy

"HEY, KITTEN!" I hear as I'm struggling to move a heavy box of donated supplies.

It's nearly as tall as me—though that's not hard to do—and feels like it's full of bricks.

Though, likely, it's just kitty litter and food.

I'm never entirely sure what these pallets are loaded with, not until I've opened and taken stock of everything, especially when it's from a new donor.

But it's free.

And the cats need it.

So, a little sweat equity is a small price to pay.

Footsteps echo off the concrete, and I release the box I'd been dragging, look over to see Rome easily clear the narrow strip of planter beds between our two driveways, his strong, leanly muscled torso almost at odds with those thick thighs and round ass.

Hockey players.

Swear to God.

The *best* asses.

"Whatcha doing?" he asks as he closes in on me.

Ignoring the pulse between my legs, I lift my brows, jut my chin toward the box. "Moving boxes."

"Moving out?" His question is a little sharp...and maybe a little disappointed.

Or maybe I'm a little delusional.

"No," I say. "Moving supplies in."

His brows pull together then almost immediately smooth back out. "For the kittens."

My lips quirk, and I agree, "For the kittens. Also for our foster families, and the care packages we send home with our newly adopted cats." I tap the side of the box I was struggling with. "We got a huge delivery at the rescue last week, and didn't have room for this stuff there, so my garage is our newest storage unit."

His eyes flick from my open—and thankfully, mostly empty—garage then back to mine. "That's nice of you."

I shrug. "That's the nature of a rescue owner."

"I bet." A flash of a smile. "Want some help?"

"You're offering?" I ask, my brows lifting in disbelief even as my belly warms.

"That's what *want some help* generally means," he points out. But then he pauses, considering. "Why do you sound surprised?"

"Maybe because you're randomly offering to schlep boxes for your neighbor you hardly know?"

He leans an elbow on said box, reclining against it as though he has all the time in the world. "You run a rescue and you're surprised that someone would want to volunteer their help?"

Yes.

Yes, I am.

And maybe I'm mostly surprised that *this* sexy, hockey-playing neighbor of mine would want to help.

Because my father's hockey players...

Well, they leave a lot to be desired in the social nicety department.

A few are okay.

The rest...well, let me just say, an eagerness to volunteer to help me move shit wouldn't be high on their priority list.

Something he seems to read on my face, since he nudges the box, says, "It'll take me five minutes." A beat. "Consider it repayment for the kitten time last night."

My heart squeezes, and I remember his concern when I fell from the tree, his gentle touch when he bandaged my cuts, his lost expression in the bathroom, how patient he was later with the fluffy terrors. A nice man, clearly, and one with a big heart. But I still feel obliged to point out, "Your season is starting soon. Don't you need to keep your body in prime hockey-playing condition?"

One half of his mouth quirks up, and fuck, that's sexy. "Consider it my off-ice training for the day."

And then he picks up the box as though it's filled with feathers, tilts his head toward the garage. "Just tell me where you want it, Kitten."

Against the garage wall.

On the hood of my car.

The bathroom counter.

From behind, my knees perched on the edge of the mattress.

"Chrissy?"

I blink, realize I'm standing there, staring at his fucking perfect, hockey-playing ass. He's brought the box into my garage, but stopped on the threshold, gaze coming back to mine.

The other half of his mouth quirks up.

"Along the far wall," I manage to rasp out.

"Anything you want, Kitten."

And then he turns for the far side of the garage, giving me another glimpse of that glorious ass...

And the notion that I so totally have the hots for my next-door neighbor.

IT'S LATER that week before I see Rome again.

Not that I've been watching for him (lies).

I've been busy with my own life (more lies).

I haven't had time to look for his car in the driveway, or the lights on in his kitchen—its window mirroring mine—or to search for his yummy hockey body sitting on his back deck, eyes on the sky as he watches the stars overhead (even more lies).

In fairness, the rescue—and Petal—*have* taken up a lot of my time, and that, along with working with the training staff to review conditioning programs, means that I've been pulling long hours (the first truth in this delusional conversation with myself).

But in all that time at the rink, I haven't seen Rome.

Not that I was looking for him (back to lies).

Still, we're both home today, and I'm—

Staring.

I shake myself, realize the garage door has finished opening, and tear my eyes from Rome holding a shovel, digging in the planter bed, to pull inside. I grab my stuff, get out.

But I don't go directly into the house like I typically do.

I linger, trying to find some reason to go and talk to him.

I just...I don't have one.

Maybe I can bring him a bottle from my father's winery as a thanks for moving those boxes?

He seems like a beer guy. What if he doesn't drink wine?

I guess I could offer to cook him dinner?

No, that's a dangerous proposition. I can do a lot of things, but actually creating something palatable in the kitchen isn't in my skillset.

Okay, so what?

He just moved in—maybe a house-warming gift of some kind?

Only...what would I even bring him?

A cranky senior cat?

"Jesus, Chrissy," I mutter, turning for the door to the house. "Enough." But the moment I grip the handle, determined to get on with my evening, I hear—

"*Fuck!*"

I don't think, just drop my purse to the concrete step, shove my phone in the pocket, and run out into the driveway.

Then stop.

Because...I can't quite believe what I'm seeing.

Water is shooting out of the planter bed—a huge geyser reaching for the clouds in the sky—and Rome...well, Rome is standing beneath that stream, soaking wet. His white T-shirt is almost see-through and plastered against his chest, his jeans sopping, clinging to those strong thighs.

I skid to a stop, feeling the mist of the water on my cheeks, mouth falling open, pussy going slick.

Fucking gorgeous.

Fucking *trouble.*

"Fuck!" he says again, finally moving, bending for the earth, for the source of that stream of water.

I unstick. "Rome?" I call over the din.

He jerks, eyes coming to mine.

"Are you okay?"

His curls are plastered to his forehead. "No, Kitten. I'm not okay."

"Did you—?" A shake of my head. "Were you—?"

He shoves a hand down, only succeeds in spraying more water into his face. "Was I what?" he manages to ask with remarkable calm.

"I just..." I bite my lip as his shirt creeps up, revealing a narrow strip of naked skin, then I manage to get it together. "Are you going to shut off the water?"

"I would," he says, still wrestling with the gushing water. "If I knew where that was."

"I know where it is."

A slow blink, a drop of water sliding down his temple, catching in the strands of his beard.

God, he's pretty.

He lifts a dripping brow. "Want to tell me where it is?"

I jerk. "Oh. Right."

That would be helpful.

I dodge around the water, that mist clinging to my cheeks, my hair, my nose, then hurry down the path, stopping at the box buried just to the right of his driveway.

A mirror image to the box on *my* property.

I pull open the lid, reach inside for the valve, tugging... but unable to move it. I wrap my fingers a little more firmly, tug again, then gasp when a warm—and wet arm—shifts past mine, wrenching the handle up.

There's a *whoosh* and then...

The spray stops.

Silence except for the sound of water still flowing down the driveway, draining off into the street, the drips falling from Rome's body, his hair, his clothes to the concrete beside me.

One lands on my head and I jump.

"Sorry," he murmurs, straightening and rubbing a hand over his face.

"It's okay." I try—and I'm not sure I succeed—to keep my eyes on his as I ask, "What were you doing?"

He sighs, shoves that hand through his hair, sending curls every direction. "Trying to find the broken sprinkler line."

Oh.

My lips twitch.

"Well," I say. "I think you found it."

"Yeah, Kitten." He smirks. "I'd say so."

We stand there for a minute before he sighs, nods toward his garage. "I should get to the hardware store, grab the stuff to fix that water line before it gets completely dark."

"Yeah." I start to walk by him but pause when I see those droplets cascading down his face.

And *that's* when I do something stupid.

I wipe away one that's dripping down his cheek.

He stills.

I still.

Hot brown eyes. Gorgeous body I want to stroke.

"Kitten."

Focus.

I swallow, whisper, "Can I get you a towel?"

He shifts, body coming closer, hand settling on my waist, the damp heat of his palm soaking through the material of my clothes, sinking into my skin. Water droplets hit my shirt, my hair, my...lips.

"I'd rather *you* be my towel," he murmurs.

I would like that.

I would very much like that.

In fact, I open my mouth to tell him exactly that—

When my phone rings...

With my father's ringtone.

And if anything could suck the desire out of this moment, it's a phone call from my dad.

Damn.

I slide back a step, pull my cell from my pocket. "I have to get this."

Blazing brown eyes on mine.

Then he nods, blows out a breath, mouth hitching up on one corner. "Thanks for the assist, Kitten."

I bob my head and hurry away, swiping a finger across the screen and answering my father's call.

"Hey, Dad," I say as I snag my things from the garage, hit the button to close the door behind me.

And then I listen to him give a rundown of his day.

And then I give him a rundown of mine.

And *then* I get talked into dinner and staying at his place again.

As the sun sets and I back out of my garage, my overnight bag in the passenger's seat—Joan's carrier safely buckled into the back seat—I catch a glimpse of that strong, hockey-playing body as Rome fixes his sprinkler line.

Then I think of what my dad would do if he found out I had the hots for one of his hockey players.

And sigh.

Then attempt to put Rome Dawson out of my mind.

Because...

Not for me.

ELEVEN

Rome

"YEAH, YEAH!" I call as I streak toward the net, cutting hard, trying hard to get open for the pass.

Which is the precise moment I make my first mistake.

I take my eyes off the asshole in front of me—just for a heartbeat—and glance to my right, checking the lane, trying to make sure my timing is right.

Perfect.

Kingston's there, big body moving fast.

I look back—

"*Fuck,*" I say, slamming on the brakes.

But it's too late.

Pat's stopped, dropped his shoulder, braced his body, and the huge fucking defenseman is grinning.

Just fucking *waiting* to lay me out.

Even though it's practice and we're teammates, and, really, we shouldn't be doing open ice hits on each other because...

It's fucking *practice.*

And we're teammates.

And it's unnecessarily dangerous.

But—

It's happening.

"Fuck!" I groan as our bodies make contact, as Pat's much bigger, much better prepared for said contact frame collides with mine, laying me the *fuck* out.

My only consolation is that I manage to stay on my feet long enough to ensure he goes down with me.

But I still get the worst of it, the impact shooting through my limbs and torso in a painful rush, stealing all of the air from my lungs. I fall backward to the ice—hitting ass to head—all of it hurting, but most especially my ass.

And my ego.

And my ass.

Whistles blow.

Coach starts yelling.

"—it's not my fault Golden Boy can't stay on his feet!" Pat yells, pushing himself up onto his skates.

If I had any air in my lungs, I would snipe back. Unfortunately, I'm just trying to regain control of my breathing when Kingston skates over and extends his hand. "Easy, man," he mutters, all but hauling me upright.

"Pat's...a...fucking...asshole," I gasp out.

"Yup," King says, still muttering, but this time giving me a nudge alongside it, sending me back towards the lines of skaters who are waiting to take their turn at the drill. "Pat *is* a fucking asshole." He nods toward the line nearest the boards, the one he'd been in before, then hops in front of the center line—the one *I'd* been in—indicating with a jerk of his chin that I should cut too.

Cool, cool.

My lungs are barely working and my body feels like I got run over by a freight train, but I'll jump right back into the drill.

Good times.

"Let's go again!" King yells, cutting off Pat's bitching, nodding at me to scoop up the puck, and taking off down the ice.

I grit my teeth, snag that puck, and get my ass in gear.

Down along the boards, beating the player between me and the net, cutting in, looking for that pass across.

Almost, almost—

There!

I flick my wrists, send the puck flying, and—

Boom!

Kingston makes it clear he doesn't give one fuck about my pass.

It sails right on by as he drops his shoulder and rocks Pat with a hit that's hard enough to make everyone on the rink freeze.

Then wince.

Then, *"Oooh!"*

The collective groan fills the air, but King doesn't acknowledge it, just scoops the puck up, skates around Pat—prone on the ice and groaning like a little bitch who can dish it out but can't take it—then buries the puck in the back of the net.

Ignoring Coach's renewed yelling, King skates my direction, lifts his fist for me to bump.

"Enough of this asshole's shit," he says. "Let's fucking go, yeah?"

Something settles in me for the first time since the trade.

Because I think...maybe we can do this.

That *I* can do this.

I nod, bump my fist against his. "Yeah, let's fucking go."

I WINCE as I stretch my legs out in front of me, body sore and aching, my ass throbbing.

The only consolation is that Pat was moving just as carefully as he undressed after practice, the hit he took from King clearly continuing to punish him.

Couldn't happen to a nicer guy.

Which is probably why I'm not all that wrapped up in the fact that every part of my body is still hurting.

I'm more focused on the fact that I haven't had any more surprises over the last week—neither in the form of broken water lines nor sexy neighbors falling out of trees.

In fact, I haven't seen Chrissy at all.

She's been busy with her rescue, I suppose, and, for my part, it's always fucking nuts being a hockey player this time of year—all the extra off- and on-ice training to get ready for the season, a heavy practice schedule, meetings with our coaches and back-office staff, everyone from trainers to equipment guys to the social media team.

Long days.

An exhausting push.

And all the while, trying to get ready for the truly exhausting part—eighty-two games and four rounds of playoffs.

My phone buzzes, and I glance down at the screen, at the pictures popping up in the Gold group chat.

Brit and Roxie, hanging out, eating banana splits at the team's preseason barbeque, a soccer game happening in the background. Players and their significant others, their kids, all just hanging out, enjoying a warm summer evening.

I should be there.

I was invited, had planned to go.

But...something kept me here—maybe it was King joining me running stairs after practice, shooting the shit for a couple of minutes afterward while we both decided that cardio is the worst sort of evil.

Maybe it was—

Screech!

I glance to the side, see Chrissy walk out onto the back deck next door.

Maybe it was a certain brunette goddess who gently brushed water from my cheeks and who has the most kissable mouth I've ever seen.

She strides to the railing, rests her hands there, and looks up at the sky.

I watch her shoulders rise and fall on a breath, my own breath catching as I witness the tension leaves her body.

Then she turns and startles when she spots me, her gasp of surprise reaching my ears.

I push up slowly. "Sorry, Kitten," I call. "I didn't mean to scare you."

She's so still that for a long moment I think she's not going to unstick.

But then she does. "Rome," she says, her voice barely audible. "I'm sorry. I didn't see you there."

That much is obvious.

Only...I can't help but think it's more than her just being startled.

"You have a good week?" I ask instead of probing there. She's far enough away that I can't really see her face, and... honestly?

I know I haven't earned the right *to* push this.

Not yet.

My fingers tighten around my bottle of beer. Determination blooms in my belly.

Not. *Yet.*

"My week's been good," she says. "Busy with the rescue and stuff for the team." Her smile is a flash of white. "But you'd know something about that too, wouldn't you?"

I grin. "Just a little bit."

She laughs.

I laugh.

And then I find that I'm just staring at her, committing her face to memory in the waning sunshine, trying to think of something to say.

Anything to say.

Anything to keep her out here.

With me.

"How's Joan?"

She walks closer, footsteps quiet as she approaches the railing, leans on it, and smiles over at me. "Cranky as ever."

I chuckle.

"And your water line?"

"Not leaking."

Her eyes dance with mirth. "That's good."

More silence, long enough that she turns to look out at the canyon, that the whistle of the wind rises up to fill the quiet between us.

I feel like I'm standing on a precipice.

Stay quiet. Let her go about her evening.

Or—

"You hungry?" I blurt, and watch as her head jerks, turning my way, her expression filled with surprise.

Or...find a way to spend more time with her.

Find out what makes her smile and laugh and *burn.*

Earn that right to learn each and every one of her secrets.

"Yes," she says, seeming to surprise herself.

My heart kicks into overdrive, but I try to keep my tone even. "Well, I've got a shit ton of snacks inside"—because I'd planned on going to that barbeque and my contribution was going to be everything salty, fatty, and carb-loaded (fatten 'em up, slow 'em down, and maybe the Eagles would have a shot at beating the Gold, muahaha)—"and I'm more than willing to share."

She pauses, eyes on me, and I wait for her to decline.

Wait for her to say *anything* as the moments tick by.

Her gaze slides from mine down to my hand clenching my bottle of beer. "I'm afraid my pantry is pathetically empty, so I can't top that offering—"

I open my mouth to tell her that doesn't matter.

"—but my wine fridge is full."

My teeth click together.

Then I grin.

"Grab a bottle, Kitten."

TWELVE

Chrissy

MY HEART IS POUNDING as I walk through the gate that Rome's propped open, carrying a bottle of wine and two glasses.

I wasn't lying about my pantry being empty.

Nor my wine fridge being full.

I'd been planning on ordering something in—and pretending to adult by doing some grocery shopping tomorrow—and instead...I'm walking up the stairs onto Rome's back deck, setting the bottle and glasses down as he emerges from inside, his arms laden with snacks.

A *shit ton* of snacks.

Bags of chips, a bakery container of brownies, candy, cupcakes, pretzels.

"Christ," I mutter. "How are you in the shape you're in with that amount of shit in your cupboards?"

He freezes.

Then smirks. "You like my body, Kitten?"

Heat floods my cheeks, but I can't think of a quick response.

Because I *do* like his body.

"*Um...*" I murmur.

"That's a yes," he says with a cocky smile.

"Oh please," I manage to say—even though I'm melting a little inside.

That confidence on him is beyond sexy.

He drops the snacks onto the table, comes close. "I like *your* body," he murmurs, and as that's settling between my legs, he straightens away from me, tone turning casual. "Just in case you were wondering." Then he points to the bottle I'm clutching like a lifeline. "Want me to open that wine, Kitten?"

Wine. Junk food. A hockey hottie.

This is a dangerous combination, and I know I'm playing with fire.

Fraternizing with one of my father's players.

Flirting with the hot hockey player next door.

Part of me wants to retreat, wants to run home, wants to grab Joan, go back to my dad's, and hide out.

Where it's safe and comfortable and *familiar*.

But the rest of me doesn't want to allow fear to take over, allow the memories of the past to draw me back, suck me under.

I'm beyond that.

Or maybe it's just that I want something different.

Something *more*.

So, instead of retreating, I nod at Rome. "Wine and snacks please."

His mouth curves, and he slips the bottle from my grip, pulls an opener from his pocket—a good thing because I've left mine back at my place.

"Snacks, Kitten," he orders softly, tilting his head at the table as he gets to work on the wine, cutting through the foil, starting in on the cork.

Brownies.

Yes, I definitely want a brownie. Or six.

And a cupcake.

And one of those cake cookie things with the pink frosting and sprinkles.

Because...sprinkles.

But I manage to restrain myself—somewhat—as I grab two brownies and a cupcake.

And a cookie.

Then Rome is handing me a glass of wine, settling into the chair next to mine, not shy in the least as he starts in on the chips.

Salt to my sweet.

I...like that.

What I *don't* like is the way he winces as he finds his seat, the soft grunt of pain as he leans back into the chair.

"What's hurting?" I ask, concern rippling in my belly.

He snags another handful of chips. "Is this question from an Eagles employee who can affect my game play?" His brows lift. "Or from my concerned next-door neighbor whose cat I saved?"

I wrinkle my nose. "I'll just remind you that Joan and I were perfectly fine until you nearly sent us toppling from the tree."

His mouth tips up. "I stand by my statement." A flick of his brows. "And my question."

I sigh, shake my head. "From your next-door neighbor," I say. "Who happens to have a degree that can help with your soreness."

Rome studies me, those deep brown eyes almost black in the fading light. "Pat took a cheap shot at me on the ice."

I pause, wineglass positioned near my mouth. "Anything serious?"

He sighs, shakes his head. "Just bruises and sore muscles. I'll be good in the morning."

My glass hits the table with a soft *plink*. "What hurts the most?"

Still again.

Rome goes very still.

I expect him to be stubborn. To ignore me. To dismiss my question and go back to wine and snacks.

But he doesn't.

He glances over at me with a bemused smile. "Pushy."

"It's my—"

"Job," he finishes for me. "Yeah, Kitten, I get that." He sets the chips down, points to his back. "Here," he says. "It's sore the worst right here."

My phone rings, and I reach into my pocket, silence it.

"Do you—?" He nods at my cell.

"No," I say, pushing out of my chair, moving over to him. "Lean a little more forward," I order, lightly palpating the taut muscles on either side of his spine. He hisses out a breath—

Just as my phone rings again.

With my dad's tone.

The universe reminding me this is a bad idea.

But I still don't pick it up or go home.

Instead, I silence it a second time, dig my fingers into Rome's back, pressing, searching, and—

He curses.

Freezes.

Then lets out a relieved sigh. "Jesus, Kitten, you have magic fingers or something?"

I grin, coax him to sit back. "I'll grab you an ice pack and heat pad. I want you to alternate between the two."

"I'm fine—"

But I'm already moving—down the stairs, through the gate, zipping into my house and grabbing the necessary gear. I pop the rice-filled heating pad into my microwave for a few seconds, knowing that the long-lasting warmth will soothe some of that tension in his spine, then fill a bag with ice.

Less than five minutes later, I'm back through the gate, settling the now warm pad on the spot he needs it the most, plunking the bag of ice on the table for the switch in twenty.

My phone buzzes as I sit back down.

Sighing, I pull it out, knowing it's a text from my father, knowing that he won't be happy after the two missed calls.

And sure enough, just the preview of his message on the screen makes that clear.

Check in.

I bite back another sigh, type a reply.

I'm good. Just busy. Talk later.

"You don't have to hang around," Rome says, making me jerk, making me realize that I'm staring at my phone like it's a cobra instead of partaking in wine and junk food. "If you need to go, feel free to go, Kitten." He smiles. "I'll even send you off with snacks."

"It's just my dad," I tell him. "He's more than a little over-protective."

Rome's brows flick up, probably because my tone is bordering on miserable. "Want to talk about that?"

I force a laugh and sit back, taking a glug of wine. "God, no."

"Want to eat snacks and get drunk and talk about bad TV shows instead?"

More laughter sneaking off my tongue, only it's real this time.

I hold up my glass. "That sounds perfect."

He clinks his wineglass against mine, asks me about a trash TV show the entire world seems to be focused on right now.

And then it *is* perfect—sitting on his deck, eating junk food, drinking my father's wine, watching the sky grow dark overhead.

Making sure he swaps the heating pad for the ice pack.

And then ice for heat again.

Finishing the bottle of wine and feeling that pleasant haze of drinking just a little too much.

Sitting there with my belly full of brownies and cookies and cupcakes and a few handfuls of ranch-flavored chips (clearly the best flavor, even if Rome doesn't agree).

I'm tempted to go home and snag another bottle when my timer goes off, signaling the return to ice on his sore muscles.

I get up, wavering the slightest bit as I snag the bag from the table, shift it to his back.

Only I move a little too fast.

And I've drunk a bit too much wine.

And I...

Somehow end up in Rome's lap.

"Oof," he grunts quietly, hands going to my hips, catching me before I slide off and hit the deck.

"Shit," I say, pushing against his chest, grip loosening on the bag, sending it down to the wooden planks. "I'm sorry. I—"

But his fingers tighten, staying me when I would have pulled away.

Hard, hot man.

A firm, but confident hold.

Spice and male in my nose.

Curls that I want to run my fingers through.

He slides his hand up my side, and my breath hitches. "Rome."

It's a plea—I know it is.

It's fucking dumb—of course it is.

But I can't stop myself, same as I can't stop myself from leaning close, from feeling the heat of his breath on my lips.

"So fucking pretty," he murmurs, cupping my jaw, tilting my face, bringing our mouths a mere millimeter apart.

I want him to kiss me.

I'm almost desperate for it.

And then...my phone rings.

"Fuck," he growls, hand on my waist tightening.

"Ignore it," I murmur, reaching down, silencing my father's call, and leaning even closer.

His hand on my jaw shifts to my hair, fingers tangling in the strands. His lips press to mine, the barest featherlike touch, and—

My phone rings again.

He curses again, hand tightening for a heartbeat.

Then he sighs, fingers slipping out of my hair, hand dropping to my side. "I think you'd better take that call, Kitten."

I don't want to.

Like really, *really* don't want to.

But...

My father isn't going to stop.

"I'm sorry," I whisper. "My dad..."

Rome's mouth curves into a half smile, half grimace. "I can't say that I love the interruption"—he cups my jaw for the barest moment—"but we have time."

I inhale sharply.

"And," he says softly, "I've learned that you should soak in all the time you can with the people you love."

My heart squeezes. "Rome—"

But there my phone goes again, and this time, he moves, setting me back onto my feet, taking my hand and walking me down to the open gate between our houses.

"I'll wash the glasses, bring them over."

I like the idea of him coming back to my house, so I don't argue that I can wash them myself. "Thanks," I murmur instead, and then hesitate for a second, feeling suddenly awkward.

Luckily, my phone ringing—*a-fucking-gain*—solves that for me.

"Bye, Rome," I whisper, extracting it from my pocket, hurrying through the gate, up onto my deck.

"Kitten?" he calls as I reach the top step.

I pause, glance back. "Yeah?"

"I know you raided your physical therapist supplies for me"—a nod to the heating pad, the ice pack on his table—"but did you get yourself a first aid kit yet?"

My heart skips a beat.

He remembers that?

"Chrissy?" he presses when I don't immediately answer.

I shake my head in reply.

His eyes lock with mine, and I squirm, just a little.

Because I really should know better.

But before I can tell him I'll pick one up during my adulting tomorrow, my phone goes off again.

"Answer that phone, baby."

"I—"

He reaches for the gate, starts to swing it shut.

"Goodnight, Kitten."

I'M HALF-ASLEEP as I stumble out to my car the next morning—my coffee clenched in my hand like the lifeline it is—and hit the button to open the garage door.

I need to stop by the rescue center to check on the cats—and Petal. Then I have a meeting with my dad, and after that I'll spend my day reviewing the reports the team's trainers have put together for injured or rehabbing players and coming up with plans for those who aren't injured but need a little extra help.

If I'm being truthful, I don't mind that part of working with my dad.

I like the body—learning how to move it properly, understanding how to build muscle and endurance and power.

It's part of what gave me back *my* power.

It's why I got my degree in kinesiology in the first place, harnessing that strength, doing something positive with it.

I like watching the way the guys move on the ice and in the weight room, clocking stiffness or a lack in mobility, favoring one side.

All the little pieces that can be tweaked to make for a better quality of life.

Or better players, as is critically important to my dad and the coaches and the GM.

All of which means I have a job and an office at the practice facility, along with one at the arena itself. And I have people to help. I can work and do something that makes me happy while giving me enough to live on, and then I can use my trust fund to keep running rescue centers.

Technically, I could live off my trust fund *and* pay for rescue centers if I really wanted to.

I've always known that was an option (albeit not one I'd take).

Unfortunately, I wasn't the only one who knew about my father's money.

Nightmares and fear.

Bobby and his—

I exhale, shake off that old, creeping, poisonous shit, set my coffee in the cupholder, and start to climb in the driver's seat.

Then stop.

Because something's caught my eye.

I glance behind my car—or well, to the opposite side of it, to the planter box sitting next to the far corner of my garage.

"What the—?"

I get out, round the hood and hesitantly approach the bag sitting on the edge of that flower-filled planter.

Peek inside.

And feel something deep inside me melt...

As I pull out a small, red first aid kit.

FINDING the proper spot to stow my new first aid kit means that I'm now running late, and I only get limited cuddle time with Petal after I finish with my other responsibilities—one of which is helping coordinate some resources with my best friend Aurora's dog rescue organization.

Limited cuddle time is probably for the best because it'll only be a couple more weeks before Petal's off to a new home, so I shouldn't get too attached.

Of course, it's too late for that.

But...life.

And, anyway, Petal and my heart aside, I need to help

Rory. She called me in a panic this morning after her crew showed up at a hoarder property and stumbled upon dozens of cats and kittens in various states of need.

Heartbreaking—for the owner and the animals who dealt with living in that state.

Now, though, we've gotten creative with my space and several others within driving distance, and the cats and kittens (and puppies and dogs) are on their way to a better future.

And...I'm slurping microwaved coffee as I rush into the arena, digging into my purse again, fingers searching for the edge of my notebook, just grasping the metal spiral edge when—

"Kitten—"

Slam.

My coffee goes flying. My purse flops down my shoulder to my wrist.

But this time when I crash into the big, broad body of a hockey player, I don't freeze, seeing the concrete floor sweeping up toward my face, anticipating the inevitable pain of impact.

Nope. This time, I'm drawn to a halt right away by a pair of strong hands.

And I'm back on my feet a heartbeat later.

"Shit, Kitten," Rome mutters, "we have to stop meeting like this."

"I know," I whisper. "I'm so sorry."

I'm safe—thankfully without the side of face meets pavement—though I can't say the same of my coffee.

Or the floor.

The lid of my travel mug has busted off and the silver metal is sitting in a puddle of milk-loaded coffee.

"Dammit," I mutter. "I need to grab some paper towels.

Can you stay here and make sure no one slips until I get back with them?"

He tilts his head to the side, studying me closely. "Are you late?"

I frown. "What?"

"You were rushing. Was it because you're late, Kitten?"

I don't know why the answer to this question is so important to him, but I find myself nodding. "Yeah," I whisper. "I'm late for a meeting."

His fingers brush my cheek. "Then go," he says, nudging me forward. "I'll get this mopped up."

"I can't have you cleaning up after me," I whisper.

"*Go*, Kitten."

"I—"

My phone buzzes, and I know—*know*—it's a message from my dad, asking where the hell I am.

And because one of Rome's hands is on my arm, I know he feels it too.

"Go," he orders gently. "I've got you."

"I—"

But I can tell by the flex of his jaw, the stubbornness in his eyes that this is like that first night with the bandages. Me insisting I'm fine, him not going to allow me to help him. Not going to do anything except continue asserting I hurry along.

And...I *am* late.

And...I don't want my dad coming to track me down and stumbling upon Rome and I standing close, looking chummy.

Jean-Michel Dubois isn't exactly reasonable when it comes to me and the opposite sex—something I get. But Rome is nice and he's...well, *nice*. I don't want him to get onto my dad's bad side, not with him already worrying about his place here on the team, and—

Well, I guess part of me just wants to keep his *nice* between him and I for the moment.

"Thank you for the first aid kit," I say instead of continuing to argue with him about cleaning up my mess.

He tugs a strand of my hair. "My gorgeous goddess needs to make sure she has the proper supplies on hand."

My mouth quirks up. "For all my Rapunzel-like hair?"

He winks. "How else am I going to climb it in order to rescue you from treetops and cranky cats?"

"I don't know"—I tap my lip—"I suppose I can save myself." A beat. "*And* my scalp."

He grins, leaning in so closely that I can feel his breath on my lips, can feel the heat of his body radiating through my clothes. "I want to kiss you right now."

I inhale sharply. "*Rome.*"

He touches my cheek. "But I'm going to be good and clean up your coffee after I send you off to your meeting, and when I bring you a refill in a couple of hours—after I've finished my workout—I'm going to taste you, Kitten. I'm going to taste those lips and that mouth and that coffee on your tongue."

Heat blooms in my belly, gathers between my thighs. "R-Rome."

He leans in, nuzzles my throat, tongue flicking out, raising goose bumps on my flesh.

My knees shake and I have to lock them in order to stay upright, but I don't lose myself, don't lose the parts that make me...*me.*

I rise on tiptoe, cup a hand over the back of his neck, brushing my fingers through the curls there—curls that feel like silk, and whisper into his ear. "What if I want you to taste me all over?"

Still.

His big body goes so still.

Then he growls, "*Fuck*."

I shiver, fingers tightening in those curls, wanting to keep him close, but then he's stepping back, pulling out of my hold, his eyes molten, warning in their warm brown depths. "Dangerous woman."

I grin.

He bends so his words are damp puffs of hot air against my skin. "But you should know," he rumbles, tongue flicking out and making me gasp, "curious pussies get pet."

I shiver. I would like to be pet by him, by those thick, blunt fingers. I would like that very much.

"And eventually, Kitten, I *am* going to taste every inch of you."

THIRTEEN

Rome

I KNOCK on the open door and watch Chrissy's head pop up, her eyes a little unfocused, until she blinks, shakes her head slightly, and then...

Then she smiles.

My heart thuds hard against my rib cage and I'm thankful that I didn't ask one of the guys where her office was, that I used my sneaky skills to suss it out.

Last thing I need is my teammates seeing me staring at a woman dopily and giving them more fuel to be assholes.

Because team bonding is going great.

Which is why Duncan and Pat almost came to blows again because they both wanted to use the same set of fucking dumbbells.

So goddamned stupid.

But I got my workout in, made sure they didn't take their stupidity out on Cam by working out with the young'un.

Now, though, I've scoped out the location of Chrissy's

office (okay, fine, I asked one of the girls who works in maintenance), washed and refilled her travel mug, and tried to match the color of the coffee I'd mopped up from the floor by adding copious amounts of milk (hence me meeting the girl from maintenance), and...I'm here.

Watching her smile at me.

Feeling my heart roll over in my chest.

"Rome," she says. "What are you doing here?"

"I told you I'd bring you a refill."

Her...face. *Fuck.*

Yeah, I like how soft it goes when she looks at me, like I've both surprised her and touched her someplace deep inside.

And that's where she's touching me.

Or where I want to be touching her—deep and hard and fast.

Heh.

Which—

Right. *Focus.*

Especially because she's now looking at me like I've lost my mind—probably because I'm standing there like an idiot, staring at her.

"Did you...want to come in?" she asks after a moment.

Yup. *Definitely* staring like an idiot.

But—

"Are you okay?" she asked.

"Just stunned still by a beautiful woman," I blurt. Like an idiot.

"I don't know about beautiful," she murmurs as I finally push off the door frame and get my shit together enough to walk into the office, to close the wooden panel behind me.

"*I* do," I say.

She rolls her eyes. "You think you're smooth, don't you?"

"No, I know I'm not smooth." I hold up the mug. "I just know how to bribe a beautiful woman with caffeine."

A flash of bright white teeth, and then she's closing the folder she'd been reviewing, pushing back her chair, rounding the desk until she's a foot away from me. "You really didn't have to bring me coffee," she says. "Especially because it was my fault for trying to take you out."

I lift one shoulder, drop it. "I probably deserved it."

She laughs, leans back against the edge of her desk. "Oh, I know how you hockey players roll. You *definitely* deserved it."

"Rude. Maybe I'll just drink this coffee I so generously brought." I raise the mug like I'm going to take a sip, even though I can't stand coffee with milk in it.

Black, all the way, baby. None of that dairy shit to water down the flavor.

"No!" she gasps, leaning forward and reaching for the carafe. "I am so very thankful for the caffeine sustenance you've brought me. I will be *forever* grateful."

I waggle my brows. "And how will you show that gratitude?"

I'm going for cheesy, but somehow it comes out...

More.

Especially when her cheeks flare bright pink, and she bites her bottom lip, eyes going molten.

"Kitten?" I ask.

More pink. More heat. "I might have a few ideas."

Need arrowing for my dick, but I don't get out *my* ideas—or discover hers—because then she's closing the gap between us, her body brushing mine.

And my brain shuts down.

Or my big one, anyway.

My little one has many, *many* thoughts.

Including bending Chrissy over her desk, tugging off those tight black slacks of hers, and giving her tempting ass a paddle until it's as red as her cheeks.

"Drink your coffee," I rasp, shoving the mug at her. "And stop trying to get us both in trouble at work."

She gladly takes it, lifts it to her lips and downs a sip, finishing with a soft moan that does nothing to soothe the ache in my dick. "*Ah.*" She sets it on her desktop. "That's really good. How did you know how I take my coffee?"

"If I tell you all my secrets then I'll just be a boring hockey player."

She tilts her head to the side. "I don't think you could ever be boring, Rome."

I cross my arms. "Try me, Kitten."

"What have you been doing the last week?"

"Besides gorging on snacks and wine?" I wink at her. "And before that, fixing my water line? And before *that,* rescuing a Rapunzel and her cat from her tower?"

"Technically," she says, swinging out a hand, nearly knocking over a picture frame sitting on her desk, "it was a tree, not a tower. And second, as I've mentioned, I didn't *need* rescuing. If you hadn't distracted me, I would have been in and out—or up and down—that tree in seconds."

"Yeah?"

She narrows her eyes at me. "*Yeah.*"

"Did you forget I saved you and Joan?"

More glaring. "I haven't forgotten that you also were responsible for me nearly slipping out of the tree in the first place."

I grin. "Are you this argumentative always, and I just saw the sweet side of Chrissy the other nights we spent together? Or is it because you haven't had your coffee yet?" I snag her to-go mug up and hold it out to her again. "Need another hit of the caffeinated stuff?"

Her bottom lip sticks out, but I don't miss that she grabs the carafe. "I always need coffee," she grumbles. "I *live* for coffee, and yeah, maybe my dad says it makes me palatable for human consumption." A breath before she takes a big glug. "But mostly I'm annoyed because I fell from that damn tree in the first place. I shouldn't have."

I tilt my head to the side. "Why?"

A sigh, but she doesn't it hold back. "I've been climbing for years," she says. "I've practiced and practiced with my coach and—" She shakes her head. "Ignore me."

"What?" I ask softly, cupping her jaw.

"I thought I could do it," she whispers. "I've climbed routes that scared the shit out of me, that were so freaking hard I thought I couldn't do it...and then I nearly fell out of a stupid tree."

"It *is* fair to say I distracted you," I murmur. "And Joan too."

"I know." She wrinkles her nose and seems to shake off her irritation. "Sorry," she says. "I know it's ridiculous, to care about something like this."

"You're talking to a man who makes his living shooting tiny discs of vulcanized rubber around the ice to win a giant silver cup. I get what it feels like to be competitive, to want to do well at something for no reason other than just wanting to do your best."

She softens, lips turning up at the edges. "Yeah," she teases lightly. "I know you and you stick slinging buddies know *all* about being competitive for no reason."

"Well," I say. "It *is* for my name to be engraved on that silver cup."

"You have it on there once already, don't you?"

"Twice," I say, barely resisting the urge to puff up my chest.

Something she evidently picks up on, considering how her smile grows. "Twice," she repeats. "So, why do you need to get it on there a third time?"

I flick my brows up. "Do you ever climb the same mountain more than once?"

"I don't really do mountains," she says. "I just like to get out on local spots, to challenge myself on the routes around home."

"So, do you ever do those routes more than once?"

I know I've caught her because her cheeks go pink again. "Maybe."

"That's a yes," I say, tugging at her hair.

She makes a face. "But that doesn't mean I go out and carve my name in the rock face."

"Eh," I tease, "you know us men, always needing to mark things."

She giggles and then sighs. "What really has you creeping at my office door?"

"Besides providing you with caffeine?"

Another giggle. "Yeah."

"I wanted to see if you wanted to grab dinner tonight."

She stills for a heartbeat then pushes off the desk, sending a picture rattling and toppling backward as she turns away from me, and I have the feeling that she's just instantly erected a six-foot concrete wall between us.

"I don't think that's a good idea," she says quietly.

I frown, wondering if it's possible that I could have misread her interest, could have misread everything so completely.

Except...we talked about licking.

And kissing.

And tasting.

And—

"Because we work together?" I ask, hoping that it's something simple like interoffice politics. "There are ways around that if this ends up being something we want to pursue."

God knows I can take a page out of the Gold playbook on *that* one.

"No, it's not that," she says. "I—" A shrug. "I know my father wouldn't punish *me*."

I frown again, trying to make sense of those words.

"But my dad *is* super protective, so I don't think it would be a good idea for us to get involved. I wouldn't want to do something to affect your career and..."

She's rambling, but I'm not really hearing her, not anymore.

Because my eyes have slid down to her desk, to that picture that's toppled over.

It's of her and Jean-Michel Dubois.

It's of her and the *owner* of the Eagles.

It's of her and a man who is practically the spitting image of her—dark hair to blue eyes to regal nose.

I. Am. A. *Fucking*. Idiot.

"...and I know I wasn't exactly giving you clear-cut signals," she says, guilt written into the lines of her face. "And honestly, I probably wouldn't turn down a night together. But that's all it could be because my dad will make your life miserable if he finds out. And dinner, I think, is a surefire way to get caught and he'll find out and—"

"You're Christina *Dubois*?" I ask, interrupting her flow of words, interrupting her explanation of why the two of us going on a date is a bad, *bad* idea. "As in Jean-Michel's...?" I trail off.

Because I don't *want* it to be truth.

Because if it *is* true and Jean-Michel is her father, and he sees me this close to her, if he catches even a hint of me lusting after her, if he knows that I promised to taste every inch of her...

I'm fucking dead.

D.E.A.D.

Dead.

"Wait?" she asks. "You didn't know?"

My throat is threatening to close up. "Know what?"

I need to hear her say the words.

Because I cannot be *this* stupid.

"Rome?"

"Know what?" I rasp.

She goes still, chest expanding and retracting on a breath, and then she tells me, her voice so quiet that I have to strain to hear her, "My father is Jean-Michel Dubois." A beat. "The owner of the Eagles."

Fuck. Fuck. *Fuck.*

I'm so totally fucked.

FOURTEEN

Chrissy

HE'S SO STILL that I think he could play a respectable statue.

Or maybe he's holding himself together so tightly, that grasp on the pieces so brittle that one push from me will send him to the floor and shattering into pieces.

"You used to come to the Gold events," he murmurs.

My heart skips a beat, my brows pulling together. "What?"

"The ones that your dad used to do for the Gold's charity. The wine tastings and Meet-a-Player nights and—"

I inhale so sharply that my lungs protest.

Because I *remember*.

Rome—years ago, smaller, leaner, a boy in a man's job. Conversations that were sweet and quiet and more than a little awkward.

Not filled with charm and silky encouragement, confidence that he can play my body to very pleasurable results.

Just a boy who liked me.

A boy who I was in no position to connect with.

Because I was still trying to figure out who the hell I was after my peaceful world had been blown to pieces.

Years out from the night when everything changed, trying to pretend I was fine, but still suffering.

Jumping at shadows.

Having nightmares.

Panic gripping me with every creak and groan of the house.

It wasn't until my dad took me in hand and signed me up for self-defense classes, taught me how to shoot a gun, helped me feel safe in my own skin that I started coming out of that.

And the panic buttons helped, along with the security team on call.

I wouldn't be caught unaware again.

I wouldn't be scared and alone and in the dark...with people who took pleasure in scaring me, in hurting me, in making it clear that I might not get out of the situation alive.

I could save myself.

And my dad gave me the skills to do that.

Not rescuing me like that princess but giving me the tools to break out of the tower in the first place.

It's why I can't hold his protectiveness against him.

Not when I understand where it comes from and how quickly things can go bad and how high of a standard he holds the men in my life to.

It's also why I can't subject Rome to that same protectiveness.

Because—for all intents and purposes—he's working for my father.

"—you look different," he says. "Your hair is dark now. You were blonde before."

"I dye it now," I whisper.

Because—

I shudder, push that memory away. I've faced a lot of the darkness from that time, but...

Some things just need to remain tucked away.

"Oh," he whispers.

"I remember you," I say softly.

And really, how could I have forgotten him? Even though he's bulked up now, has a man's body that's put the kiss of youth behind him, I don't see how I hadn't recalled those deep brown eyes, the curls that scream for a woman's touch. How I hadn't remembered the charity work, the hockey player flirting with me, hadn't put the pieces together of him coming over on a trade from the freaking *Gold.*

Probably because my dad does a *lot* of charity work.

Probably because those memories from that time are slightly fuzzy because I was struggling to glue the pieces of my life back together.

Yeah, there's that.

"My hair *is* different," I say, my gaze drifting away from his eyes, sliding down to his toes and back up, not missing a single muscled inch. "But you've changed too."

That sexy, confident smile flashes again—no sign of awkward and quiet in this conversation. "You like what you see, Kitten?"

My lungs freeze.

"Because"—he reaches forward, brushes his fingers over my cheek—"you were beautiful then, but now? You're a fucking goddess."

Heat in my belly, shooting down between my thighs, making my knees shake. "This is a bad idea," I say, but my body drifts toward his.

"I know." His head drops, and I hold my breath,

wanting him to kiss me, even though I know this is just going to end badly—starting something with one of my father's players, starting something with my sexy neighbor next door, starting something when I'm not sure I will be able to finish it.

His fingers flex on my cheek, tilting my head back, aligning our lips so that if I move forward the slightest bit, our mouths will meet, and...I'll get that kiss.

I *want* that kiss.

Enough that need is burning through my veins, scorching through me, making me desperate for the touch of his lips, his teeth, his tongue, his body, his—

Cock.

"We're so fucking stupid," he says.

"Yes."

"Your father is going to kill me."

I pull in a breath, release it. "He won't," I say, even though I know it's delusional thinking, know that I need to put an end to my dad's overprotectiveness, but almost desperate to not have to, desperate for him to realize, "I'm a grown woman."

"Maybe, but you're his baby girl."

My throat tightens. "He wants me to be happy."

But I also know that he will do anything to protect me— even if that's protecting me from a relationship he thinks won't work out.

I...

Just a bit longer.

I lean a little closer, allow my breasts to brush across Rome's chest.

"*Fuck.*"

His growl reverberates through my flesh, and his free hand drops to my waist, fingers clenching on my hip, spiking my need, my arousal, my desire, until I know my panties are soaked.

"Tell me to stop, Kitten," he whispers.

"No," I whisper back.

"Fuck," he growls again, his forehead resting against mine, breaths glazing my lips. His palm rests flush against my cheek for a heartbeat before sliding back to dive into my hair, fingers tangling in the strands, tips pressing against my scalp.

I lift a shaky hand, allowing it to drift forward, to rest against his chest, settling on the spot over his heart, feeling that the organ is pounding beneath.

Knowing mine is launching itself against my rib cage, leaving me feeling breathless, my head spinning.

"Kitten," he murmurs, his other hand tugging me forward, bringing me flush against him as his knee parts mine, his big body presses close—

Fuck.

He's hard.

And big, and—

He's shifting again.

Only this time, it's to align our mouths.

Sensation explodes the moment our lips touch, a flash-bag along my nerves. His tongue slips into my mouth, sliding right between my open lips, tangling with mine.

He groans, tugging me closer, and I wrap my legs around his waist, feel another shock of sensation when the hard length of his cock presses against my clit, even through the layers of our clothes.

I can come.

Literally, thirty more seconds of this and I'm *going* to come.

And that's when there's a knock on the door.

And my father's voice echoes through the wood.

FIFTEEN

Rome

"CHRISSY?" There's another knock, concern clinging to the questions. "Why is the door locked?"

I freeze, glance over.

Then fucking thank the hockey gods that I engaged the lock.

Because I recognize that voice.

Jean-Michel Dubois.

Fuck. My. Life.

"Just a second, Dad," Chrissy calls, confirming that I'm right when I really, *really* don't want to be. When I spent the last five minutes going around and around in my head until I decided that maybe we can do this, that I can see Chrissy, can be with her, can see what this feeling of right between us means, and not end up in Jean-Michel's crosshairs.

Because he respects me enough to trade aggressively for me—so, naturally, he would have to see that there's *some* good in me.

And because I'll treat Chrissy like the goddess she is.

"Chrissy!" More knocking, loudly enough to draw attention to her office, to bring all the nosy Nellies out of hiding.

"Shit," I mutter.

She widens her eyes, slants a look at me that tells me clearly to, *Shut the fuck up.* "I'm...um...changing," she calls.

Then she's shoving me back, pushing me into the corner behind the door, eyes wide, finger pressed to her lips.

I nod, telling her I've got it, that I'll be quiet.

That I'll shut the fuck up.

Which probably shouldn't amuse me, considering I'm one panel of wood away from finding out if Jean-Michel would kill, maim—or much less likely—not care upon finding me in his daughter's office.

"Changing?" Jean-Michel asks as she backs away from me. "Why the hell are you changing? We're supposed to go to dinner."

"I spilled coffee on my shirt," she says, going to a cabinet and yanking open the door, pulling a sweater off the hanger. "Just give me a second, and I'll be right there."

A look over her shoulder at me—one that sends flames burning through my insides.

Then she spins her finger in the air, indicating I should turn around.

I just lift my brows, teasing her, fully intending to rotate to the wall, to give her privacy, but she shocks the shit out of me by smirking, shaking her head...then reaching for the hem of her blouse and tugging it up and over her head.

Tits. Lush tits overflowing a plain blue cotton bra.

Strong arms—but I knew that already.

A slender waist, a slightly curved belly, hips that flare out and call a man to hold on to them as he fucks her deep and hard and fast.

My dick, already hard from that scorching kiss, twitches, and when I glance up from her naked flesh—which, okay, doesn't actually happen until she pulls the sweater down to her waist, covering herself, it's to find her mouth quirked up into a sexy smile, her eyes dancing with humor.

"Christina?" her father bellows.

"All right," she calls, rolling her eyes. "I'm finished and will be right there."

She goes to her desk, snags the folders, her purse, keys, and phone then moves over to me, pressing her hand to my chest. "We need to think. No," she whispers. "*You* need to think."

I lift my brows in question.

"You need to decide if what we might have is worth the trouble he'll bring your way." The amusement leaves her gaze, and she shakes her head, sad creeping into blue eyes. "Because...I'm not sure if it will."

"Kitten—"

A shake of her head. "Just...think about it." A glimmer of humor in her eyes. "You know where I live."

Then she's turning away, opening the door, and flicking off the lights. "Geez, Dad," she says. "You can't wait for a girl to get cleaned up for her dinner date?"

"I..." But I don't hear the rest of Jean-Michel's words because their voices are fading, along with their footsteps as they walk away from Chrissy's office.

I wait until I can't hear them any longer (and then I wait a few more minutes, just for good measure) before making my way out of the office.

And nearly run directly into Pat the moment I clear the threshold.

We both skid to a stop.

His eyes flick over my shoulder, and his brows shoot up,

seeming to correctly read the situation—not that I'm going to admit as much to him—especially with that gleeful smile emerging on his face. "The owner's daughter?" he asks. "*Really?*"

I frown, play dumb. "What are you talking about, man?"

A nod toward Chrissy's office. "I'm talking about you sniffing around Jean-Michel's daughter." That grin expands, one big shoulder rises and falls. "Oh, he's going to kill you, and it's going to be great. I can't fucking *wait* to watch the Golden Boy implode his career."

My eye still throbs from this fucker's elbow hitting it yesterday, and I want to punch him back, bruise him like he did me. But I also understand that I can't let him know he's on to something. So, I lie. "You've lost your mind. She's working on a rehab program for me." I lift my leg, nod down at my knee. "Tetchy ACL and all."

He opens his mouth, but I press on, playing dumb.

"Hey, you should ask her to help you," I say, even though I know that I don't want him anywhere near her *and* that he's too much of an egotistical asshole to actually go to a *woman* for help with hockey.

Taking care of his dick, sure. But something to do with his game? Absolutely not.

Fucking moron.

"I know your back is shit," I add.

He scowls, but I push my advantage.

"So," I ask, "have you seen her for it?"

Pat scowls. "No," he snaps. "And my fucking back is fine." He glares at me before he spins on his heel and stomps down the hall.

I release a breath when he's gone.

Then rub the pulsing throb in my temple.

One fucking kiss and the shitstorm of my life is already

growing, gaining strength and wind speed and...threatening to sweep me up into its treacherous currents.

And I know Chrissy's right.

I need to figure out what the fuck I'm doing.

And what I want.

SIXTEEN

Chrissy

"DINNER, THEY SAY," I mutter, glad I grabbed my laptop from my office and all the files.

Because I've been sitting here, in the lobby of my dad's high-rise, waiting for him to finish up an emergency meeting that's taken precedence over dinner.

Not an unfamiliar feeling.

I've learned to adapt and be flexible and—

Get things done while I wait.

Like arrange an adoption fair—during which all of the Flower Kittens, including Petal, will be available to find their forever homes.

Like finish with the rehab plans that need updating.

Like think about a certain hockey player...and the potential logistics of a dinner date.

Something that has me finding my feet, ignoring the way my heart pulses with longing. I bring a lot of baggage with me

—and that's not even considering my father. I need to give Rome time to decide what he wants to do.

If he wants someone else.

Which...hurts.

It shouldn't. We've spent a couple of hours together. We've shared one kiss.

And yet...the heart doesn't follow logic.

If it did, I wouldn't have been out that night in the vineyard trying to meet Bobby.

And I wouldn't feel adrift and worried now.

"Ugh," I whisper, grabbing my stuff, going to the elevator, getting on, and hitting the button for the floor that was the reason I started finding my way back to myself, all those years before.

The car moves fast, the doors dinging open only a couple of moments later, and then I'm stepping into the gym, smiling at the girl manning the desk, moving into the locker room.

I change, using my spare set of clothes I leave there for exactly these types of situations, lock up my stuff, and then head to the rock wall.

I put on a harness and tie off—because safety first, and honestly, my dad would throw a conniption if I didn't.

Am I an adult woman who worries about what my dad thinks?

Yes.

Does that make me an immature weakling?

Maybe.

But—

I exhale, approach the wall.

I can only be who I can be.

I'm smart and kind and—

I reach for the holds on the medium section, wanting a

nice, easy warm-up to get my muscles loose and ready for a harder exertion.

And then I start climbing, puzzling out the tangle in my mind about Rome, focusing on what I'll need to do next for my cats, the staff I need to bring in so they're properly cared for, the supply shipment of food, checking in with those who are in foster homes, ensuring that they're developing properly and ready to progress to adoption next—or a permanent home with someone like me, who can handle their extra needs.

Organizing. Planning.

My teenage self would likely be disappointed.

But…I'm happy and fulfilled and—

"Am I, though?"

My grip slips and I barely catch myself, fingers and wrists and shoulders burning as I struggle to stop my momentum, and then as I draw myself slowly back to the wall, hooking one foot in, then the other. I rest for a second, heart pounding, upper body on fire, but so near the top that I just shake both hands out—one after the other—and continue climbing, touching the spot we've marked to signify the end.

Then I'm descending back down, walking over to the bin of extra supplies that we keep stored to the side, picking up a bag of chalk and covering my hands in it.

Pretending that the reason I slipped was clearly because I didn't have enough chalk on my hands, and not because I was distracted and unfocused and not paying attention as I should.

One more reason for the safety of the belay.

I roll my shoulders, head back to that same path, and as I start ascending again, my thoughts are drawn back to Rome.

And my teasing him about wanting to win the Cup a third time.

My mouth quirks.

My competitive streak might not be as overtly out there as a certain hockey player's, might not be driving me toward hefting a huge silver cup.

But it has me making deliberate moves as I climb my way up a second time—without any mistakes—before moving my way, one at a time through each of the harder courses.

And I do it wondering what Rome would think if he saw me.

Some part of me knowing already—because I saw his expressions when I was in the tree with Joan.

Pride and surprise. An urge to get up here with me, to compete, to try his hand, to excel.

Because that's the kind of man he is—or maybe the one I hope he is.

It's the type of man he's shown me so far.

The type of man—

My father is.

I slide down to the floor, the slight jolt of gravity reminding me how fun it is to be in the air, and I smile, wondering if Joan had wanted to feel the same thing.

The flow of air through her fur, the slightly mind-bending moment of looking down at the ground far below. The adrenaline rush of making it as high as you dare.

I hope so.

Because my pain in the ass, stubborn kitty deserves that.

I'm smiling, thinking of the trouble she causes—and how much I love her anyway—when I turn around to face my dad.

Who's watching me, pride on his face. No phones. No underling trying to get his attention.

When he's with me (and in the absence of any emergency meetings), he's *with* me.

"You done?" he asks, and I know he's not rushing me.

He's patient, knows that I've waited for him, so is willing to wait for me to be finished.

It's why I put up with his nonsense sometimes—okay, *most* of the time. From the outside, it seems like a very rigid, he-tells-me-what-to-do-I-do-it relationship. But it's not like that. We've been the Dubois Duo for as long as I can remember.

In most things.

It's just men that…complicate our dynamic.

"Yeah, Dad," I say, wiping my face with a towel.

"You want to shower, baby girl?"

I nod. "Definitely. Otherwise, you won't be able to stand to sit across from me."

His mouth quirks. "Never going to be the case, honey."

I toss the towel into the bin, start to undo my ropes. "Did you handle the crisis?"

A cocky grin as he takes over. "Don't I always?"

It's warranted, but I don't call him on it, not like I normally would. Because I have more important things to ask him about. "Is the fire very bad?"

"It took out an entire section of the vineyard." He shakes his hand. "Will probably cost us almost the entire harvest."

I wince. "That's not good."

"No"—he coils the rope, sets it to the side—"but that's why we make contingencies." He nods to the locker rooms. "Take your time, baby girl. I'll be waiting."

That's my dad.

Always there.

Always watching.

Always seeing.

And…always waiting to step in.

Whether I need him to or not.

SEVENTEEN

Rome

"HEY," Kingston Bang says as I give my shaking legs a rest by sinking down onto one of the steps, "I thought you were going home."

I grind my teeth together, but only for a second because I'm still trying to catch my fucking breath. "No," I mutter. I'm trying to figure out what in the fuck I should be doing.

With Chrissy.

Though not necessarily *doing* Chrissy.

Even if my dick would be happy to oblige.

King drops down onto the step next to me, long legs sprawled out in front of him. "What's the matter, pipsqueak?"

Swear to Christ.

Just because the man has four inches and thirty pounds on me...

I shake my head, knowing he's trying to piss me off so I'll spill my guts.

This is a common hockey interrogation technique.

But it's not going to work on me.

"I don't know, *King* Bang—"

He scowls and I shove to my feet, preparing to make another circuit because I would rather kill myself on these fucking stairs than talk about the bullshit swirling around and around and fucking *around* in my head.

"—maybe I just wanted to get some extra exercise in."

His scowl transforms into a grin. "That's a fucking lie—"

But I don't hear the rest of his sentence because I start jogging up the steps, glad the practice facility is empty at the moment—well, empty except for the Bang brother joining me in my assent.

Yup. *Brother.* As in, King is one of the six Bang siblings—five hockey-playing brothers and one former-figure-skating sister.

Unfortunately, King catches up with me before I reach the top of the first section and continues keeping pace beside me. "So, you do this every day?"

"So," I say, moving faster, "You this annoying every day?"

He grins, shakes his head, keeps matching my speed. "You know I've got a sister and four brothers."

"Yeah," I say.

"You know Annie went to PyeongChang."

I sigh. "Yeah."

"And you know they all play in the league."

I exhale, trying to settle my heart rate because it feels like I'm going to die. "Yeah," I push out a third time.

"So, you must also know that we Bangs are competitive."

"Yeah," I say dryly, nodding to him jogging right beside me. "I've gathered that much."

He smirks, picks up his pace, and I begrudgingly do the

same. "Which means that you must know that we all grew up in locker rooms."

I draw in air, grind out, "Yeah."

"So, you must also know that all of that means that I've perfected my annoying sibling skills."

Christ.

Exactly what I want to hear.

Ignoring him, I grit my teeth, keep running.

Unfortunately, he also keeps talking.

"And with four brothers and a sister," he says, his tone like silk. "My detecting trouble with the opposite sex skills have grown significantly."

I slant a look his way as we reach the top of the aisle, round the metal banister, start to make our way back down. "So says"—I inhale to please my aching lungs, let it out again—"the man who's made it very clear that although he's a confirmed bachelor, his mom keeps trying to fix him up with every single female in California between the ages of twenty-five and forty."

He rolls his eyes, and swear to fuck, I don't think he's even the least bit tired.

Or out of breath.

Bastard.

"I'll have you know," King says, "that forty-year-old was hot. It was just unfortunate my mom didn't know that she had kleptomania until after my computer and Rolex disappeared." A beat. "Luckily, I was able to buy them back off eBay."

"Jesus," I mutter, wiping sweat from my brow.

"Also"—we start climbing again—"this is more evidence for me knowing exactly what trouble with the opposite sex looks like."

"Right," I mutter. "So, if you're such an expert, is your mom going to stop trying to fix you up now?"

Kingston laughs, shakes his head. "Of course not. She raised five NHL players and an elite figure skater. She's stubborn as fuck."

I lift my brows as we jog down the next set of stairs.

He slants a look in my direction. "And she told me she's refining her matchmaking skills and won't make the same mistake twice."

"More skills," I say, and I'd feel sorry for the fucker—if only he didn't deserve whatever his mom could dish out.

He shakes his head, mouth tugging at the edges. "Yup."

"So," I ask, "how are you going to get her to stop?"

He shrugs. "You come from a big family too. You know how it is. Sometimes you just have to suck it up and endure."

My family loves me.

But...we're not like that.

We support each other and show up and cheer on, but we also all have our separate lives.

My experience with the Gold, however...well, from that I understand putting up with nosiness, pushiness, and no little amount of irritation when family butts in.

"And *then*," King says, "you just throw another sibling under the bus to save yourself."

"Brutal."

"A Bang's gotta do what a Bang's gotta do." He shrugs. "Plus, she's coming to visit soon, so I'll get mine."

I can't help but notice the warmth in his tone when he speaks of her. "You love her."

"Yup." He swipes his forearm across his forehead. "Loads. You know my dad played—"

I nod.

"He's great, but when you're on the road for half the year,

it's hard to be there for the day-to-day stuff. She made it a point to be there for us—even though there are six of us and one of her—and she also made sure that Dad was involved. I still don't know how she managed it."

"Superwoman."

He nods. "Basically." He slows as we round the top of an aisle, shrugs. "So, I put up with the romantic notions of a happy ending because I know she feels like she needs that, and in exchange, every time she visits, she makes me an apple pie."

My brows flick up. "It's that good to be worth the other bullshit?"

"It's fucking great." A beat. "She puts white cheddar in the filling—"

I wrinkle my nose.

Which makes me think about Christina.

Which is...problematic.

"Trust me, man," he says. "I'll share a slice next time around. It's fucking great."

"If you say so."

"More for me if you don't like it," King says and then shakes his head.

"Definitely."

"And if I could just find her a hobby that's *not* setting me up with women now that she's retired, I'd be golden." A flick of his eyes to mine, gauging my reaction. "No pun intended."

I shake my head, ask as we circle back down, "How about knitting?"

He laughs and nearly misses a step.

Which has *me* nearly missing a step because I'm laughing at him. "Why is that funny?" I ask after I manage to not break my ass.

His mouth is tipped up. "If you knew my brother, Tanner, you would think that's hilarious."

I slow to a stop, contemplate the next rise of stairs.

King pauses next to me, and he's out of breath. *Finally,* the bastard.

"Now," he says. "We've chatted. We've done manly exercise things. I've shared. It's your turn to open up. Think you can stop punishing both of us, and just tell me what sort of female problem you're having?"

Christ.

Dog to a bone.

"Are we so close of friends that we're sharing shit that's deep in our hearts now?" I ask, rolling my aching shoulders.

Cunning creeps in dark blue eyes. "So, you're admitting there is a female problem?"

I grind my teeth together, realize that I'm an idiot.

Because I've fallen for interrogation tactic number two—something I also know courtesy of the Gold—and I've been lulled into a sense of false complacency.

And then having questions sprung on me, which make me reveal too much.

"And I also know that whatever you're feeling, you're doing it deeply." He lifts his brows. "In your *heart.*"

I growl.

Then take off running again, glad to hear him groan as he follows me. I hit this stretch of stairs hard and fast, so hard and fast that I know I'm going to regret it later, going to regret it tomorrow (and likely the day after that).

The only consolation is he's going to be hurting with me.

King comes up beside me, matching my pace easily. "More punishment, huh?" he says, puffing now. "She must be in really deep." A beat. "In your heart."

I glare at him.

He just grins.

And keeps up with me as we run, keeps up with me until I literally cannot take another step, until my lungs are sawing and I'm fairly certain I'm going to eat shit and tumble down these stairs, Humpty-Dumpty style.

Only it's just going to be my head cracked open, not my whole body.

Maybe that will excise Chrissy from my mind, free me of this all-encompassing feeling that if I let her go, I'll regret it forever, and that if I don't—

Fucking stop.

I do.

Physically, if not mentally.

I give into my swirling mind, into the fatigue, and sink down onto a step, leaning back, trying to give my lungs as much room as possible to get oxygen within them...and also because I can't hold myself up any longer.

Kingston drops down beside me, breathing heavy, but not like me, not like if he doesn't get air into his system soon, he's going to pass out.

Or puke.

Or maybe both.

I groan.

He chuckles roughly. "This is your own fucking fault," he mutters, wincing as he stretches one leg and then the other. "Tomorrow's game is going to suck, you know that, right?"

"Because our legs are going to feel like they're getting repeatedly jabbed with flame-tipped spears?" I rasp out.

A pause and he looks over at me, mouth curved. "That's quite a description."

"I might not have excelled in school," I say, my breaths still coming rapidly. "Mostly because I was too busy slinging pucks to truly put the effort in, but I've never forgotten Mrs. Henderson's lesson on similes versus metaphors."

King pauses. "Was she hot?"

I grin up at the rafters. "*So* fucking hot."

"I fucking knew it." He laughs then nudges my shoulder with his hand. "So, was that thing about the flame-tipped spears a simile or a metaphor?"

Laughter in my chest. "No fucking clue."

Just that it's one of them.

Another shove of my shoulder, but he's grinning. "Fine," he says, climbing to his feet with a groan. "You win. Keep your confidence about the woman and all your deeply seated, heartfelt desires."

I make a face.

He sticks out his hand.

I grab it, let him drag me up to my feet.

"Come on," King mutters, clapping me on the shoulder. "I'm hungry. Let's go save Cam from the assholes in the weight room and drown our sore muscles in some beers."

EIGHTEEN

I DON'T KNOW if the universe has a sense of humor, or fate is just fucking with me for my subterfuge earlier, but I do know that I spot Rome the moment I walk through the restaurant doors.

He's sitting with Cam Jackson and Kingston Bang, two hockey players I easily recognize—because I know they're on the roster, have looked at their health reports, and I don't have any random past interactions with either of them, years ago, when I was putting myself back together or recently, after my father bought the team and acquired their talent.

Neither of them makes my heart skip a beat either.

Not like the third man of their trio with his curls and yummy body and pretty eyes.

And gentle soul and lips that provide the most sinful kisses and —

"This way, sir," the hostess says, picking up two menus,

smiling and leading us to a table that is comically close to the trio of Kingston, Cam, and Rome.

The latter of whom notices, doing a double take as I walk by, our eyes connecting in a way that makes my heart pulse hard.

So, yup, the universe is definitely fucking with me.

My dad is focused on food, apparently, and misses that three of his players are sitting within ten feet of us.

Though, in fairness, he's seated with his back to their table, while I'm given the full, glorious view of three hockey hotties, only one of whom actually makes my heart go pitter-patter.

Yup.

I just said *pitter-patter*.

Clearly, I'm losing it.

Pitter-patter.

How old am I?

Five? Or a hundred?

Maybe both, somehow, at the same time. Because I let my *Daddy* control my life—or parts of it, big, giant swathes of it—while also using terms like *pitter-patter*.

Rome's eyes catch mine, and I suck in a breath so quickly that I choke on my own spit.

My dad's head flies up as I reach for my water glass, glad someone already came by and filled it so I can stop embarrassing myself in front of the trio of hockey hotties.

"You good?" my dad asks.

I nod, clear my throat so I don't start choking again. "Something caught in my—" The tickle starts up and I take a big glug of water, probably looking like an idiot to the next table over.

That'll teach me to choke on my own spit.

I shake my head at myself, finish off the water, glad when the guy comes by to refill it.

"Thank you," I murmur.

He smiles at me, then sweeps away again.

My dad lifts his brows in question.

"I'm good. I promise." I take one more sip to clear that final tickle. "I can climb cliffs, but I can't swallow correctly, apparently—"

My eyes drift over my father's shoulder, I see that Rome is blatantly listening in. He waggles his brows and I frown for a moment before my words process, helped along when he mouths, "That's what she said."

I have to clamp my lips together to swallow down the hysterical giggle rising in my throat, and I know I'm not entirely successful because my dad's head comes up again. "Baby girl," he says. "Maybe you need something besides water."

"Wine," I rasp. "Pick me out a good glass?"

He winks at me, snags the wine menu, and starts perusing options.

Rome is watching me again, but I glance away before he can mouth something else dirty to me, and I start the whole cycle of choke-chug-choke—

Okay, that's so not helping my dirty mind.

And when, inevitably, my eyes go back to his, it seems like he has a line straight into my mind and is able to read every dirty thought.

My cheeks flare hot, and I press my palms to them, know they have to be bright red.

But I still can't tear my gaze away from his pretty brown eyes, especially when he opens his mouth and—

"What do you keep looking at?" my dad asks.

I jerk, ripping my stare away from the hockey hotties (or

the hockey hottie, *singular*, since the others haven't held a lick of my focus), and dart it back to my dad's, whose penetrating blue eyes are fixed on mine.

And...

Really, I shouldn't be using words like *penetrating* right now.

Not with my dad sitting across from me, and Rome—

Far too close for these thoughts to be swirling through my head.

I reach for my water glass, drink half of it down, and try to come up with a lie.

Too late, though.

My father twists around and I know the moment he clocks the hockey hotties—and how close they are, and how they are inevitably in my line of sight—because his shoulders stiffen.

"I saw some guys from the team," I say dumbly.

My dad spins back toward me, eyes fixing me in place. "*Some* guys?" he asks.

"Yes," I say, trying to play it off like this is all no big deal, sitting ten feet away from a man I want to get horizontal with, a man I really like and want to know better...with my overprotective father perched in a chair that's directly between us. "I've worked with Cam a little bit," I say, adding quickly when my dad's eyes narrow. "His hip was bothering him so Jeff"—the team's head trainer—"and I worked out some exercises. And Kingston seems to be settling in after the trade—at least according to the medical report I reviewed."

A pause. "And Rome?"

My throat tightens, and I barely resist the urge to start squirming in my seat. "And Rome," I say, faking bravado. "Well, he's my new neighbor."

His fingers seize on the wine menu. "Your *what?*"

I take another glug of water, set the glass down with a plunk, and it's immediately topped off by my water-filling friend.

Who I could kiss for buying me some time to settle my voice, so that I'm not squeaking out my explanation like a guilty teenager.

"My new neighbor," I say. "You know how the house next door sold not long ago?"

He nods.

"Rome is the one who bought it."

And then—before I have to summon even more nonchalance—my phone rings.

I pull it out of my purse, glance at the screen.

Then send many thanks up to the universe.

"Sorry, Dad," I say. "I need to take this. It's Rory."

He nods, opening his mouth, but I don't let him reply—though, I'm sure it would be in the positive, because he knows Rory, knows that she's a good person—

Even if she prefers dogs to cats.

I don't let him reply as I hop to my feet, swipe my finger across the screen, lifting it to my ear as I rush out of the dining room.

Leaving my father behind.

With the trio of hockey hotties.

Heaven help me.

NINETEEN

Rome

SHE'S FUCKING BEAUTIFUL.

Every time I see her, I feel that fact deeper and deeper, until it feels as though it's branded on my heart.

So, when I see her walking through the restaurant, her father a couple of feet in front of her, I know that the waffling I felt all afternoon was for naught.

I can try and ignore the draw I have toward Chrissy.

But I'm not going to be successful.

Especially with her right next door.

She looks up and our eyes connect, and I know she feels exactly the same thing that I do. Her cheeks go pink, her lips part, and she misses a step, nearly running into a chair.

I watch as she shakes her head slightly, straightens her shoulders, focuses on her surroundings and the weaving path they're taking through the restaurant's tables...

To the one that's right next to ours.

I feel my heart skip a beat, watching as she clocks her

location—and thus, our proximity—and nibbles at her bottom lip, obviously debating.

But then she sits in the chair her father's pulled out for her.

The chair that's facing mine.

I exhale, resisting the urge to rub a hand over my heart, feeling it roll over deep inside my chest.

She's right there.

Close and I can't do shit about it.

But...she's *right there.*

"So, what do you think?" Cam asks.

I keep my mouth shut, wait for Kingston to answer. Which he does, thankfully, and they start talking about an idea for a set play during an offensive zone face-off.

Which, actually, sounds pretty fucking good, not that I'm fully listening.

Mostly because I'm focused on Chrissy, and putting every bit of what is in my head, what's been in it since I tasted her in her office, into my eyes.

Which lock with hers.

She starts choking.

Shit.

My body tenses and I almost leap out of my chair, prepared to give her the Heimlich, but she's already reaching for her water glass and drinking deeply, her coughing slowing, her eyes coming back to mine.

Seeming to say she's fine.

I still keep an eye on her, shamelessly listening in on the conversation she's having with her dad, barely paying attention to my two teammates as they talk shop.

Whatever.

I've got more important things to worry about.

Like hearing her say—

"I can climb cliffs, but I can't swallow correctly, apparently—"

Our eyes lock again, and I'm a child because the first thing that comes to mind is, "That's what she says."

Luckily, I only mouth it and don't actually say it out loud.

Yup.

I'm definitely a child.

But seeing the mirth and heat gather in her eyes—and feeling the need her presence conjures coiling through my abdomen, sliding down, wrapping its fingers around my cock —and I can't give two shits.

Mine.

"And then we can—" Kingston is saying and I nod when they look at me, but I'm not paying attention, not in the least.

"Oh!" Cam says. "If I swing it around to the outside and I cut deep—"

"Yes," King says, drawing it out with a finger on the table, one of our beers acting as the net, players of both teams being represented by sugar packets—blue for us, pink for our opponents. "See? If we can draw them out, he'll have a free lane to the net and we might be able to slip in and score. Don't you think, Rome?"

My eyes have drifted from the uninteresting sugar packets representing hockey players back to Chrissy.

Who is so much more interesting than a face-off.

I can talk hockey anytime.

Which is why I just say, "Yeah, sounds good," and then continue taking my time studying her, committing every facet of her beautiful face to memory.

"I don't believe it," Kingston mutters. "Your woman troubles involve Christina Dubois?"

I tear my gaze away from the table, away from the woman who's now talking earnestly to her father, shove down the urge to scoot my chair closer, to find out what's got her so enthusiastic, and look at my teammate. "No," I tell him. "It doesn't."

Not a lie.

Because I don't consider her trouble.

I just consider her...*mine.*

"Don't even fucking try it, man," Cam says. "You've been staring at her for at least the last five minutes."

"No, I haven't." But even as I try to peddle that bullshit, my gaze slides back to the side, back to that table next to us, and I can just make out the soft tone of her voice over my teammates' blabbering.

"Dumb. Fucking. *Ass,*" Kingston grumbles. "I would seriously take a klepto over potentially having Jean-Michel Dubois as a father-in-law—"

My heart convulses, but I focus back on my teammate.

"—and that's even saying if you make it that far. Which you won't because he's either going to find out and you're going to meet an untimely end, or he's going to find out and your fucking career is going to be over."

King shoves my shoulder, and I realize that I'm staring again.

At Chrissy.

Christ.

He's right.

I've probably lost my goddamned mind.

I need to focus, not blow my load on revealing this all too soon. I need to figure out where we are, if we really work, and then...sort out how to win over the man who holds my career in the palm of his hand.

But even as I think that, I track Chrissy getting up from her chair, winding between the tables, disappearing out of sight.

And I actually have to dig my toes into the souls of my boots in order to not stand up and follow her.

Right in front of her father and my teammates.

Jesus fucking Christ.

If that's not indication enough that I need to slow down, to think this through, to be calm and measured in my decisions—because that's what I always do—I don't know what is. I'm trying to build a solid foundation with the team, not open myself up to criticism or bullshit or an owner's retaliation.

I need to focus on why I'm here.

And that's hockey.

But it's also...*that woman*.

I pull in a breath, release it, then open my mouth to tell King to back the fuck off, that I'll deal with my own shit—whether or not it involves Chrissy—when I feel a hand on my shoulder, clapping down roughly, driving me into the cushion of my chair so deeply that I can feel a spring jabbing me in the ass.

I look up, prepared to tell the asshole who's dared touch me to get lost.

But then I see whose hand it is.

And...fuck my life.

TWENTY

Chrissy

"OH MY GOD," I whisper into my cell, speeding down the hall and out onto the patio. "You have the best timing."

There's a long pause. "I don't think you're going to say that when you know *why* I'm calling."

Well...that's ominous.

But, also, it's—

"Well, whatever favor you need," I tell her. "It's yours."

Another pause that's...well...*ominous*.

Fueled by her next words. "You may regret saying that."

"Rory," I say softly. "What the fuck is going on?"

"You tell me yours first."

I scowl, but if I've ever met another person more stubborn than my father, it's Rory. She's a warrior for her animals, and she does it holding down a full-time job doing design work for my father's winery. Branding. Labels. Boxes. Pamphlets for tastings. Banners for the events that bring people in. She's in charge of everything domestically.

So, I don't argue with my friend, demand that she give up the goods and tell me exactly what favor she's about to ask.

Because it doesn't really matter.

Rory is one of those people who's proven her loyalty over and over again.

I'll bend over backward to make sure I get whatever it is done for her.

Which is why I say, "You gave me an escape from a tense dinner conversation with my dad."

There's a blip of quiet. "You guys only fight about two things—hiring a manager to take over the rescue—"

I inhale, because even the mention of that hurts, especially when I'm not as involved in the day-to-day operations as I feel like I should be, but there's so much to do, so much responsibility that comes with being the face of it, the main funder, the person with the connections to bring in other funding.

It started off with fostering, with playing with cats all day, with cuddle time and finding the toys they like the most.

Now...it's more.

I love it. I wouldn't do anything else.

I just...it's *more*.

"—or you guys fight about men."

I inhale sharply and she laughs, the sound soft and tinkling like bells in my ears, and if Rome accused me of being Rapunzel (and I'll take that, so long as it's the badass brunette with the shoulder-length hair and the mad frying pan skills) then Rory is...Aurora.

As in, literally, her name *is* Aurora.

And she's as beautiful and fragile as Sleeping Beauty.

Luckily, she's already found her Prince Charming—or Phillip, rather.

"So, which is it?" she presses.

The wind gusts and I push my hair back from my face. "I have the hots for my next-door neighbor."

"I—" She breaks off and I picture the shock sliding across her expression. "That's...convenient?"

It *is* convenient.

It's also...neither of us can reasonably get away if it all goes bad.

But that's not the tetchiest part of this whole thing.

"He plays for the Eagles," I admit.

Rory's pause this time is long enough that my gaze is drawn up to the sky, that I've started trying to pick out constellations.

Then rip-roaring laughter hits my ears.

"Oh my God," she says. "This is just too good. You know I love your dad, but he is as interfering as one of those meddlesome grannies in a Hallmark movie." She laughs again, back to bells tinkling. "But how is he going to be a good old-fashioned cockblock when his hockey player lives right next door?"

I groan, rub a hand over my face. "First, please don't mention the word *cock* and my dad in the same sentence. Second, did you miss the part when I said he *plays* for the Eagles?" I grit out. "My dad can interfere a whole-freaking-lot. What if he benches Rome? Or trades him to another team? That would be my fault and I can't ask him to risk—"

"Rome Dawson?"

I snap my teeth together.

"Your hot next-door neighbor is Rome Dawson?"

"Yes," I whisper miserably. "And he kissed me, and I don't know what to do."

"Well, considering he kissed you, I think you already know how he feels about the risk."

I'm not so sure about that.

"My dad doesn't know," I say miserably, explaining about the tree and Joan, the Band-Aids and the refill of coffee and the first aid kit. The kiss and...the knock on the door, and how I hid Rome, how I told him to take time to think.

"Oh."

"Yeah," I mutter. "And now he's here at the same restaurant as us and..."

"Is he avoiding you?" Rory's tone is deadly.

"Kind of hard to do when he's sitting at the next table over," I say dryly.

"Whoa. Really?" A beat. "You think he planned that?"

"No," I whisper, considering we came in after they already had their drinks.

"They?"

"Rome and Kingston Bang and Cam Jackson."

"The hot hockey trio."

"I've been referring to them as the trio of hockey hotties."

She giggles. "Well, neither of us is wrong."

I groan again. "What am I going to do, Ror? I don't really know how I'm feeling"—except that some part of me is feeling like I can't let him go—"and my dad's here and his teammates and..." I sigh. "My dad caught me looking at him."

"It'll be okay, babe." Her voice is calm, assured, like she's talking to a spooked animal. And she basically is, I suppose.

"Of course it will be," I lie, pushing down my angst and redirecting the conversation. Enough about me and my silly problems of the heart. Rory called *me*. "So, how about you tell me this favor of yours I'm going to be doing?"

"It's a lot less exciting than what you've got going on," she says. "I was just hoping you could take in a couple of puppies for a few days."

Joan is going to *love* that.

Luckily, this happens often enough with cats—or dogs—

that I have a completely secure room so my dear, *dear* Joan of Arc won't be inconvenienced and the cats or dogs can remain safe.

"Of course, I can take them," I say. "For as long as you need, you know that. Are you guys full up again?"

"Yup." She sighs. "Apparently, this is the season for it, and Phillip says he'll divorce me if I bring home another dog."

I frown, not liking that threat, especially because it sounds less joking and more...well, *serious*. "But you're not even married yet."

"We're as good as married," she says. "Our wedding is next month." A sigh. "And he's right, we've got a lot happening. I don't really have the mental space to take on more dogs until after that's done."

"That's fair," I tell her. "But does he get that the rescue is important to you?"

Bells tinkling. Soft laughter reaching my ears. "I think he'd be completely dense if he didn't get that at this point."

Yes. He would be.

But...

"Ror?" I ask. "Are you two okay?"

"We're fine. Though I might scream if I have to discuss one more flower arrangement style with his mother." She sighs. "Now, don't try to turn the tables and avoid circling back to all the juicy details about Rome Dawson. What did he do when he saw you and dear old Dad sitting at the next table over?"

"Well," I whisper, as though my father might somehow hear me, even though my eyes are on the door and he's nowhere in sight. "We couldn't keep our eyes off each other."

"That's good."

"*Is* it?"

"How is it not?"

"I...Ror," I say softly. "My *dad*."

She falls quiet for long enough that I open my mouth to break the silence, but then she blurts, "How was it?"

I frown at the question that makes no sense before I piece together the only thing she could want to know. "The kiss?"

"No," she snaps. "Joan's latest A1C. *Of course* I want to know about the kiss."

I nibble at my bottom lip, sigh softly. "It was...incredible."

She goes quiet for a beat then, "I think that tells you all you need to know."

"Ror—"

"He's seated at the next table, and he's making eyes at you," she says. "He's an incredible kisser and doesn't appear to care what your dad might throw at him. He's interested in you and brings you coffee and first aid kits."

My throat goes tight again. "It was just one first aid kit."

"Chrissy, honey," she murmurs. "For once in your life, will you stop worrying about what everyone else wants and go for what makes you happy?"

Ice in my heart.

"I did that once."

She falls quiet. "This isn't like what happened that night when you snuck out to meet Bobby."

I inhale sharply.

"You're not a teenage girl rebelling against your dad," she says. "You're a grown woman and allowed to make your own decisions about your love life. And your dad will get that if you just set a boundary and stick with it."

My breath slides out in a hiss. "You make it sound easy."

"No, it's fucking not," she says. "But I want you to be happy."

My eyes sting and I swallow hard.

"So, what do *you* want, babe?"

If I'm sharing—and I suppose I am, considering all I've told Rory—all I've ever wanted was someone interested in me, and *only* me.

Not my father.

Not his money, and whatever chunk of it I might one day get.

Not my trust fund.

Just me.

And maybe my cats.

And maybe all the little pieces that make me...well, *me*. My abhorrent cooking skills and my penchant for climbing trees. My passion for my rescue and that I'm more of a home-body than a party girl. My coffee addiction and the fact that I can't stand anchovies. And all the other things I haven't noticed, things my partner will, things that will make him love me more.

Because I want someone who isn't scared of the baggage I bring—my dad and his overprotectiveness, my nightmares and journey to healing that is still partially in progress, Joan and her sharp, *sharp* claws.

Because...maybe I even deserve that.

"Chrissy?" she presses gently. "What do you want, babe?"

"I think," I whisper. "I think I want to see where things go with Rome."

Pride through the airwaves. "That's my girl."

I nibble at the inside of my cheek, fighting a smile, ignoring that my heart is going a million miles an hour. "Yeah."

"Now," she says. "What are you going to do about it?"

"Go inside," I say, and it's not necessarily because my newfound clarity has brought me loads of courage but rather because I've suddenly realized what I've done, what I've given my father the opportunity to do.

I left him and Rome within ten feet of each other.

Without me to run interference.

Shit.

"Ror?"

"Yeah?"

"I need to go."

"Yeah," she says and I can hear her grin through my cell's speaker. "I bet you do. I'll text with details about the pups."

We hang up.

And...I brace for what I'm going to find inside.

TWENTY-ONE

Rome

HIS EYES ARE ALMOST identical to Chrissy's, except Jean-Michel's have specks of gray amongst all of that cerulean blue.

And they're frost-filled, like icy daggers are going to shoot out from within them, fly through the air, and sink into my chest.

Goodbye expensive hockey player.

Don't let the skate blades slice you on the way out.

Or do, I don't fucking care.

His fingers tighten and I feel a sharp dart of pain through my arm.

Fuck, he's really going to murder me.

"Rome," he says.

Fuck.

He knows I kissed his daughter, knows I wanted to fuck her on her desk, that we might have very well gone that far if not for the fact that he was knocking on her door.

"Mr. Dubois," I return because my parents taught me to be polite with my bosses, even if they're tossing frosty, murderous icicles my way, and—

"I understand you've moved in next door to *my* Christina." It's a statement.

But also, somehow, a question.

And also...threat of murder, his hand not moving from my shoulder, fingers clenched tight.

"Yes," I say...and then run out of steam.

Because, fuck, this man is scary.

"Hmm," he murmurs, just staring down at me, our eyes locked, his still as cold as fucking Antarctica. "You like the area?"

My stare flicks to King's, and I see that he looks like he's going to shit himself.

And Cam isn't much better, sitting there, white as a ghost, like he doesn't know whether to get up and run out of the restaurant or stay and confess each and every one of the misdeeds he's committed in his young life—not that there can be all that many. He's a good kid.

But neither of them is going to rescue me from this shit.

And it's not their job to do so.

So, I need to pull it fucking together.

"Yes," I say. "I like the area a lot."

Jean-Michel's brows flick up and I find myself elaborating, even though he probably doesn't give two shits about my childhood—or already had people to research all of us and our pasts to suss out every detail—bland to sordid—of our lives, if that was what he wanted.

Still, I tell him, "Where I grew up was pretty populated —our neighbors practically on top of us. I wanted some space—quiet, but not too far from town, so I waited to buy until I found somewhere I really liked. Luckily, where I ended up is beautiful and the commute to the rink isn't bad."

"Hmm," Jean-Michel says again, but at least he releases my shoulder.

Blood flows back into my body in a rapid rush of sensation, and I'm not sure exactly where the sudden burst of confidence comes from, exactly, but I nod to the empty chair at our table.

"Do you want to sit down for a couple of minutes?" I ask, making Cam choke on his beer. "You and Chrissy are welcome to join us."

"*Chrissy* and I?" There's disapproval in his tone.

But, look, I like Chrissy, and this is me being deliberate and measured and thoughtful. I live next door to her. I want to soak in her smiles, watch the way her face softens when she's with her cats, and I want...to see where things go with us. I want to taste her again, want to feel her in my arms. No, I *need* to. And I figure the only way to ensure that happens is to make peace with her old man, and further that, I figure the only way to deal with a man as powerful as Jean-Michel Dubois is to fake that I'm completely confident in my own skin and decisions, and just hope that, someday, it'll be true.

I'm cool. I'm confident. I'm unaffected by tiny, murderous eye daggers.

Greater miracles have happened in my life.

Including playing in the NHL.

And maybe...maybe coming to this team.

I exhale softly and push on. "Chrissy mentioned she prefers that over Christina."

I hear Kingston hiss out a breath.

And I almost do the same. Because Jean-Michel's expression has gone from frosty and murderous to...skin me alive and wear my flesh like a Halloween costume. "*Christina,*" he emphasizes, stare daring me to argue, "and I are having dinner together." A beat, leaving absolutely no doubt of the importance of his words that follow. "As a family."

Which doesn't include us.

Which doesn't include *me*.

I nod, conceding that point, eyes flicking over his shoulder, wondering where she is, knowing it's been at least five minutes since she left (even though it feels like a fucking eternity since Jean-Michel approached our table). How long does it take for someone to go to the bathroom? What if someone—?

I'm being an idiot.

She went to the bathroom. That's it.

I return my focus to the table, see something strange has come over Jean-Michel's face.

Like, maybe, he doesn't hate me quite so much.

Unlikely.

Probably, he's coming up with new and painful ways he's going to torture me because I dared look at his daughter and—

Screech!

He pulls out the chair and sits down.

"Christina is very important to me," he says in such a calm, placid voice that it takes a moment for me to actually process his words. "She is *so* important that I will personally hunt down and calmly dismember anyone who dares to hurt her. Now," he adds as I'm absorbing the threat, changing the subject as easily as turning a page in a book. "What's this?" he asks, pointing at the sugar packets.

Silence and wide eyes all around.

But I grind my teeth together. "Chrissy is an adult and can make her own decisions."

Jean-Michel goes still.

King kicks me. *Hard.*

Cam twitches like he's going to run from the table.

But I ignore the bolt of pain through my bones, ignore Cam's shit fit, and hold Jean-Michel's eyes.

"Christina doesn't always understand the consequences of her actions," he tells me.

"She seems to be doing just fine," I point out. "She's doing good work for the team and her rescue is amazing. She is fully capable of making her own choices."

Stillness in Jean-Michel's frame a second time, but he doesn't acknowledge the words, doesn't admit that I'm right. He just glances down at the sugar packets and the carefully positioned beer on the table and asks again, "What's this?"

Silence—me looking to Cam, Cam looking to King, King looking back at me.

And then Cam Jackson slides into the conversation, effectively turning it from threats of murder—and dismemberment —to hockey.

"Set plays," Cam says. "For face-offs."

Another "Hmm," Jean-Michel tilting his head to the side, focus solely on those colored packets now. "Tell me about it."

So Cam does.

He explains his thoughts for the O zone and a couple of variants based on winning or losing the draw, who's on the ice. And his ideas for a couple of defensive options.

Smart. Analytical.

And I have no doubt they'll be effective.

Cam Jackson was definitely a good add for the roster.

And I can tell Jean-Michel thinks so too, the pride shining in his eyes.

So, Chrissy's dad is a hard ass, but he also has a streak of *not* asshole somewhere under the tough exterior.

Good to know.

I glance at King. He looks back at me, eyes wide and filled with warning.

But I don't heed it.

I just get up, walk over to the table where Chrissy and her dad had been sitting, and snag a chair, carrying it to our table, plunking it down right next to mine.

TWENTY-TWO

Chrissy

I KNOW my dad said something.

Because Rome is looking at me like...like whatever we had been forming between us has...

Changed.

Likely lost to the ether.

My heart pulses and I turn my focus away from him, something that's hard to do considering they've joined our table—or well, that *we've* joined theirs, my father taking up their empty chair, another having been brought over for me to sit in...next to Rome.

Who's acting...

Different.

They're *all* acting different...

As though I'm a leper about to take them all down and—

I bite back a sigh, pick up the glass of wine my dad ordered for me, and sip, the tart and fruity notes proving exactly how well he knows me.

"Good?" Rome asks softly.

"Yeah," I say back, fighting the urge to lean into him, to drag my chair closer to...

Take his hand.

I deliberately keep my gaze turned from his, refuse to get lost in eyes that are going to tell me I'm not worth the trouble, and I blow out a quiet breath.

"What's the obsession with sugar packets?" I ask quietly.

My eyes catch Kingston's, and half of his mouth turns up. He nods encouragingly, like this is a safe conversational topic.

And I suppose it is, because it gets Cam to unstick and start talking about the packets and how they relate to some plays, and then my dad is asking questions, moving the packets around, and then...

My gaze is drifting back to Rome's.

Those deep brown eyes are unfathomable.

Have we ended before we've even begun?

I think...I think that maybe we have.

My heart squeezes and I look away, shoving that down, shoving it away with all of the other things I want but can't have—a mom, a man who loves me for just me—and turn my focus back to the four men sitting with me at the table, instead of the one I want but likely won't ever have.

More shoving.

More pretending it doesn't exist.

And then I cheerfully ask, "Have we ordered dinner yet?"

ADMITTEDLY, I'm feeling sorry for myself.

Because dinner was...pleasant.

And uneventful.

And Rome was...what?

Polite. Considerate. Pulling out my chair, helping me into my jacket, holding the door for me...and leaving with a smile.

Ugh.

It's not like he was going to pull me into his arms and declare his undying love for me in front of his teammates and my dad.

I'm being far too dramatic and angsty for my own good.

"Meow!" Joan warns as I move by her, swiping out a paw.

With claws out.

I shake my head at her. "Stop being so grumpy."

"Meow," she growls, and then hisses at me for good measure.

And I know that she's accusing me of being grumpy too.

I bare my teeth at her, continue on to the back deck, after having checked the spare room to make sure I'm ready for puppy central tomorrow—because watching a *few* dogs for Rory for a few days has turned into looking after an entire litter of eight-week-old puppies until they're ready for adoption—which, thankfully, should only be for a few weeks.

I push through my back door and step outside. The air is cool, but not unpleasant with my sweater on.

"I was wondering when you were going to come out here, Kitten."

I startle, heart pounding, fear closing in for a second as I nearly upend the generous glass of wine I poured for myself, but the voice isn't close by and that distance gives me a second to process. To breathe.

To save my wine.

I set it carefully on the table before I allow my gaze to go to my tree.

Or *Joan's* rather.

Rome is sitting on the bottom branch, one leg on either side of it, his back against the oak's thick trunk.

"What the heck are you doing?" I say, marching across my lawn, heart in my throat.

At dinner...

Well, I thought that things were done.

He lifts a bottle of beer to his mouth, takes a long sip, then rests it on his thigh and smiles over at me. "I figured I'd try this whole climbing thing out, considering that the girl I like enjoys it."

I start picking through my planter bed, careful to avoid the flowers and in-ground lights, not stopping until I reach the base of the tree and look up at the hockey hottie. "The girl you *like?*" I barely suppress my scowl as I cross my arms.

"Why do you ask that like it's a real question?"

I just flick up my brows. "Maybe because it is?"

He flicks his brows right back. "I figured I made myself pretty clear."

"By ignoring me at dinner?"

"Ignoring—?" His scowl deepens. "What in the fuck-all are you talking about?"

"I'm talking about—" I groan, rub my hands over my face. "Nothing," I say. "I'm losing it. Ignore me. I'm—"

He sets the bottle on the branch and jumps down, the reverberation of his impact vibrating through the souls of my shoes. "What are you talking about, Kitten?"

I look away, but he cups my jaw, turns my face back to his. "Nothing," I say again.

"Such a pretty little liar." His hand slides from my jaw to my hair. "I was aware of every single breath you took, every bite and sip, and every fucking time you laughed at one of King's dumbass jokes." His fingers press into my scalp. "And I was also aware of every single time you didn't allow yourself to look my way."

My eyes shoot to his. "What?"

"You didn't look at me, Kitten. Not once after you ordered your dinner, and I don't know if it's because you know your dad threatened me with dismemberment, or because you don't want the others to know that we've been sniffing around each other, or—"

"Wait. What?" I ask. "My dad did—" I shake my head, heart sinking. "He threatened you with dismemberment?"

Rome's fingers flex, tilting my head back. "It's not a big deal, Kitten," he says nonchalantly. Yup. *Nonchalantly.* As though my dad hadn't said he would tear off Rome's limbs.

What the fuck is wrong with the men in my life?

"Not a big deal?" I say. "Not a freaking *big deal?*"

I want to grab him by his sweatshirt and shake some freaking sense into his dumb, hockey-playing brain.

But I like how he's holding me more.

"Yeah, Kitten," he says, dropping his forehead to mine, his words ghosting over my lips. "It's *not* a big deal." He brushes his mouth over mine.

I gasp, but he's already pulling back.

"So, why did you ignore me?" he asks softly.

I frown, shake my head. "You're the one who was ignoring me."

"Ignoring you by asking your dad if he—and you—wanted to join us for dinner?" he says, drawing my body flush against his.

My mouth drops open. "You *what?*"

He shrugs. "I suggested we combine tables."

"My dad came over, threatened dismemberment, and y-you suggested we all sit down for a *meal* together?"

Another shrug.

My head starts to throb. "What is wrong with you?"

"Kitten, I like you," he says, and there's a thread of annoyance in the words that has my insides twisting. "But I'm also not sure what you want from me here? We spent a night together and shared a fucking kiss that tells me we can burn the fucking bed sheets up. I want to explore that—I think I made it pretty fucking clear in your office and at dinner." He bends a little, our eyes connecting. "And I think I've made what I want pretty fucking clear because I'm standing right here."

He's not wrong.

He's showing me what he's feeling.

And I'm messing it up—because *I'm* messed up. Maybe that's why I say what I say next, "Don't tell me you're not worried about what my father might do."

He pauses—minutely—but that hesitation is still there, and it's like a knife sinking into my gut.

Because some part of him *is* a little worried.

I can feel it.

And what if he takes a risk for me and it doesn't work out?

What if we explore this connection, he deals with threats of dismemberment, and...

We're wrong for each other?

TWENTY-THREE

Rome

I HAD HER FOR A SECOND.

I could almost feel the shift, the panic in her settling.

Then it's rising again, and doing it fast, screaming toward a crescendo, and she's throwing up walls between us, pulling back again, her eyes skating away from mine, settling in the darkness.

But I know she's not looking there, not really. Her thoughts are just...really far away.

"Look at me, Kitten," I order softly.

She doesn't turn back, just keeps looking into the dark.

I step close again, intending to draw her into my arms, making her stop and think and *be*.

But then she *does* look back, her eyes returning to mine, and I see the grim resolution in them. She likes me too—she wouldn't have been upset about me "ignoring" her at dinner if she didn't—but she doesn't like me enough to take a chance.

"Kitten—" I begin.

"It's too risky for you," she whispers.

My heart pulses. "I know what I'm doing," I tell. "Know what the risk is, and I still want to see what this thing is between us."

But she's already shaking her head, already pulling back from me, martyring herself for me...

Or maybe she's just scared.

Either way, it gives me a moment of doubt. If it's *this* hard and we haven't even started...

Only the really hard things are worth doing.

Brit's voice in my ear when I injured my knee a couple of seasons back, when I was rehabbing without hope of getting back onto the ice any time in the near future.

And she was right.

I'm stronger than ever. *Better* than ever.

And...so I say something that's not measured. Something that doesn't make any logical sense. Something that's holding on to the fight and not letting go just because things are hard.

Because it's from the heart, and it's all I fucking have right now.

I cup her face in both palms, wait until her eyes come to mine. "What if we keep it a secret?"

She jerks, but I hold her fast.

"Hear me out, Kitten," I say. "We try this out. We figure out if this draw between us is something worth risking dismemberment for"—I force my lips to curve, to keep my tone light, even though my heart is pounding a million miles a minute, frantically trying to think ahead, to barter and beg and convince her to take a chance on me—"and we take the time we need to decide if we want to go public with this."

"You want to keep us a secret?" she whispers.

And I fucking hate the thread of hurt in her voice.

"I don't, Kitten. I think you're too fucking wonderful to

hide in the shadows. But," I add as she opens her mouth, as I watch the protest form on her lips, "I think keeping this between us gives us a chance to take things slow, to figure them out, without..."

"Without my dad attempting to tear you limb from limb," she says softly.

"Yeah."

She nods.

And I'm holding my breath, waiting for her answer, knowing that the stakes—and how fucking important this all is to me—are beyond high.

"I—" She breaks off, presses her lips together, looks away.

Fucking *killing* me.

I start lining up arguments in my head because every fucking cell in my body is saying this is important, this is one of those hard things, this is one of those times I need to power through and make sure I get the right result in the end.

The right result being that I'm going to keep her.

Forever.

But...she has to agree first.

Before I pass out from lack of oxygen.

I open my mouth, draw in air, prepare to let those arguments fly...

Then she whispers, "Okay."

"Okay?" I blurt, roughly, sharply.

Probably because I've been standing here like an idiot, not breathing.

"Okay," she says again. "We'll try this." A beat, her eyes flicking away from mine then back. "In secret."

Relief flows through me, so heady I nearly pass out.

Then I reach for her again, and before she can change her mind, I kiss her.

She goes stiff, but it's only for a fraction of a second

because then her lips are parting and her body is melting against mine. Fucking nirvana, tasting her mouth, the plump softness of her lips, the bite of wine on her tongue, the vibration of her moan as it slides up from her mouth and into mine. Fucking perfect, having the soft curves of her breasts pushing into my chest, her arms wrapping around my shoulders.

But it's a stretch to reach her mouth.

I spin us, pinning her flush against the tree trunk, coaxing her legs up, encouraging her to wrap them around my waist.

Luckily, she's good at climbing.

Our lips connect again, and then her tongue is in my mouth and she's taking charge of the kiss, driving me freaking insane as she undulates against me, as she slides her hands into my hair and tightens her legs around my middle, aligning our pelvises and—

Christ.

She's. So. Fucking. Right.

I groan when she bites at my bottom lip, losing patience and taking back over, pressing her harder into the tree, rocking against her until I find the right angle, the right motion that makes her gasp into my mouth, that has her hands tightening in my hair. I grip her waist, slide my hand along her side, up until it's positioned right beneath the lush curve of her breast, until I feel the weight of it against my fingers.

And then I move my thumb, just the slightest bit, caressing the underside of one breast.

She moans, head dropping back so quickly I barely get my other one behind it, barely stop her skull from colliding with the tree trunk.

Fuck.

She is so fucking pretty.

Skin flushed, lips swollen, eyes dilated, tendons in her neck standing out sharply in relief.

"Again," she whispers into the night, making me realize that I've stopped, that I'm staring at her, holding her.

But I'm not *doing* anything.

I bend my head, taste her again—long and deep and wet—and then I'm breaking away, speaking against her skin as I trail my way over to her ear, "God," I rasp, "we are *so* going to set my sheets on fire."

She gasps again, but I don't know if it's my words, or because I've sucked her earlobe into my mouth, tonguing it lightly, or because I've moved my hand.

Not brushing the curve of her breast.

But cupping it, molding it in the palm of my hand, massaging her flesh, running my thumb over the hard bead of her nipple.

Her legs tighten, her pelvis rocks, and—

I pull away.

I don't want to. I want to strip her naked and fuck her right against this tree.

But—

I also want her to remember, to feel what our bodies do together, to ache for me as I'm going to ache for her.

I want her to ache so intensely that she's desperate to have me back in her arms.

So...I pull my mouth from her skin, drop my hand from her breast, coax her legs down from around my waist, settling them onto the ground.

"Wh—?" She grabs for me when I remain close to steady her, eyes hazed and body shaking. "What are you doing?"

I grind my teeth together, sweep her up into my arms when she wavers, and carry her to the house, snagging her glass of wine from the table as I move by it.

Into the house.

Up the stairs.

Through her bedroom door.

I set the wineglass on the nightstand and her on the mattress.

And then...

I turn and walk away.

"Rome!" she cries as I move through the open bedroom door. "What are you doing?"

I glance over my shoulder at her, wanting nothing more than to stride back across the room and get inside her.

But this is more important—the long game and logic and reason.

So, I just start walking again, tossing over my shoulder,

"Dream about me, Kitten."

TWENTY-FOUR

Chrissy

DREAM about him

I'm going to murder him.

I dreamed about him, all right. *All* freaking night, until my eyelids were gritty and my body was aching, and I'd finally taken matters into my own hands—or toys, rather.

Two orgasms hadn't even taken the edge off.

So yeah, I'm going to murder him.

Especially because it's the buttcrack of dawn and I'm still aching and wanting and my clit feels raw...and I'm about to take charge of six eight-week-old corgi pups from Rory's hoarder house.

She's sent pictures—they're freaking adorable.

She's sent videos—they're complete and utter terrors.

I groan and rub my face, hating my life. Then I move downstairs, completely intent on my coffeepot. Which is probably why I miss the man peering into my sliding glass door, watching me.

Waiting for me.

I flick the switch to start brewing, turn to look out my windows, wanting a glimpse of the orange and red and blue sky, the sun just beginning to rise in the east.

And then I see him.

Watching and waiting.

Coming for me.

I scream, knees giving way, my body collapsing to the ground. I huddle in a ball, hands over my ears, eyes slammed closed. "No! *No!*" I wade through the fear, try to pull myself together, distantly knowing I'm panicking, but unable to stop. "No. Don't! I—"

This is nothing like that night.

But it's brought that night right back, and I'm drowning in the darkness, feeling hands on my skin, the barrel of a gun pressed to my temple.

I lurch toward the panic button, fingers scrabbling on the tile floor as I crabwalk my way to where the knob is located.

Ignoring the knocking.

Ignoring the voice.

Just trying to breathe.

Trying to survive.

Like that night.

Until...I get my fingers around the fob for the panic button, glance back out the windows, and hesitate long enough to...

Realize it's Rome.

He pounds on the door. "Let me in, Kitten," he orders through the glass. "Let me in right fucking *now.*"

For a second, I can't move.

Then I manage to peel my fingers away from the panic button—thankfully not pressed—and I push up to my feet, walk to the back door on, albeit, shaky legs.

The moment I flick the lock, he's pushing open the door, and doing it so quickly, it almost smacks me in the face. He catches it before it can then he's moving into me, crowding me back, until I'm pressed against the kitchen counter. "Kitten, what the fuck was that?"

My heart is pounding so hard and fast that it feels like it's sitting right in the back of my throat, feels like I have to force the words out. "Nothing," I whisper. "I just—you startled me."

And I crumpled like a wet paper bag.

Acted like a total fucking baby.

My heart rate is slowing, but my embarrassment is growing. No, I didn't expect Rome to be on my back porch, staring at me through my windows as I stumbled toward my coffeepot.

But I also didn't expect him to be in my back yard the other night, and I handled that with aplomb.

This...*this?*

I thought I was over this type of reaction.

So, yeah, embarrassment doesn't begin to cover it.

I want the floor to open up in front of me, to swallow me whole, and—

"No," he says then stops, shakes his head. "Yes, I startled you. But also"—his eyes come to mine—"that's not why you reacted the way you did."

He's right.

Because while a normal person might have jumped or even shrieked, collapsing into a blubbering ball and crawling frantically toward safety on the kitchen floor isn't a typical reaction.

And it's not typical of me.

Of the person I've worked hard to become.

"This is why your dad is so protective," he says.

I still, the reaction giving me away when I would have continued holding this in, shoving it down, pretending it hadn't happened. Move on. Move forward toward the person I want to be. Keep doing that and all will be fine.

Except that it isn't, apparently.

"Tell me, Kitten."

"We don't have time for this," I say. "My friend Rory is going to be here soon with the puppies I agreed to foster and—"

"Tell me, Kitten."

I can't. I don't want to.

And...I don't *not* want to. Because if I keep hiding behind it, I'll never escape. And...because if I keep hiding it, then I just keep giving those nights, those men power.

It's just—

"Tell me, Kitten."

What if he looks at me differently?

Fuck it.

That's what this is supposed to be, right? Seeing if we fit? Seeing if my baggage is too heavy?

If he can't carry this, then what the fuck am I doing trying at all.

I lift my chin, and...

I tell him.

"I was kidnapped when I was sixteen."

He rears back so quickly that I nearly lose my balance, but even as I waver, he's there again, body close, hands gentle as he wraps them around my waist, as he holds me up, as he stares down at me so gently, I want to cry.

Only...

I may have freaked out, may have allowed some old demons to knock me down for a moment, but I will not shed another fucking tear over the men who took me, who hurt me, who destroyed my childhood.

"You know," I whisper, blinking rapidly, blinking back those tears. "I used to have blonde hair."

His fingers tighten slightly, but not enough to hurt.

"I...um...started dyeing it a few years ago."

"Yes, Kitten."

I blink again. No more tears. Not now. Not ever. "I did it because the blonde reminded me of them. Because when I was with them, they cut it off and sent it to my dad."

He flinches and I reach up, touch his cheek.

"I kept it for a while, grew it back even longer, but every time I looked in the mirror—" I exhale. "It was a reminder and I wasn't doing well, not for a long while after I got home. That's why I don't remember those Gold events when I was in college and you were there all that well. My dad got me back and I went to therapy and I dealt with it—or so I thought." I sigh. "Except, it kept coming back up and even though I was trying to focus on my classes and being more independent, I kept...failing," I whisper. "I needed him there until I was more stable. And then, after, I didn't have the heart to tell him to back off, not when during the days I was taken—" I inhale through my nose, release it slowly. "He was unhinged, and when I came back, he was as messed up as I was."

Rome's hold is gentle. "Because it's always been the two of you."

I nod. "Yes, because it's always been the two of us." And since I'm dropping baggage, I just...give him the rest of it. "My mom left me on his doorstep when I was a baby"—his eyes widen—"literally on his doorstep, and we were able to confirm that I'm biologically his, but she didn't leave any identifying information about herself. I don't know who she is, and I probably never will, and..." I shake my head. "I think I've finally gotten to a point where I'm at peace with that."

He tilts his head to the side, studies me closely. "Okay, Kitten," he says, and I know it's not that he's trying to move me along, but rather that he accepts I'm at peace with it—and also probably that he knows we have bigger things to talk about.

"So, I...um...well..."

He waits while I get my thoughts together, patient and gentle and—

The words come.

"I was doing my best to move forward, but eventually it all caught up to me and I had a breakdown. My dad was there, and while he helped me get the resources I needed—more therapy and medication and, then, self-defense classes—I don't think he ever forgave himself for what happened that night when I was taken and how it affected me afterward."

A gentle hand on my cheek. "What did happen?" he asks. "When you were taken?"

"Me," I say. "I was reckless and stubborn that my dad wouldn't let me go on a date with a boy I liked, and sixteen-year-old me didn't recognize that I was being used, not until I snuck out to meet him and he wasn't there." I clench my teeth together, swallow down the bile that's rising. "His uncle was instead."

"Shit, baby," he whispers, tugging me close, hugging me tight. "I'm so sorry they did that to you."

"It's why I'm such a pushover when it comes to my dad," I whisper. "I did that to him by being a stupid hormonal idiot, and I paid the price. They didn't rape me, but they made it very clear they could, and—" I suck in another breath, holding it like my therapist taught me, then releasing it slowly. "And they hurt me in other ways."

He touches my cheek. "God, Kitten, I'm so fucking sorry."

"I'm okay," I say. "I'm healed and alive and happy, and I'm not perfect, but I'm...okay."

"You're my gorgeous goddess," he murmurs, "and that's way better than perfect any day of the week." He leans in, brushes his lips over my forehead—just as the doorbell rings.

"I have to get that," I murmur.

"I know." He touches my cheek. "You are so fucking beautiful and strong and I'm in awe of you."

"Rome—" I begin, but then he's handing me the carafe of coffee he brought over, the reason—I presume—he showed up at my back door in the first place, and he's slipping out into the morning sunshine.

"I'll see you tonight," he promises, closing it behind him.

I nod, and heart pounding, I leave the kitchen, answer the front door, and pretty soon I'm inundated with cute, fluffy corgi butts.

But even though the cuteness is overwhelming—

I don't forget the way Rome looked at me as he left.

TWENTY-FIVE

Rome

CONSIDERING I started the day by scaring the hell out of the woman I care a fuck-ton about then finding out some heavy shit, *heavy* shit we would need to revisit later (so I can understand how to never fucking scare her like that again), I would have expected my morning to improve.

At least a little bit.

But the shitty start to the day has extended, flowing over the rest of my day, tainting anything positive with disgusting, awful—

Shit.

First came the torture of Media Day—being in front of the camera, having to pose like an idiot, smile like a goober.

Look sternly into the camera, Rome. Yes! Just like that! Now, smile! Chin down. Hold. Hold. Hold. Now, stick up and—

It doesn't stop.

Pretending to shoot, to stop suddenly, to glare at an opponent.

Posing next to a fucking eagle.

Posing next to the stuffed eagle that is our mascot, Blaze.

Stupid name. Stupid mascot.

Stupid—

Media day.

Especially when it's already dumb and uncomfortable and I feel like an idiot in front of the camera, and Pat keeps walking by, Duncan his moronic shadow, their smirks wide and dumb and—

God, it feels like high school.

Especially when they snicker as I get off the ice.

And when they decide the best course of action is to keep fucking with me.

Starting with deflating the ball I brought in for some backstage soccer, a way to keep us warm and engaged as we rotate through our turn playing model.

It was an "accident."

But I know what it is.

I interfered in their spat, and now they're going to make me pay the price.

Duncan is an idiot, banding with someone like Pat, apparently forgetting that *I* was the one who saved his ass and stopped him from getting choked out.

But po-tay-toe, po-tah-toe.

Apparently, he doesn't think that attempted murder is a bad thing.

Regardless, I ignore their antics, reinflate the ball, and bring it back into the hall.

And...they decide to join in.

Of course, joining in means fucking with the game,

missing balls they can easily get, or sending them off way too hard for no reason.

Or, for *a* reason—that being to frustrate any of the guys who are coming together, succeeding at keeping us apart, at being a roadblock to something that might develop into camaraderie.

Dumb, right?

I think so.

But I'm not in Pat's head. I don't get the motivation. Nor Duncan's.

And I can only...

Sigh as I bend over and pick up another piece of glass from the shattered light overhead—the one that Duncan "accidentally" broke with a too-strong kick.

"You want to grab a beer?"

I look up, see King and Cam standing there, having cleaned up plenty of shards themselves, and...things might not be going well with the team, but at least the three of us are figuring our shit out, and I know I can count on them to be decent.

Maybe we'll be able to rope in a few more and form a decent chunk of the locker room to counterbalance the assholes.

"Yeah," I say. "I want a beer."

***

"So," King says, as we wait for those beers, his brows lifted expectantly.

"So what?" I ask.

Cam snorts, shakes his head.

King punches my shoulder. Hard. "So, what the fuck are you doing about Christina—*Chrissy*—Dubois?"

I should have seen this coming.

Beer. Bonding. And interrogation.

"Nothing," I mutter. "She's my neighbor. I'm being neighborly and that's it."

Cam snorts again.

King just studies me for a long moment. "You are so full of shit."

Secrets.

I hate them.

Especially when I'm trying to make friends—which makes me sound like a goddamned grade schooler.

"Think what you want," I say, leaning back slightly, "but we talked, decided we're better off as neighbors, mostly because we're not going to do anything to rock the boat with Jean-Michel."

"Is *talking*"—he does goddamned finger quotes—"code for fucking?"

I glare at him, but don't take the bait. "It would be stupid to start something with my neighbor. No matter how beautiful she is—"

Their brows come up, but I force myself to press on, even though I probably just undermined all the bullshit I was trying to spout.

"—I have enough crap to deal with. Pat and Duncan in the locker room, management wanting me to somehow pull us all together, trying to win a game when most of us can barely stand to be within five feet of each other. I don't need to add the owner's daughter into the mix."

"*Need* and women sometimes get tangled up," King says, taking a sip of beer.

"Is that advice from you or your mom?" I ask.

Cam cackles, and scowling, King punches my shoulder again. *Harder.* "You're hilarious."

"How's that Rolex fitting?" I tell him, earning another punch.

King pulls back his sleeve. "Fitting great."

"What about your mom's new pick for you?" I push. "Is that fitting great too?"

King glares.

I glare.

"Children," Cam warns.

I don't want to back down, but I have all of two allies on the team, so I let it go, settle back onto my stool, extend an olive branch. "How about we stop talking about shit that neither of us want to discuss and focus on something more important—hockey?"

King studies me for a long moment, likely seeing right through my bullshit, but eventually he nods.

And we stop talking about women.

And start talking about hockey.

Thank fucking God.

Because keeping secrets sucks.

But it's not *all* bad, having that beer with Cam and King.

Mostly because we *do* talk hockey—and also because Hudson and Levi end up joining us.

I have hopes that the non-asshole numbers have grown to five.

Only seventeen more to go!

I shake my head, clench the steering wheel so I don't rub at the throb in my forehead, and drive back to my place.

We're dating secretly, so I can't just take Chrissy out to dinner, but I *can* order us something, can cook if I have any food in the fridge.

But first, I have to convince her to come over to my place.

I turn into my driveway, relieved to see the lights shining through her front windows, and pull into my garage, closing the door behind me. I grab my shit, make my way inside, and scope out the contents of my fridge.

And I make plans.

Make plans for a secret first date.

Make plans to woo a woman in the shadow of her father's protective gaze.

Make plans to win her heart.

Because that might be the most important game of my life.

And it's a game I can't afford to lose.

TWENTY-SIX

Chrissy

HE KNOCKS at the front door this time, and when I see his face peer through the side pane of glass, I don't drop into a sniveling, sobbing mess of a woman.

I just exhale, move to flick open the lock, and—

Try to ignore the embarrassment twining through my belly.

"Hey," he says when I pull open the door.

"Hey," I say back, biting at the side of my tongue, trying to hold in my apology. But it starts to escape anyway. "About this morning," I begin.

"No."

Just *no.*

And then he's pushing into the house, nudging me back, gathering me into his arms. "Don't you dare try to apologize for this morning," he says as he tucks the top of my head beneath his chin and holds me tight. "I was the one who scared you, and your past is not something you have to apologize for. What those fuckers did to you—" His hold tightens for a moment and then it's as though he has to force himself to relax, to gentle his grip. "That was on them. Not you. It's not your fault, and if I find out who they are, I will—"

I press a palm to his front, lean back enough to meet his eyes. "My father took care of them."

There's a pause, his broad chest expanding and then contracting on a long, deep breath. "Considering the threats of dismemberment he tossed my way so casually, I'm guessing he took care of them permanently?"

"They—" I do some breathing of my own. "I don't have to worry about them bothering me. Not ever again."

"Good," he says, and I can tell he genuinely means it.

But then we're both standing there awkwardly again.

"I find that I don't really know how to start secret dating someone," he finally says.

Which has a hysterical giggle bubbling up in my chest. "Me neither."

"I thought..." He shrugs. "We could start by having dinner?"

I grin. "Dinner sounds great."

He grins. "Good, Kitten."

"See?" I say. "I think we're already kind of crushing the whole secret dating thing."

His brows lift. "By nearly getting caught in your office and then sitting across the dinner table from your dad and making him suspicious of me?"

"Ding. Ding. Ding." I tap my nose. "*Totally* acing it."

His grin is so beautiful it has my heart skipping a beat, but his next words have it convulsing with tenderness, especially when he gently cups my cheek. "How about you come over to my place and tell me about your day as I cook you dinner?"

That sounds...perfect.

Only—

"No?" he asks, seemingly reading that word cross my mind.

"I have the puppies," I say, nodding my head toward the spare room where I have the gaggle of corgis confined. "I can't leave them for too long, or I'm worried they'll create mischief."

"Mischief?

"The couple of dogs I'm watching for my friend Rory—she runs a dog rescue—has turned into a litter of six eight-week-old corgis." I smile. "And turns out they create quite the amount of mischief."

"*Six?*"

I nod. "Their rescue is full up and she's desperate, otherwise she wouldn't ask me to disturb Queen Joan." I nod to my cranky kitty, who's glaring at us from her perch.

"No," he says. "We can't disturb Joan of *freaking* Arc."

"Meow," she growls quietly.

"Exactly, baby," he says, moving over to her, lifting his hand—

"Be careful," I warn.

But he's already within Claw Distance, and I wince, start moving toward him.

So, color me surprised when Joan of *freaking* Arc allows his hand to cross the invisible threshold she keeps around herself and the rest of the world and lets him scratch her between the ears.

What the actual fuck?

She doesn't even let *me* do that.

I take another step toward them, and she tracks my movement, green eyes narrowing, low growl filling the air.

"Traitor," I mutter.

She hisses.

I shake my head.

Rome continues scratching, crooning softly at my cranky cat for a few more moments before he's turning back toward me. "Okay, so"—he taps my nose lightly—"let me go raid my fridge and bring my supplies here. We can both be on puppy duty while I cook."

"*This* is your idea of a first date?" I ask. "Cooking for me while we puppy-vise?" I'm not upset. I just...men aren't— they *don't*...well, they don't want to cook for me and sit home with my cranky as hell senior cat and foster puppies.

Rome just grins and brushes his lips over mine. "A beautiful woman, Joan of *freaking* Arc, and six corgis? I can't imagine anything better."

I sigh and pat my belly, leaning back on my elbows on the floor.

I'm full—probably too full, all things considered, but Rome is an excellent cook.

(Much better than I am, that's for sure).

It was simple fair, but that's perfect for me. I can't stand all those fancy, tiny plates of food—a sip of foam here, a bit of roasted vegetable topped with caviar there, all for the cost of a car payment.

Luckily, my dad only eats at those types of places if he's required to for work.

But that also means, I'm usually right alongside him, stuck eating the fancy food that isn't filling...and ending up at In-N-Out afterward.

I smile, thinking about milkshakes and extra-crispy fries.

The world would probably get a kick out of Jean-Michel Dubois chowing down on a Double-Double.

A finger sliding down my cheek. "What?" Rome murmurs.

Murmurs because there's currently a puppy on his chest —a puppy named Athena.

Because Rory loves a name theme as well, and this litter is inspired by Greek and Roman gods...which is fitting because I think a certain *Rome* god may have been claimed by this one's big, puppy eyes.

"I was just thinking about how my dad hates fancy restaurants, so much so that we would often hit up an In-N-Out after some long business meeting we were forced to attend."

"We?" he asks, slowly smoothing a hand over Athena's back, turning her into a drooling mess—and considering I know exactly what it feels like to have that hand trailing over my skin, I can't help but feel a pang of jealousy.

"You know my dad was overprotective before"—I glance over at him and he nods, hand reaching out and carefully taking mine so as not to disturb Athena (or the crew of pups surrounding me)—"afterwards, neither of us could stand to be separated for long. He was my safe space," I say.

Another nod, his fingers flexing.

"And, for a while, I thought that I might want to be in business like him, so I asked to be included in everything." I shrug as well as I'm able, considering I'm flat on my back, surrounded by sleeping pups. "That notion resolved itself quickly in my mind, even though my dad hasn't necessarily changed his."

"He wants you to take over his businesses?"

I nod. "I don't mind helping out with the team," I say. "At least that's applicable to my degree. But it's just that in my mind—*helping*. I don't want to be on the board. I don't want to be responsible for making the tough decisions about the roster. I don't want to be stuck in an office every day when..." I sigh, bite back the rest of the argument I've given my dad countless times over the last couple of years.

Since I've begun to figure out who I am.

And what I want.

"Don't want to be stuck in an office when you could be at your house in a literal dog pile?"

I freeze then giggle. "Yes," I say. "Exactly that." I sober. "And I know it sounds like I'm a spoiled brat, but I'm taken care of. I'm beyond lucky. So, why can't I pass along some of that to these animals who are suffering?"

His eyes are warm. "I think you can." His fingers flex. "And I think you are."

"I think I am too," I whisper. "I just don't know how to make my dad see reason."

Rome sighs. "I think that getting Jean-Michel to see anything that's not *his* idea isn't going to be easy."

I still, my hand in his, our bodies surrounded in floofy corgi butts.

And I know he's right.

But I also know...I still have to try.

TWENTY-SEVEN

Rome

"WOOF!"

I look down at the little face of Athena, and I'm lost.

Almost as lost as the woman who's fallen asleep next to me.

"*Woof!*"

"Shh," I whisper, slowly sitting up and taking her with me. "You don't want to wake the human who's responsible for feeding you."

"Woof."

It's quieter now, like she knows what I'm saying.

"You need to sleep through the night and go potty outside and make sure to unleash those puppy eyes on her any chance you get, all the better for extra treats."

Athena tilts her head to the side, big old bat ears almost bigger than her head, dark brown eyes—with *all* the puppy magic—pointed in my direction.

Then she licks my chin.

And I *know* I'm as lost for this little pup as I am for the woman snoring softly on the rug, a trio of passed-out pups surrounding her.

The other two (and Athena), are looking a little...perky, and considering it's bedtime, I figure I'd better do my sleeping woman—and myself, since I won't leave her by herself to clean up the mess wrought by a half-dozen mischief making corgi pups—a favor and let them stretch their legs in the pen Chrissy set up out back.

I grab Athena, Diana, and Zeus and creep from the room, carrying them out, setting them in doggy jail, and waiting while they sniff every inch of the space before they, eventually, use the bathroom. Then I'm carrying three now sleepy again pups inside, putting them in their indoor pen, and repeating the process with Hermes, Apollo, and Neptune.

Chrissy doesn't move as I come in and out, just continues with that adorably soft snoring, even as I turn on the sound machine and off the lights, even as I'm scooping her up, inhaling the soft, floral scent of her as I walk upstairs with her in my arms, bring her down the hall to her bedroom, as I settle her into bed.

I stand there for a second, debating.

And I know...

I'm not strong enough to deposit her on the mattress and walk away. Not this time.

I need more time with her, need the settling force of her nature, need...

Her.

She rolls over, lips parting slightly as she breathes out a long sigh—and on that sigh, I hear my name.

"Rome."

It's a whisper of a sound.

But that does it, strangles the final bit of control I have.

I tug down the blankets, crawl into bed beside her.

I draw her into my arms, and...

I hold her close as I fall asleep.

I WAKE to the smell of...

Something not good.

Something very *not* good.

And a wet tongue licking my chin.

I frown, cracking open sleep-heavy eyes, seeing a tiny adorable puppy face in mine. "Hi, precious," I murmur, cupping the back of Athena's head, wondering how she made her way to my chest. "Is there a reason you're in my bed and a certain curvy brunette isn't?"

I sit up further, tucking the pup against my chest so she doesn't tumble off, and look around the room for the other woman I'd been holding before I nodded off.

Only, the bedroom is empty and morning light is beginning to stream through the windows and...

Chrissy is nowhere in sight.

What the fuck?

Athena's nose starts working.

And—*that's right*—there's a smell in the air.

Like something's burning.

It's tart and clogging the air and...there's *smoke* in the air.

"What the fuck?" I mutter, tossing the blankets to the side and pushing up to my feet, keeping the pup close and going to the windows, wondering if flames are closing in. This is California after all, and fires aren't uncommon this time of year, what with the dry hillsides and lack of rain. Fucking October, man. But the sky is clear, and the sun is out. In fact, it's a beautiful fall morning.

Which means...the fire is likely coming from *inside*—

The dogs.

The grumpy ass cat.

"Shit." I move to the door, hustle down the stairs, ignoring Athena's licking of my chin, the puppy seemingly not worried despite the thickening smoke as I hit the main floor, as I sniff, pause, trying to determine the source. *There.* I move toward the kitchen, and...

Find Chrissy standing on the kitchen island wearing the shortest pair of shorts I have ever seen...

Waving a towel at the ceiling.

"Shh," she coaxes the smoke detector. "Just stay quiet and I promise I won't ever attempt to cook again. Just don't wake up—"

"Whatcha doing?" I ask, leaning back against the wall, Athena snuffling closer, sticking her cold nose beneath my chin.

Chrissy freezes, slowly turns in my direction. "Rome," she whispers.

I set Athena on the floor, cross over to her, resting my hips against the island and looking up...right beneath the loose leg holes of her shorts.

Fuck.

Lush thighs.

A plump pussy pushing against soft pink lace.

I don't think.

I just wrap my arm around the back of her knees, drawing her slightly forward until she gets that I want her to shift forward, that I want her to slide off that counter.

I back up...barely. Just enough to let her down, so that her body fits in the gap between mine and the counter, but it has to brush against mine the entire way down—inch by inch by luscious inch.

"What are you doing, Kitten?" I ask.

Her lips are parted, her eyes are slightly glazed. Which is a good thing because it matches what I'm feeling—my dick growing hard, my pulse speeding, my body filling with need. "What?" she murmurs, her hand lifting, pressing lightly to my chest.

I lean against her a little heavier. "I asked what you're doing, baby."

Her teeth press into her bottom lip, and her lids go half-mast, lush curves melting against me. "I—"

I drop my head, press my mouth to her throat, needing to taste her.

And she's fucking delicious.

I suck lightly, leaving a pink mark on that creamy skin. She shudders, her hands diving into my hair, holding me against her. "Mmm," she whispers, arching her neck, digging her fingers into my scalp. "Keep kissing me."

A soft order that I have no issue obeying.

"Here?" I ask, dragging my lips along her throat. "Or here?" Back along her jaw, heading for her ear. "Or here, Kitten?" I murmur, lightly tonguing her earlobe, hand at her waist, keeping her flush against me.

She moans softly, head falling back.

"Oh," I say silkily, "maybe here?" Ghosting over her cheek, dancing along the edge of her mouth, almost a kiss, *almost* what she wants...

Just not quite.

"Rome," she protests, arching against me, head coming forward, trying to align our lips.

"Here?" I ask, bypassing her mouth, dragging my tongue along the other side of her throat. At the same time, my hand at her hip is moving, sliding up her side, taking the material of her shirt with it.

Up. Up. *Up.*

Until I have to pull my mouth away from her skin in order to get it off her.

A pity, but worth it.

"Why aren't you wearing a bra, Kitten?" I murmur, my gaze taking a long, slow perusal down, my cock going from hard to granite when I see those pink-tipped breasts, her nipples hard and pouting, calling for my lips and teeth and tongue.

Her flush spreads down from her cheeks, over her chest. "It was uncomfortable."

I slowly lower my head, inhaling the scent of her, mouth a millimeter from her skin. "Because you fell asleep in it?"

A nod, those tits bouncing.

My cock throbs. "Do you want me to kiss you here?" I lightly cup one lush mound in my hand, her flesh overflowing my palm, her nipple hard against my skin.

She gasps and nods again, her tits bouncing a second time, and fuck I could watch that all day, especially when she arches slightly, pressing into my hand, the movement lifting her other breast toward my mouth, begging me silently to taste.

So, I do.

And it almost makes me come in my pants.

I seal my lips over her flesh, drawing deeply on the tight bud, making her sigh and then gasp, those fingers tightening further in my hair.

It stings like a motherfucker, but I'm not stopping, no fucking way. Not when it has my name dancing off the tip of her tongue, her body undulating, her grip relentless. I suck and nip, draw that bud deep, sliding my palm up her back, placing it between her shoulder blades, coaxing her to arch further, to give me better access, and then, when she does, feasting on her until her skin glistens, until I can't resist the call of that neglected breast and I find myself kissing my way over to her other nipple, drawing on it deeply, rolling the hardened tip on my tongue, dragging my teeth over the sensitive bud.

No mercy.

No relief.

Just me and those fucking gorgeous tits.

Until she shudders. "Rome," she whispers, body trembling against mine.

I look up, see her eyes wide and her head tossed back, dark hair cascading down her back in shining waves like a fucking goddess. Never have I seen anything more beautiful than her in this moment—cheeks flushed, tendons in her throat standing out in sharp relief—until those deep blue eyes come to mine.

Glazed with need.

Close to completion.

I want to slip my hand beneath the waistband of her shorts, want to feel the slick heat of that cunt.

But I want to make her come *this* way first.

TWENTY-EIGHT

Chrissy

I SHIVER when something changes in his eyes, heat and arousal mixing with just the slightest bit of wicked.

My knees tremble, and I know that if his body wasn't flush with mine, if he wasn't pressing me back against the island, I would be in a puddle on the tile floor.

But he *is* pressed against me.

And he's big and strong and his mouth is...

Fucking *divine.*

Almost as good as that rough hand on my breast, massaging and caressing, gripping tightly, rolling my nipple between thumb and forefinger.

My head is spinning, my body feels as though it is a single live wire.

One touch and I'll explode.

"Kitten?"

"Mmm?" I manage to get out.

"Are you going to come?"

A full-body shiver rips through me, and I know—*know*—if I don't come, I'm going to die.

So, I nod.

And, thankfully, it's the right answer because that wicked gleam in his eyes grows and he bends his head again, taking my nipple into his mouth.

Pleasure explodes through me, a huge wave that threatens to suck me under. It's sneaky, those waves, having splashed and splashed against the shore, creeping up toward me, starting at my toes then my ankles, my knees and thighs and pelvis. Up my torso, closing in around my throat—

He nips.

Hard and sharp and—

I explode, shatter into a million pieces of sand, that wave crashing over my head, sending me under deep, dark water for one long moment.

And then I'm breaking the surface, finding his hands moving on my skin again, gripping the waistband of my shorts and tugging them down, taking my underwear with them.

"Ro—*ah!*" His name ends in a squeal because he's stripped me naked and settled me on the counter.

Which is cold.

But I'm only able to focus on that for a second before my legs are spread and—

"Should I kiss you here too?" he rasps.

But, thank fuck, he doesn't actually expect me to answer because he's already leaning in and then his mouth is on me.

"Oh, God," I groan, head falling back, losing sight of the lights overhead—the same lights that are hazy from my attempt at making breakfast. "Oh, my *fucking* God."

His lips are soft against my pussy, but his tongue is a glorious amount of firm, sliding slickly through my folds, circling my clit, pressing the flat of it to the bundle of nerves, making me jerk and moan and...*fucking melt*. And then he's sliding a finger inside me, that blunt intrusion exactly what I need.

Only...it's a tease. It's not enough—nor is the second finger plunging deep, stretching me until my entrance burns, until I crave the burn of his rock-hard cock.

"Rome," I whisper.

Or maybe it's a plea.

One he hears because he lifts his head, but only slightly, the heat of his breath, his words a damp brush of sensation. "Come like this first," he rasps.

And there's that full-body shiver again.

Something he doesn't miss, I know, because his mouth curves up into a sexy, cocky smile before his tongue and lips and fingers get back to work.

Every nerve in my body is on fire, coiling tight, winding and winding and—

Then there's pressure in the tight rosebud in the cleft of my ass, one roughened fingertip drawing moisture from my pussy, back along to that crease, coating it, and then...

Pressing.

Thick and hard and another slight burn, the tight muscle there resisting.

But then it gives...and it's fucking *great*.

I fall back onto my elbows, my legs splaying wide, his fingers sliding deeper. And all the while, his lips and tongue don't stop their relentless assault on my senses. They're building that orgasm into me, and if the first was a rogue wave, this time it's a freaking tsunami.

Rolling in. Decimating my awareness of anything but that pleasure *right there*. Just out of reach. Almost—

"Fuck!" I groan.

Because then it *is* there, hitting with the force of a

runaway train, and my elbows give way. I feel him move—faster than I can track—and before my head can hit the granite, his palm is beneath my head, cushioning me before I can concuss myself.

Cushioning me as wave after wave of bliss rolls over me.

"Christ, Kitten," he rasps, kissing his way up my body, tongue dragging over my skin, his beard damp and leaving a trail of moisture as he makes it to my breasts, to my throat, to my mouth.

I can taste myself on his tongue when he kisses me, but I like it.

I fucking *love* it.

Love how there's no hesitation, how he's just fucked me with his lips and fingers and tongue, but he isn't shy about tasting me.

Then he's pulling back, slipping his hand gently from behind my head—and I'll be fucking honest—it takes me a minute to settle into the loss of the heat of him and how right it feels and how I don't fucking like it going away to realize that *he's pulling back.*

As in, reaching for my clothes.

As in, making me come twice and then going to play staid and moral hero by backing away and—

What the actual fuck?

I lurch up from the counter.

The movement isn't the least bit graceful, but I manage to make it upright.

Rome freezes, shirt pulled tightly around his torso as he's bent, picking up my clothes, head swiveling, deep brown eyes going wide. "Kitten—"

I move again—still ungracefully—sliding off the granite, feet hitting the cool wooden floor. "What are you doing?" I ask, moving close to him.

He straightens, and the movement brings his mouth so fucking close to my skin that I feel the heated glaze of his breath. "Easy," he murmurs, setting my clothes on the counter, one hand dropping to my waist when those orgasms go to my head, and I waver.

I narrow my eyes. "*Easy?*" I ask, and my tone is deadly. "You're telling me *easy* when you gave me two orgasms that practically set my hair on fire, and now you're just going to walk away?"

I see it in his expression then—that was *exactly* what he planned.

Because...Rome is honorable. It's why he cares about the team so much, why he works so fucking hard on and off the ice. It's why he would help me with puppies and keep our dating a secret so I won't feel guilty about putting him at risk with my overprotective father.

It's why he's—

"No, Kitten," he murmurs. "I'm not going to walk away." But he does just that, taking a couple of steps back, turning and glancing into the sink, lips twitching—likely because he's spotted the remnants of the breakfast I had been trying to make him.

The *charred* remnants.

He spins back, mouth still curved. "I'm going to cook you breakfast and then we'll—"

But he doesn't finish that sentence because I've launched myself at him.

He catches me—because of course he does—even though he's clearly shocked by my actions, one arm wrapping around my middle, the other beneath my ass. "Kitten—"

I kiss him.

Mouth open, tongue parting his lips, tangling with his. Kissing him deep and long, until my lungs are protesting, until my head is spinning, until all of my focus is reduced to solely this man, and only when I can't stand another second without breathing do I break away. I grip his jaw as we both breathe heavily. "Don't back away from me," I say. "Don't deny yourself because you're worried I'm not ready. I'm not a precious vase to be placed on a high shelf and protected. I'm a grown woman who's decided what she wants."

The irony of my words don't escape me.

I'm a woman who's decided what I want.

And I'm hiding it from my father.

But I don't have time to focus on that. Not right now.

I bring my forehead to his. "If you're not ready—because I know we're moving fast—that's fine," I say. "I can wait. I just—"

"I don't want to wait," he says.

The words are spoken in a rush, and they take my breath away. Or maybe that's because I suddenly find myself bent over the counter, ass in the air. I glance over my shoulder and watch as Rome's shirt is ripped over his head. He tosses it to the side and hits the floor at the same time as he flicks open the button on his jeans and shoves the material down those thick thighs of his. A moment later, I watch his underwear join the party on the floor and—

"Oh," I whisper.

Because that cock of his...

It's big and thick and my pussy convulses, remembering the burn of his fingers inside me, knowing this will bring more of that, and desperate for it.

He bends, snags his jeans, digging out his wallet from the back pocket, and I thank God he's thinking enough to extract a condom from the depths, to tear it open and roll it down the hard length of his erection.

Then he's close, his warm and naked front pressed to my

back. "Like this, Kitten?" he asks, skating a hand down my side, drawing my hips back so my ass is higher in the air. "Or should I take you to bed?"

I lift my brows as I glance over my shoulder at him. "If you don't get inside me, I'll have to take matters into my own hands."

He grins, notches the head of his cock at my entrance. "Can't have that now, can we?" he murmurs, pushing inside in a steady stroke that—fuck, yes—brings that slight burn, the risk of overfilling. "I almost dropped you the last time."

I groan, arch back against him, take his cock a few inches deeper.

He hisses out a breath, and his teeth press into my shoulder, all signs of teasing forgotten.

And then he's pressing into me, long and thick and hard, bottoming out and pausing, his head dropping to my shoulder, his body wrapped around mine, his groan sending shivers down my spine.

Fucking *perfect.*

Especially when he draws back out, a long, slow slide that has my breath catching, my hips following his, not wanting to lose him.

And then back in.

Again. And again. And *again.*

"You feel so fucking good," he rasps, hips moving fast, cock driving deeper. "The way that cunt of yours is clasping me like a fucking fist." A groan. "Fucking hell, baby. So." A thrust. "Fucking." Another. "*Good.*" He smacks my ass and I gasp, the sting warming my cheek, spreading out along my belly, dipping phantom fingers in between my legs to rub my clit.

Oh.

"You like that?" he murmurs, leaning in, his teeth coming to my ear.

"Y-yes," I stutter, gasping again when he smacks me a second time.

And then I realize it's not phantom fingers on my clit.

It's *his* fingers.

Rubbing and circling, pressing firmly.

The waves are lapping at my toes again.

My ankles and knees and thighs.

My throat. My—

Another *smack!*

"Rome!" I shriek, thrusting back against him.

And the water has me, yanking me under, taking him alongside me.

"*Fuck!*" he groans.

One thrust, sending that pleasure spiraling. Another as he shouts my name. One more before he's slumping against me, breaths coming in rapid gusts.

My knees give way.

But he catches me.

Of course he does.

TWENTY-NINE

Rome

I DON'T KNOW how the fuck I'm going to play tonight when my legs feel like fucking Jell-O and my lungs seem as though they've stopped working.

The plus is that I've just had the best orgasm of my life.

The negative is that I legitimately don't know how the fuck to rally my leg muscles in order to get us both back onto our feet.

Because...circling back to that best orgasm of my life.

So, maybe I'll just sit here for a minute with this woman in my arms and soak that in.

There. Good plan. Go team.

Break.

Only, just as my eyes are sliding closed, my arms full of lush, beautiful woman, Chrissy goes stiff.

"What?" I ask, nape prickling, lids peeling back, pulse that had been settling picking speed back up again.

"*Athena,*" she says, sitting up so quickly she almost

tumbles out of my hold. I snag her before she faceplants on the hardwood floor.

"What about Athena?"

And then *I* go stiff, remembering that I put her down to get close to a certain scantily clad woman standing on the counter.

Which was...a long time ago.

She could be getting into all manner of mischief, including...

With Joan of *freaking* Arc.

Who isn't friendly with other animals.

"Shit," I whisper, summoning a herculean effort and finding my feet, bringing her up beside me. I grab my shirt, yank it over her head, snag my jeans and wrestle them on. "Let's go."

She grabs my hand, fingers wrapped tightly around mine. "Her perch in the office," she whispers, drawing me forward. "Joan likes the morning sun." And then we're hustling down the hall, moving through the door into an office filled from floor to ceiling with lavender shelves. There's a desk along one side of the space, placed between two large picture windows, and a cozy-looking armchair pushed into the opposite corner. Next to which...is a tall cat tower.

With a large, striped, pissed-off looking cat sitting on top of it.

And...

A tiny corgi puppy somehow having made it all the way to the top...

To curl up next to Joan of *freaking* Arc.

Chrissy stills.

I still.

"She's..." Chrissy turns wide eyes in my direction. "She's just lying there."

"She doesn't look particularly happy about it," I point out.

"That's"—a shake of her head—"that's her normal expression," Chrissy says softly. "If she was unhappy, we would have come in here and found Athena—" She shivers. "Well, Joan is a big cat, and she can do a lot of damage to a tiny puppy. Especially one who's as good at climbing as Athena apparently is."

"Should we get her down?" I ask softly.

She looks back at Joan, then at me, teeth worrying her bottom lip...

"I guess so." She takes a step toward the perch.

Joan hisses.

Chrissy freezes, looks back at me with eyes that are beginning to gleam with amusement.

Then takes another step, earns another warning yowl.

"I can't believe it," she murmurs, slowly backing away, moving into the circle of my arms.

I touch her cheek. "I think this means I have to keep her."

Which *her*, though I'm talking about...

I don't know.

Lies.

Because I already *know* I mean both of them.

"ARE you sure they'll be okay?" I ask quietly, lacing my fingers through hers, holding her hand tightly.

Chrissy smirks over at me. "You're already acting like a worried parent."

Well, yeah, because I adopted a puppy today.

And now I'm responsible for her, and she's fucking cute—and a goddamned menace when she's awake—and I spent the day outfitting my place for all things puppy and helping Chrissy with those other menaces and her cat rescue responsibilities and well...just spending the day with her.

Fucking nice.

So nice I don't want it to end.

Just being with her and learning what makes her laugh, what annoys her, what she likes to eat...

I don't want it to *end*. As in ever.

Even though it's just beginning.

Stupid, probably. But also...I've been around enough people who've found the people in their lives they're supposed to end up with to know that the beginning is sometimes the end, and to treasure every fucking moment of it.

So, I followed her car to the grocery store parking lot several blocks away from the arena, and we snuck in a quiet moment like a couple of teenagers because we've spent most of that *quiet moment* making out like said teenagers. The rest we spent like adult pet parents, watching the puppies and Joan—who willingly strolled her way into the puppy room as we were getting ready to leave—on the camera Chrissy set up in the space.

Likely, because we couldn't turn Athena loose in the house, and Joan's decided that Athena is hers, so she'll tolerate her corgi siblings.

Who are currently sleeping piled haphazardly in their pen.

With Joan sleeping in front of the entrance.

"They'll be okay," Chrissy says, squeezing my hand and leaning close. "But you won't unless you get going to the arena."

For the first time ever, I'm not looking forward to getting on the ice, nor to the thrill of the crowd or the feel of the puck on my stick. Not looking forward to connecting a tough pass or making a good play along the boards.

I want to stay in this car, holding hands with this woman.

But…that's not conducive with keeping this a secret.

An idea I fucking hate, even though it's barely twenty-four hours old.

I bite back a curse, then press a kiss to the back of her hand. "You're right." I exhale. "You'll be there?"

She touches my jaw. "I'll be watching." Then she slips out of my hold, tugs the door handle, and waves before getting out of my car.

I watch her in the rearview until she's safely in the driver's seat, watch as her headlights come on and she pulls out of the spot behind me.

And then I follow her to the arena.

And…

I miss the car following me.

THIRTY

Chrissy

"TELL ME FREAKING *EVERYTHING*," Rory says the moment I walk into the owner's suite.

I widen my eyes at her, telling her silently to shut the hell up.

"We're alone," she says, moving over to me and taking my arm, drawing me further into the room, showing me that—indeed—we *are* alone.

"Where's Phillip?" I ask, glancing around like her fiancée is about to pop out of the ground whack-a-mole style.

She grimaces then sighs.

"What?" I ask, concern pooling in my belly. Rory has been a good friend for years, and she doesn't get worried about much—aside from dogs, that is.

"He wasn't happy I missed his work event to go to that hoarder house, and he was even less happy that I brought the puppies home, even though it was just for the night." She sighs again. "We got in a fight about it again on the way here

—which is annoying because the only reason *I'm* here, watching a sport I don't understand and that bores me to tears is because my fiancée loves it." She wrinkles her nose. "And he's not even really thankful that I brought him, that *I'm* the freaking reason he's able to sit in the box in the first place."

Phillip is...

Well, I used to think that he was Rory's perfect match.

Now I'm worried that with all the years they've been together, that he's not the man for her.

God, anyone can see that she works to pay her bills, but she lives and breathes for animals.

And if Phillip doesn't get that?

I don't know if this wedding is going to actually happen.

"It's fine," she says, brushing back her long blonde hair, tucking it behind one ear. The action shows off her sparkling dog bone earrings.

Earrings that Phillip bought for her.

Because he used to understand.

"It's all fine," she goes on. "He's taking a walk to get a beer, I'm cornering my bestie to figure out why a certain hockey player from her father's team was at her house long enough to bond with our little Athena, and then we're going to figure our shit out like two grown adults."

"That sounds awful," I grumble.

"So says the woman with the secret *luv*-a," she says, drawing out the word and generally being ridiculous.

The problem is that Rome *has* become my lover.

A very, very good one who's left my legs shaking and my pussy aching with the reminder of him fucking me hard and fast and deep and...well, senseless.

He fucked me senseless.

Which is why my cheeks flush a bright red, and...why my friend sees that.

Why—

"You whore!" she exclaims gleefully, grabbing my arm and practically bouncing on the balls of her feet, she's so excited. "You goddamned *whore!*" She leans in. "Tell me everything so I can live vicariously through your whorish ways."

I swat her. "Bitch."

She just grins gleefully. "I'm so fucking happy for you!"

I clench my back teeth together tightly enough to send a bolt of pain shooting through my jaw.

It's *supposed* to be a secret.

It *needs* to be to protect Rome from my father.

"I can't," I whisper. "My dad—"

Rory's face softens. "You know your dad loves you, honey cakes. If you told him—"

I shake my head. "If I told him what I'm feeling for Rome"—how freaking big those feelings are, how deep they've dug themselves, how far in over my head I am already—"he would take it out on him. You know he would."

She grimaces, and I know I'm right, even if I want to be wrong, want my dad to be one of those super kind and supportive and understanding fathers who are just happy their daughter found someone who makes their heart flutter and their smile never want to fade from their face and—

"I know your dad loves you and wants you to be happy, but if you told him you're dating the captain of the team and the man he's brought in to elevate the Eagles to the next level..." Rory sighs, shaking her head. "I think it *is* likely that he might find a convenient way to shuttle Rome off to another team."

That's what I'm afraid of.

Because I know it wouldn't be back with the Gold—my dad wouldn't be that nice.

It would be somewhere that would make Rome even more miserable than he is now, what with a locker room half filled with assholes he's struggling to find a way to bring together.

I sigh, rub my forehead. "I know," I whisper. "It's a freaking mess and it would be better if I just backed off, told Rome I changed my mind..."

Only, just thinking that—let alone actually verbalizing those thoughts—has my stomach twisting, my mind revolting, my heart hurting so freaking much.

Because I like him.

"But you can't," Rory says gently.

I shake my head. "He's different," I whisper. "I feel different when I'm with him. Feel like I can be myself and he won't blink an eye, won't judge me, won't—"

I pause when I see a flash of pain dart across her face.

But it's there and gone in an instant, Rory taking my hand and asking, "He won't what?"

I chew on the inside of my lip, debating, wondering if it would be better off to press my friend to explain that wave of hurt in her eyes, or to let it recede a little, allow the pain to ease and then approach her about it later. "Ror—"

Her jaw hardens, a muscle flexing in her cheek.

And she might as well have planted a Do Not Trespass sign in the concrete, right in front of my feet.

"He won't what?" she asks again.

Stubborn woman.

I stifle a sigh and tell her what's in my heart. "Rome won't turn away if he sees the real me."

And he *has* seen me—clawed up and climbing a tree, hair a mess in the morning, panicked on the floor when the memories shot up and yanked me under, frantically fanning the smoke detectors because I burned breakfast, sweat on my forehead as I scooped litter boxes—and none of it has fazed him. In fact, he seemed to be committing all of it to memory.

Like he enjoys seeing the glimpses of the real me.

Because he does, I suppose.

He likes me as much as I like him.

Which is why...

"I can't let him go."

Rory moves close, her expression gentling, her hand gripping mine. "Then don't, sweetie. Hold on. Get to know him. Enjoy this time. You've been through enough in your life that you know when something is important enough to fight for."

She's right.

Of course she is.

But...I just want a little bit longer *without* a fight, a little longer with Rome to myself without having to battle my father.

I just want—

The door to the suite flies open, and my dad walks through the door, eyes immediately searching mine out, his soft and warm, like I could never do anything to disappoint him.

Never hide a relationship with a player from his team.

Never hide something important to me.

Never—

Lie to his face when he asks me what I've been up to today.

I sigh and push down the guilt.

I just want a little bit longer before my world implodes.

Is that too much to ask?

THIRTY-ONE

Rome

I'M CLENCHING my jaw together, trying desperately to not bust up at the awful rendition of the national anthem—complete with more runs and drawn-out notes than actual words, I swear to God—when Pat scoots close to me.

His eyes are shrewd. "What are you looking at?" he asks slyly.

I'm clenching my jaw tighter, albeit for a completely different reason now, deliberately slow as I shift my gaze from where I *had* been looking—the owner's suite, trying to get a glimpse of a certain Rapunzel-like woman who likes to climb mountains in her spare time and has a mouth built for sin—and turn it slowly toward Pat. "I'm trying to look at the motherfucking flags, asshole."

His mouth hitches up before I look away, look at the flags—sending thanks up to the hockey gods that they're hanging so close to the owner's suite that Pat shouldn't be suspicious.

Shouldn't.

Such a challenging word.

Because a lot of things shouldn't have fucking happened —the trade, me falling for Chrissy, the locker room that's tense before our first game of the season, half the assholes in it not giving a fuck that this *is* our first game, that we should be bringing the intensity and focus and hard work to show the fans who shelled out hard-earned cash to fill the arena the respect they deserve.

Good hockey.

Hopefully a fucking win.

And focusing on coming together instead of ripping each other apart.

The woman singing finally wraps the song after drawing out, *"the home of the brave"* for long enough that my toes are starting to get cold.

I ignore it as she and the cameramen exit and the carpet is rolled off the ice. The refs and both teams take our positions—goalie, two D, left wing, right wing, me at center, readying for the face-off.

There's a collective hush—there always is.

Or maybe it's just the way my brain and ears work in tandem before play begins, before that puck drops and I do every fucking thing in my power to win it back to my defenseman.

Quiet. Focus. *Go!*

The ref throws down the puck, sending it wobbling through the air before it drops to the ice between our stick blades.

I slash my stick forward, feel the sting in my palms, hear the *crack* as it collides with the other center's blade, and then the hard rubber disc is floating between us for a millisecond before I jerk my stick back, sweep it toward my defense, winning the draw and starting us off on the best note possible.

Unfortunately, winning that face-off ends up being the *only* positive note I can glean for the next twenty minutes.

"You're a bunch of lazy fuckers!" Coach yells, stomping around the room, shoving at the folding table set up along one wall, sending the bottles of water and sports drinks, the glucose and smelling salts rattling. "You're getting paid for this shit"—he sends a bottle flying through the air, the lid popping off, water spraying everywhere—"I don't know fucking *why* considering a bunch of fucking beer leaguers could do a better job out there."

He's not right.

He's also...not *wrong*.

We've played twenty minutes and been scored on three times.

We've played twenty fucking minutes and had two shots on their net, and one of those is because Kingston got fucking tired of his linemates screwing around and took the puck the entire way up the ice, getting our only decent chance to score.

It was also the only time that the crowd had gotten excited, cheering loudly enough that their voices had echoed around the arena, making me nostalgic for the Gold Mine, the way my former home crowd's screams used to resonate through my belly and make my ears hurt.

And now my ears are hurting for another reason—Coach's bellowing.

"I ought to bench the lot of you, bring up the Firebirds"—the minor team affiliated with the Eagles—"to take your fucking spots."

Pat snorts.

Duncan smirks.

A few of the other assholes look amused.

Me?

I feel like shit, as I always do when a coach lays into me, piling on top of my already heavy expectations, the weighty mantle of worry that I'm disappointing the people I'm supposed to be excelling for.

That this will be all over.

And then who the fuck will I be?

I'm a hockey player to the core, and I know—fucking *know*—if it's all taken away that I'll be...

Nothing.

Kingston bumps the toe of his skate against mine, waits until I look at him, then nods once. It's short. It's firm. It's fucking exactly like the one he gave me when I told him that it was time to start running those arena stairs after practice, time to push through the forthcoming pain and discomfort to get through to the other side.

Let's fucking go.

Stop standing at the bottom of the staircase, looking up at the huge distance we have to travel, and thinking it's insurmountable.

Let's take one goddamned step at a time.

I push out my breath, nod back, and turn to Cam, whose expression is drawn, his eyes wary.

Now I tap my skate against his, wait until he's met *my* eyes. "Let's fucking go, yeah?" I murmur.

He exhales, his hazel eyes filling with determination. "Let's fucking go," he repeats softly.

I lightly punch his shoulder and get up to my feet, moving to the table, snagging one of those sports drinks. I have no intention of actually ingesting it. I don't want that much liquid sloshing around my stomach while I'm helping my team dig out of this hole. But it gives me an excuse to hit up the other guys who have misery on their faces instead of amusement, who want to do well, but maybe don't know how to do it by themselves, without a team working together to back them up.

I nudge Hudson and Levi, make eye contact and nod at Kane and Dash, and receive determined nods back from all four of them. Seven. I've got seven in this room of eighteen skaters, the rest of whom are avoiding my gaze as I slowly meander back to my stall, taking small sips of that drink, seeing if any of the fence sitters are going to come to the good side.

Unfortunately, I get a whole lot of nothing.

Fuckers.

But I'm not giving up.

Because I've got a secret weapon.

Having played with Brit—a fucking force in her own right—I know that goalies are often the key to that initial uphill battle. They're weird. They volunteer to have pucks shot at them. *Willingly.* But...when a goalie's on, when they're fighting for their team, making saves they shouldn't be able to make, fiercely protecting that space between the pipes, their team can't help but respond in kind.

And I've figured out what gets Marty motivated.

I lean close, pausing for just a second before I head back to my stall to whisper something in his ear.

I watch his head fly up, shoulders going stiff, eyes narrowing.

Then I keep walking, knowing that my smirk likely rivals Duncan's.

THIRTY-TWO

Chrissy

"COME ON," I mutter, leaning forward, hands clenched into fists that I bang lightly on my thigh. "You've got to connect that pass up the center."

My father, who's sitting not far away, makes a sound of agreement, and I glance over at him, lips twitching when I see his laptop closed in front of him, his notebook and pen moving furiously as he takes notes of everything he thinks needs to be improved.

The list is long.

Though it hasn't grown much since the first period.

Rory snickers, drawing my focus back to hers.

I lift my brows in question.

"Your hockey is showing."

I narrow my eyes at her—but only for a second—because the game has gotten freaking exciting. The Eagles—led by a certain hockey hottie, by *my* hockey hottie—having come out with a fire lit in their belly after the first intermission.

They've tied things up, and now with less than ten minutes left in the third period, I can feel the tide is turning.

Maybe my hockey *is* showing.

After all, I *did* play for a couple of seasons, quite a few years ago now, enjoying the thrill of being on the ice, of scoring goals, of doing something I didn't think was possible, of skating and shooting and *winning*. It's just that I found climbing and fell in love with it, and the thrill of summitting beat out any mediocre goal I might have managed to shove past a goalie in rec league.

Still, it gave me respect for the guys out there, an understanding of the game (thanks to one of the Gold players, Josh, who volunteered his time to coach us), and...a realization that it's not for me.

But maybe having a hockey boyfriend who can do all the things I wanted to but couldn't actually make my body do is igniting my passion for the sport again.

Or maybe...I just like watching Rome out there.

Like watching him score a goal two minutes into the second. Like watching him work hard enough to inspire several others to join in on that effort, until half the team is skating like they have rocket boosters attached to their skates.

It's not everyone.

There are still guys whose playing style is...uninspired.

But they're not affecting what Rome is doing—or not so dramatically, anyway— that his leadership isn't shining through, and...

Fuck.

I clench my fists tighter because my eyes are stinging, and my heart is convulsing, and...I'm proud of him.

Because I know the locker room is rough from hearing him talk about it. I know it's rough because that's why my dad brought Rome to the team in the first place.

And Rome is making a difference.

In game one.

But...

He still needs to connect that fucking pass up the center.

I narrow my eyes at Rory. "Okay, Ms. Never Played a Day in Her Life, I would advise you to follow my lead about—"

"Taking things up the center?" she asks softly, waggling her brows.

I snort, trying—and failing—to stifle a giggle.

Phillip—who's sitting next to her—goes stiff, shooting her a glare.

"Drink your beer, honey," she tells him, ignoring that glare and leaning close, pecking him on the cheek. "You know that Chrissy and I are here to cackle over the sexy hockey players"—a wink that has me shooting my own narrowed eyes in her direction and has her grin growing—"you just focus on the guys swinging their sticks out there to hit that round thingy across the ice."

Round thingy?

Where does she get this stuff?

"You're terrible," I mutter.

She giggles, but Phillip just sighs and lifts his beer, taking a long glug as she leans close to me, lashes fluttering. "I know." A beat, wicked in her tone. "I thought you'd fallen out of love with hockey...or has something changed?"

I shove her beer at her. "Drink up, you menace."

Because she knows something *has* changed.

Knows that maybe I'm falling *in* love...with a certain hockey player.

Christ. I can't think like that...not with my dad sitting five feet away from us.

I nudge my shoulder against hers, heart pounding so hard

it feels like it's trying to crawl up the back of my throat. "I'm just proud of him," I whisper. "He's doing well, and he wasn't sure he could bring the guys together. But it's game one and" —I nod out at the ice—"look, Rors. He's doing it."

"He's certainly carrying the team on his back," she whispers.

"Cam's there," I say. "And Kingston too."

So much so that the lines have been switched up and the offensive coach put all three of them on one line.

Rory makes a face at the mention of Kingston Bang.

"What?" I ask, studying the flicker in her gaze. Like there's more to the story and I'm the stubborn reporter determined to ferret out every detail.

Her nose wrinkles further. "You know his nickname is The King, right?"

My lips twitch because I had—indeed—heard as much, usually mentioned alongside with his bedroom abilities. "You know that he's not like what you think, right?"

"With a last name like Bang and a laundry list of women he's fucked," she says so quietly I have to strain to hear. "I don't see how he can be anything *but* what I think."

I nudge her thigh lightly with my own. "I worked with him late last season when he was first traded. He's a good guy."

"A good guy." A beat, her lips pressing flat. "Sure."

"Ror—"

The crowd gasps, and her eyes slide from mine, both of us looking back out at the ice, surveying the scene in front of us. I see one of the players from L.A. on the ice, and Kingston is skating away from him, blades digging into the rink's surface, moving so fast my eyes can barely keep up as he hustles to join Rome and Cam as they gain entry into the offensive zone.

Three on two.

Three Eagles players versus two L.A. ones.

Advantage to our guys.

Because of a great hit at center ice, because Kingston is hustling up behind his linemates. Because Cam is watching, head on a swivel, eyes searching, and I know that big brain of his is calculating at rapid-fire speed.

As strong and fast as King is, Cam is equally as smart.

And Rome...well, he's a combination of both of them—strong and big and fast, but constantly thinking, looking, preparing. He's also creative as fuck—something I know thanks to his inspired actions in my kitchen this morning—but also illustrated perfectly in this moment as he receives the pass from Cam, cuts across the ice, drawing the two players from Los Angeles toward him.

Freeing up space.

So he can pass it back to Cam—

Who misses.

The crowd groans.

But I don't.

Because he hasn't missed.

Cam *lets* the puck slide by his stick—those eyes always watching, always taking in where everyone is at all times.

So he knows Kingston is behind him.

King scoops up the puck, fires it toward the net as the goalie is still reacting to the change in direction, sliding across the crease, trying to stop the shot.

He does.

But it bounces out...

To Rome.

Who just has to tap it home, sending the red light behind the goal light flashing and the bullhorn ringing and the crowd to their feet—me and Rory included.

"Woo!" she screams, fist-pumping before wrapping her arms around me. "Maybe I do like this hockey thing after all!" she shouts over the din as we jump up and down.

"Damn right, you do!" I tell her, grin so wide it feels as though my face is going to split in half as the goal song winds down and the crowd starts to find their seats.

She drops her hands on my shoulders. "That was incredible! I've never seen—"

"Jesus. Enough. Sit. The fuck. Down." Phillip's words are sharp, and I nearly teeter backward into my seat as he grips Rory's arm and yanks her away from me, cutting off our conversation mid-celebration and shoving her back into her seat.

I start toward him. "What the fu—?"

But I freeze, words stoppering up in my throat when Rory takes my hand and squeezes hard.

I glance down at her, and she shakes her head, mouths, "*Not now,*" and I swallow my words back down.

Then I look to Phillip, see his jaw is clenched tight, his eyes narrowed as he focuses on the ice.

As though he didn't just rip his fiancé out of my celebratory hug and shove her down into a seat.

As though he didn't just manhandle her in front of me. In front of my father.

"Ror," I begin as I sit beside her, fingers squeezing around hers.

"Not right now," she whispers, not looking at me, and I watch the top of her cheek I can see turn pink, know that her eyes are glimmering with tears. She's embarrassed and hurt and—

Not right now.

Christ.

I glance to my right, meeting my father's eyes, his ever-present notebook still open in front of him.

But instead of taking notes about the players, about what's happening on the ice, he's watching Phillip with narrowed eyes.

And then he flips the page and jots something else down.

Something I know isn't about the game or the Eagles at all.

Those eyes, so much like my own, flick to mine, and for once, I know that we're on the same page.

Phillip has *got* to go.

Which is why I don't push through Rory's warning, don't give her fiancée the dressing down he deserves.

Instead, I give my friend what *she* needs.

And I don't let go of her hand as we watch King and Cam and Rome lead the Eagles to their first victory of the season.

THIRTY-THREE

"YOU OWE ME," Marty says, tossing his helmet to the side, ripping off his chest protector.

I grin and go to my bag, glad that I have something inside that will allow me to pay off my debts here and now. I dig deep, know I haven't bothered to clear out some of the pockets since last season.

Since...I was with the Gold.

And played with Max—who isn't a goalie but has the same dorky interests.

My fingers brush the edge of the plastic wrapper, and I make a mental note to stock up, as I yank out the pack of Pokémon cards and toss them toward Marty.

My goalie displays his glove hand skills by scooping them out of the air, excitement filling his face as he tears into the plastic and starts flipping through the cards inside.

"Seriously?" King asks from next to me.

I grin over at him. "Whatever it takes, am I right?"

King shakes his head, but he's smiling when he agrees, "Whatever it takes."

"I'll buy the next box," Cam says from my other side as he bends to loosen the laces on his skates.

"You're on," I tell him.

"Beers?" King asks.

"I—" I break off because I was about to say yes, because I *want* to say yes, because in the spirit of the team camaraderie I'm trying to build, I should *absolutely* say yes.

But the urge to say no is fucking intense.

The urge to say no and quickly shower, to get changed and track down Chrissy, takes over every cell.

"Breakfast," he says before I come up with an excuse, his eyes glimmering with amusement. "And then I can meet this new puppy of yours."

Spy on me and Chrissy he means.

Luckily, I know my woman will be at the rescue, so there's no chance of blowing our cover.

I nod. "Deal."

"Good," Cam says. "I want Molly's, and then I want to meet Athena."

The kid has a thing for details and a memory like a steel trap.

Something to remember.

"You get the Pokémon cards," I tell him. "I'll buy the pastries."

"And we'll both get a face full of puppy breath?" King adds.

I grin, finish stripping off my gear, and shove my feet into my sneakers, turn for the weight room.

Puppy breath...and maybe a claw or two from an ornery cat named Joan of *freaking* Arc.

I MOP the sweat off my head and stop peddling as the bike finishes guiding me through the cool down.

My quads and ass are aching, and I'm fucking disgusting, dripping sweat everywhere, but I finally feel right, finally feel like the tide is turning.

I unsnap my shoes from the peddles, yank out my earbuds, and head for the dressing room.

It's empty, considering that most of the guys head out right after the game, and the others—including King and Cam and Hudson—only ran through a quick cooldown routine.

I'm not trying to kill myself, but I'm also trying to stay in the best shape of my life...

And maybe trying to delay long enough that the halls will be quiet and deserted as I search out Chrissy.

Who, of course, has probably headed home instead of waiting around for me to burn out my quads.

I shower because—here or not—I'm going to make sure I'm clean for her, but I do it quickly because if she *is* still here, I don't want her waiting any longer than she already has for me.

I wrench the shower off, snag a towel, dry, dress, and gather my shit in record time.

Then I'm in the hall—empty, thankfully—and turning in the direction of her office instead of the parking lot, walking by empty room after empty room, the lights dimmed overhead, the post-game buzz of activity having faded at least six miles ago on my bike ride.

And, yup, the emptiness continues as I make it to her office and find the door closed.

I knock anyway—because I'm not taking the chance to

miss her—and then when she doesn't answer, I sigh. "Idiot," I mutter. Because of course she will have gone home instead of waiting around for me and potentially increasing the risk of us getting caught by no manner of nosy fuckers.

Then I'm turning away, but still not toward the parking lot.

I can feel the cool lick of the ice brushing along my jaw, creeping in through my clothes, and I give into the call of the rink, walking down the hall, turning toward the entrance. It's not the one we—as a team—use, the one that's paired with lights and smoke and music when we jump onto the ice. It's the opening that leads to the Zamboni access. There are shovels and buckets, shelves lined with equipment to repair the ice, tools to keep the resurfacing machine in the best possible shape. The Zam itself is a couple of feet away, partially blocked by a huge black velvet curtain, and parked back by where the operator dumps the ice.

I inhale that distinctive hockey smell—damp and ice, sweat and propane, popcorn and the smoke from fog machines—and turn back out toward the rink, running through the plays from tonight's game—or the ones I can remember, anyway. I stand there and mentally walk through where I could have done better, what went right, what didn't, what I need to fix for our next game in two days—

"Hey."

I jump and spin around, seeing Chrissy standing behind me, looking uncertain and beautiful and...

I go to her, take her into my arms, but she goes stiff, her eyes flicking behind me.

Right.

We're standing right where anyone could see us, which defeats the purpose of keeping this shit secret, so I drop my arms, take her hand, and draw her away from the glass, guiding her into the shadows. "Sorry, Kitten," I mutter as I step close to her, backing against the metal side of the Zam, caging her in with an arm on either side of her head.

Her hand comes to my jaw, lips curving up. "You played well tonight."

That slides down my spine like silken fingers. "Thanks, Kitten," I murmur, dropping my head and inhaling the scent of her. "I went by your office," I said. "Where were you?"

"Talking with my dad about Rory."

I frown, lift my head. "Your friend? Is everything okay?"

She sighs. "No," she says. "I don't think so." Then she tells me about the conversation from earlier in the day, about what that fucker did in the owner's box, and the conversation she had with her father before coming down to the rink to think. "It's a mess," she tells me, dropping her forehead to my shoulder and sighing again. "They've been together forever, but I just...don't like the change I've seen and heard about in him. Rory deserves better, you know?"

"Yes, she does," I agree. Because I might not know her friend, but that's just fucking common sense.

"My dad is on it though," she says. "If there's anything that we can both agree on, it's that Rory needs someone looking after her, especially when it comes to dealing with an asshole like him."

"Good." I brush my fingers through her hair. "Let me know what else I can do, yeah?"

A nod. A sigh. "Yeah."

And then she's melting against me, her arms coming around my middle, her breath slow and steady on my neck, and we stand like that for a long moment. Hidden in the shadows, taking comfort in each other.

And I've never felt more certain that this is right.

I want to stay like this forever, to keep holding her

forever, but she's begun trembling and so I start to pull back, intending to get her home—and preferably to get her in bed.

And me along with her.

"No," she whispers, arms gripping me more tightly, keeping me against her. "Let's stay like this a little longer."

And what power do I have to resist her?

THIRTY-FOUR

Chrissy

IT'S DANGEROUS, holding him like this.

Here.

Especially when my father's on a hair trigger and prepared to go after anyone who might dare hurt someone under his care.

Who might hurt *me.*

Who *had* hurt me.

I shudder and Rome draws me closer. "It's cold in here, Kitten," he murmurs. "We should get you back to your place."

"I'm not cold."

"You're shivering."

"No," I whisper. "Or yes, it's cold," I add with a shake of my head, lifting it and meeting his gaze. "But I'm not cold. I just..." I trail off, but he doesn't push, just waits for me to say, "I was thinking about that night—*those* nights—after I was kidnapped and how scared I was and unsteady, and—" I blow out a breath, shake my head, lock in on what I should be focusing on. "My dad was there for me and I'm glad that he's going to be there for Rory too."

Rome's face gentles. "A hard man with a heart of gold."

My heart convulses, but my lips curve up. "Don't let him hear you say that."

Amusement in Rome's pretty brown eyes. "Noted." Then his expression goes somber again. "I really am so sorry that happened to you."

There my heart goes again, but this time I feel tears well up in the backs of my eyes, stinging and sending my vision blurry. Because I know it's a genuine response, because I know this man has a heart of gold too—I knew it from the first time he moved to catch me as I fell from that tree, knew it when he gently bandaged my hand, knew it all over again when I watched how carefully he cradled Athena.

He cares.

He's good.

He would take on a person who tried to hurt me or anyone else as fiercely as my father.

And that...

Well, it's settled deep in a place I never thought would be possible to access again.

"How did your parents make such a wonderful man?" I ask softly.

His arms convulse and his big chest inflates, and I wonder if I've crossed a line. I know only a little about his past, about what made him who he is today—because we haven't had time for more than that. And I know some about the man standing in front of me at present—his habits and what makes him laugh and a bit of those day-to-day things.

But the rest?

I haven't learned yet.

And now I'm left wondering if I've unknowingly poked a sore spot.

"Rome—" I begin, intending to tell him he doesn't have to divulge anything important or sensitive or painful. Not here. Not now. Not if he's not ready.

"My parents are good people," he says. "But I didn't grow up like you did. There were a lot of us, always on the brink of too many mouths to feed and sports to pay for and skates to buy to truly feel secure. So, when I left to pursue juniors at sixteen, left to live on the road, to find a space as a billet player, to carve out what I was desperate to make my future, I knew they would be better off. Less money to shell out. One fewer kid to drive around."

My heart squeezes and I rest my hand over his, hating he felt that way.

Which he sees, of course. "I love them," he tells me. "I've never had any doubt that they love me back, but it's different than what you and your dad have, and it's different than what I found with the Gold." He touches my cheek. "When I joined the roster, I found something...bigger than myself, and it was the first time I truly understood what a family could be like."

I inhale, eyes stinging again. "I'm so sorry my dad pulled you away from that."

"I don't blame you," he says. "Or him, for that matter."

I scoff.

"It's true." His mouth tips up on one side. "Did I like it? No. I miss those guys, especially when I'm dealing with assholes like Duncan and Pat in the locker room, but..." He exhales. "I'm also starting to think it might be a blessing in disguise." He crouches a little when I scoff again. "No, really. I think...I think I might have grown into a leader given time with the Gold, but that roster is stacked so deep, and there are so many experienced guys there, I'm not sure I would have found the courage to truly grow in that way."

"Not unless you were forced to?"

The other half of his mouth curves. "Something like that."

I rise up on my tiptoes, press my lips to the underside of his jaw, feeling the bristles of his beard on my skin. "So, how did you manage to get the guys to come together tonight?"

"Who says it was me?" he asks innocently.

I grin. "I know it was you." I kiss his jaw again. "Now divulge all of your secrets."

He hisses out a breath when I flick out my tongue, when I lightly press my teeth into his flesh. "You're playing with fire, Kitten," he warns, but he's the one who's playing a dangerous game as he slides his hands down, cupping my ass, drawing me against him more firmly, before allowing those hands to drift down to the backs of my thighs, before he's lifting me, encouraging me to wrap my legs around his waist.

"What if I like the heat?"

He grins and fuck if I don't melt, just fucking melt right there—soaking my panties, making my pussy convulse with need, my breasts tingle and my nipples harden. Then his lips are pressed to mine and his tongue is inside my mouth and his hand is slipping beneath my layers of clothing, finding my bare skin and—

"God," I whisper, breaking the kiss as my head falls back against the Zamboni's metal side, legs tightening around his waist.

I'm on sensory overload.

His slightly roughened fingertips, the warm heat of his palm, the way his hard body presses into mine, the deter-mined rhythm of his pelvis rocking against me, rubbing the seam of my jeans against my clit, sending tingles through my pussy, ramping my need nearly out of control.

"Not *God*," he murmurs against my skin, teeth pressing into my throat, making me shiver and arch against him. "Rome."

I groan.

"Say my name, baby," he orders softly. "Say it right fucking now."

I shiver again, but it's still not because I'm cold.

It's that silky voice sliding over my flesh like velvet, phantom fingers dipping between my legs and pressing at the bundle of nerves at the apex of my thighs.

"Rome," I whisper.

"Let's go home, Kitten," he says, dragging his lips along my jaw.

"Mmm," I moan, sliding my fingers into those damp curls, feeling the satiny strands tease the backs of my hands. "Just a little longer."

"Kitten—"

But I'm already grabbing onto his head, tilting it back toward mine, aligning our mouths and kissing him as though my life depends on it.

And maybe some part of me feels as though it does, my lips parting, my hips grinding, my hands...sliding from his hair down his chest, down again to the waistband of his sweat.

Thank God for elastic.

It lets me slip my fingers inside, gives me enough room to wrap my hand around the hard, hot length of his cock, to stroke firmly.

"*Fuck*," he growls into my mouth, pressing me into the side of the Zamboni before he's lifting me higher, setting me on the driver's seat. His lips are swollen and red and his eyes positively *burn* as he stares at me. "Killing me, baby," he rasps, dropping his hands onto the edge of the platform, head close enough to my pussy that I find myself spreading my thighs, practically begging for his mouth even though we have far too many layers of clothes between us.

His hands tighten on the platform, and I'm mesmerized by the way the veins stand out sharply on the backs of them. "Come up here," I order.

"Kitten," he warns.

But we're blocked by that curtain—or mostly so, anyway. And...I want him, and he wants me and...I just want to soak in this moment, to be with this man, to—

Have his cock inside me.

So, I stand up, shifting slightly to the side as I reach for the button of my jeans, kick off my shoes.

Zip! goes my zipper.

Down go my jeans.

"*Fuck!*"

And then Rome is next to me, hands on my body, one between my thighs, the other back beneath my shirt, sliding up, cupping my breast, rolling my nipple between roughened fingertips.

I gasp, knees going weak, but before I fall, he's sitting in the driver's seat and tugging me down onto his lap, coaxing me to straddle his waist...

And, *oh hey*...

There's his cock.

"Get it inside, Kitten," he orders. "Get me inside and fuck me until you come."

Heat coats me from head to toe and desire leaves my pussy slick and practically dripping as I lift up, wrap my fingers around him, and—

"Fuuuck," he groans, head falling back.

He's inside me, filling me to bursting, hot and hard and fucking...perfect.

His hands come to my hips, guiding me as he grinds up into me, deep and a little rough and more than impatient. But it's exactly what I need, and it sends sparks of sensation flying through me, filling my belly, shooting down my legs, making my toes tingle and my pussy throb and my nipples hard and sensitive as they rub against the fabric of my bra.

Fucking. Perfect.

This stolen moment.

This man who slips his hand beneath my bra and cups my breast, who rubs my nipple against his palm, who angles his pelvis just right to send me over the edge.

Just. *Fucking.* Perfect.

THIRTY-FIVE

Rome

I WANT to stay here for a thousand years, want to keep fucking her until I come inside her.

But...I'm not wearing a condom.

But...I have my dick inside her and anyone could walk up, could find us here, find *her* here and—

I won't risk her.

So, I summon my strength to pull her off me, dick hard and aching, desperate to stay in that slick sheathe, wanting nothing more than to keep grinding her down against me, to keep thrusting up into her. Then I grab her underwear and help her into them, pull on her pants, her shoes.

She's wobbly as I bring her down from the Zam, eyes glazed, expression so damned proud of herself as she leans close, as she wraps her arms around me and lifts up on her toes, brushing her lips over mine. "I think I kind of like this secret relationship thing," she murmurs.

The jolt of pain through my middle surprises me.

The feeling of *wrong* slices deep.

Because I don't want to hide her. Because I want to draw her off with knowing looks from my teammates. Because I want her to want to be with me and not give a fuck—hell to be *proud* to be with me.

Because...

Hiding this isn't right.

Clang!

She jumps and I quickly grab my bag, snag her purse, drawing us both away from the scene of the crime, back to the thick curtain shoved to one side. I tuck her behind it. "Stay here," I say, wishing that I could just take her hand and walk out of here with her at my side. "I'll text you when the coast is clear."

Her cheeks are still flushed, her eyes wide, but she nods up at me.

And then I'm walking out of the shadows, moving to the rink, seeing one of the ice technicians is near the boards.

He looks up, frown pulling his features together sharply, probably because he's not used to players emerging out of the Zamboni tunnel.

"Hey, Ron," I say.

"Rome," he begins.

"I was looking for you," I tell him, moving closer, thumbing at the screen of my cell, getting it ready. "I wanted to show you a spot near the boards," I lie. "You probably already found it, but—"

His face clears, eyes lighting up. "Right at the blue line, yeah?" he says, stepping onto the ice, jerking his chin toward the far side of the rink.

"Yeah, exactly." My thumb starts tapping. "Is it fixable?"

I ask because nothing gets Ron more excited than repairing the ice.

Ron scoffs. "Of course it is."

"How are you going to fix it?" I ask, walking down the bench, following him over to the spot.

"Aw, man, that's the easy part," he says. "It's getting the idiots who lay down the floor for the concerts in between games to not fuck it up again."

"That sounds complicated."

"Tell me about it," Ron grumbles, waddling over to the divot and squirting some water into it. "Fucking musicians don't respect the ice."

My phone buzzes and I surreptitiously glance at the screen, see that Chrissy has made it past us and into her office.

I type back a response telling her I'll meet her back at her house then spend a couple more minutes shooting the shit with Ron—a.k.a. attempting to extract myself from the conversation about proper temperature and the best minerals to have in the water they use to patch holes like this—before I manage to get away, walk down the hall, and make it out to my car.

And then I get right back to where I'm desperate to be.

Chrissy's bed.

OVER THE NEXT WEEK, I have two more Eagles' games—one a loss on the road (and a bad one), but, thankfully, another win at home.

And today is...hopeful.

"Get it, motherfucker!" Hudson calls.

Because of curses and razzing.

Cam dives for the ball—with a little too much enthusiasm probably, since this is supposed to be warming us up for practice and not risking injuries—but he gets his foot beneath the soccer ball, flicks it my direction.

I catch it on my chest, allow it to fall down to my feet, chip it over to Levi.

He corrals it, flicks it to Dash, who passes it to Kane, who heads it over to King.

Rhodes gets a touch in.

Marty resists putting his goalie skills to use and kicks it to back to Cam...

Who makes a valiant effort on the wildly bad pass, but misses, and the ball bounces from the large open space we've taken over, rolls down the hall.

"Goalie's only got good hands," King jokes. "Why am I not surprised?"

Marty shoots him a look. "Next time you fuck up the pass and send a breakaway my direction, I'm not gonna make you look good."

"In fairness, he *never* looks good," Levi chimes in.

I grin, toss out. "Maybe that's why your mom has such a hard time finding you a match."

King's smile is a razor-sharp flash. "I don't know," he says. "*Your* mom thought I was pretty good last night."

There's a collective, *"Ooooh!"*

But I'm laughing, and so are the other guys as I jog down the hall to retrieve the wayward ball.

I reach for it—

A sneaker-encased foot settles on top of it, and I look up, drawing my eyes beyond the narrow ankle, along a shapely calf I've kissed, drifting over a lush thigh, pausing on hips that

I've held as I fucked her deep, tits that I dream about...a slender throat, plump lips I've kissed, and—

Cerulean blue eyes.

That are filled with humor.

"Hi," she murmurs.

"I wish there was a Zamboni around," I mutter, making her smile.

"Move it, Dawson!" someone yells, and I shake my head.

"I've got to get back."

She smiles and I want to taste that curve of her lips, but before I can do something stupid—like actually do that—she lifts her foot.

I snag the ball, straighten, whispering, "I'm going to make you come later."

Loving that she sucks in a breath.

Loving that I got to see her, even if it's just for a second before I turn away and start for the room.

King strolls into the hall before I reach the end of it. "I know that you struggle keeping track of your balls—" His gaze flicks over my shoulder and he clamps his lips together.

Then he shakes his head.

"What?" I ask, feigning innocence.

"Nothing going on with you and Christina Dubois, huh?"

"Chrissy," I correct before I can stop myself, glancing behind me, catching a glimpse of that long brown hair as she turns the corner.

His eyes go icy. "Are you fucking dumb?"

"Dude," I mutter. "Back off."

King's brows flick up. "You really want to risk what we're building as a team for some pussy?"

I move before I realize, grabbing him by the throat, shoving him back against the wall. "What did you fucking say?"

His expression is severe. "You fucking heard me." He closes his hand over my wrist, rips it from his throat. Then leans in and hisses, "Jean-Michel's daughter? Fucking, *really?*"

"It's none of your goddamned business," I growl.

"Really?" he says sarcastically. "You mean all that team bonding out there, the leadership in the locker room, all the shit you're trying to get us on board with isn't going to be affected when we find your dismembered body in an isolated vineyard somewhere?"

I freeze.

"For some pussy," he says again.

This time he's fast enough to catch my hand before it wraps around my throat.

"It's not about pussy," I snap. "Chrissy—" I break off, grit my teeth together. "She's fucking more than that, okay?"

Much more.

She's...*everything.*

"Is she?"

This man wants to die today.

"King," I warn, flexing against his grip.

Then the bastard smiles. Widely. Like I've just told him the funniest joke on the planet.

"What?" I grit out.

"Nothing," he says. "Just had to make sure you were in deep for her before I take your back and risk dismemberment." He pushes me back, bends and scoops up the ball, then saunters off like he doesn't have a care in the world.

"What the fuck?" I whisper to the empty hallway.

But it's not empty for long because Pat comes strolling around the corner, trademark smirk in place.

Christ.

I don't have the patience to deal with the fucker.

Luckily, King—apparently—has my back, popping his head around the wall, glancing at me, at Pat who's strolling close.

Who's opening his mouth.

"Let's go, fuckers!" King calls. "Coach wants us on the ice in ten."

Saved by the goddamned whistle.

THIRTY-SIX

"MEOW!"

I smile down into Petal's adorable face, heart aching at how much she's already changed in the couple of weeks she's been at the center.

She's bigger, obviously. And taller and heavier.

"*Meow!*"

And louder.

And more curious.

But her white fur is just as white (when she stays clean, that is), and the splotches of orange and gray on her face are still there. And Petal is still the most adorable cat I've ever seen.

(Don't tell Joan of *freaking* Arc).

"*MEOW!*"

I shake the feather toy, but apparently not with enough vigor since she gives up on me, darting across the room and joining in on making chaos with her siblings. Toys scatter, water dishes get bumped, one kitty gets stuck with her rump hanging out from beneath a couch on the far side of the room, its little legs waving.

Rome, sitting next to me, chuckles. "They're tiny yet powerful." A wink at me. "Like someone else I know."

I roll my eyes. "You're just saying that because I was faster than you on the rock wall."

We went to a gym over in the city, and—my lips start to curve—I was better.

I mean, of course I was.

I've had training.

Rome has never done it before.

I just...I was faster, *na-na-na-na-na*.

He taps his finger to my nose. "I sure am—or I *was*, anyway. Now, I've decided that there are benefits to having a girlfriend"—my heart squeezes as the word settles deep inside me—"who's a good climber."

I lift my brows. "Oh? Why's that?"

His mouth curves. "Well, you'll never have trouble reaching stuff on the top shelf."

I giggle.

"And you'll be able to hang your own Christmas lights."

My chest starts to shake with laughter.

"And you'll be able to help me pick the apples from the tree in my back yard."

I'm barely holding on as Petal comes over to me, settling herself on my lap for a nap. "I'm not cheap labor," I point out through my chortling.

A lazy shrug. "I can pay off my debts with orgasms."

I tap my finger to my chin. "Hmm." I smirk at him. "You sure about that?"

"Them's fighting words, Kitten."

"I think of them less as fighting and more as—*oh!*"

Suddenly, Petal is off my lap, blinking grumpily as she's dropped onto the bed next to me, but I barely process that before Rome is tugging *me* now, tugging and rolling, pinning me beneath him on the plush rug.

"Naughty Kitten," he murmurs, dragging his lips over my throat. "How should I punish you?"

"I-I have a few ideas," I say, suddenly breathless, my legs wrapping around his waist, my neck arching so I can reach his mouth.

He slants his lips over mine for one long, slick kiss, and then his teeth are grazing over my jaw, my earlobe, down along my collarbone. "I have *more*," he murmurs.

I shudder, pussy wet, pulse going a thousand beats a second, my mouth desperate for his...

"Kitten," he rasps.

Hot brown eyes.

A hand sliding up my side.

A hard cock rocking against me.

And...a bell tinkling distantly at the edges of my hearing.

Rome goes still.

Curses and then rolls off me in a rush, yanking my clothes down, wrapping fingers around my wrist and pulling me up to my feet.

"What—?"

But then I process it all at once.

The kissing. The rug. The *bell*.

"Chrissy?" my father calls.

Rome's eyes go wide, but I...well, *I* panic, gaze swooping around the space as though I can suddenly find a way to teleport Rome out of here, or maybe hide him behind a couch, a cat tower—

But my panicking means that I don't do the one thing I could that might have potentially prevented this interaction—

Go out to meet my father.

Instead, he walks into the space to find me wavering on my feet, Rome straightening with Petal in his arms.

My dad takes one look at us and his expression turns thunderous. "What the fuck is going on?"

"One of my closers called in sick and Rome offered to help out," I tell him—which is the truth, just not all of it. "With the adoption fair coming up, I can use all the help I can get." I affect innocence. "Is that why you're here? Did you get the message I left you?"

My dad's scowl deepens. "No," he snaps. "You weren't at home or at the rink, so I came here." His eyes flick to Rome, murder in the blue depths.

"Meow?"

Petal squirms in Rome's hold and he carefully sets her down. "Jean-Michel," he says, lifting his hand for a shake. "Good to see you." Then he glances back to me, brows raised in question.

Do I want him to stay?

Or to go?

Dear God, please go.

A thought he seems to read on my face because he nods slightly, and I feel a pulse of guilt at the sliver of hurt in his expression.

"Rome," I say as he turns away.

He rotates back to face me.

"Thanks for your help," I say. "I appreciate it."

His mouth ticks up into a half-hearted smile. "Anytime."

And then he's nodding at me, scooping up Petal when she twines herself around his ankles, and bringing her to me. As he passes her over, he murmurs, "No sweat, Kitten. I get it."

Except...I don't want him to *have* to get it.

To hide this.

To hide us.

But one look at the murder written into the lines of my father's face as Rome leaves tells me enough.

It's too soon.

I have to find a way to make my dad accept Rome as my boyfriend.

And to put all thoughts of dismemberment aside.

"You're staying at my house tonight?" he asks an hour later as we finish with the cats and talk through some final details on the adoption fair.

I glance up at him…

And smother a sigh.

Then say, "Yeah, Dad, I'll stay at your place."

We stop at In-N-Out, devour our burgers and extra crispy fries, then go back to his apartment.

Go to bed.

But it's the first time I don't have a good night's sleep with him just down the hall.

Because the mattress might be the best that money can buy…

But it's still missing one thing—

Rome.

THIRTY-SEVEN

Rome

WE HAD an early start for our game today.

And I fucking *hate* early starts.

It messes up my whole pregame routine, and I have to get up early, and everything just feels...rushed.

But we managed to snag a win in the shootout, so I can't complain too much.

Especially when it means I get to see my woman after being apart for two nights—her staying with her dad for one, me on the road for the team for the other.

Especially when it means I get to spend tonight with her.

Clutching a bag of takeout, I move through the gate and into Chrissy's back yard, climbing the steps to her deck.

I spy her standing in the kitchen, sipping a glass of wine—probably from her father's winery—knock on the glass door.

She jerks and spins around, hand coming to her chest, some of that wine tipping over the top of the glass.

I bite back a curse, but before I can really worry, she smiles, hurries over to me.

"Kitten," I murmur, after she's unlocked and opened the door, stepped back so that I can move inside. "We need to talk about this."

She goes stiff.

I wrap an arm around her shoulders and draw her to the island, set the bag of takeout on the counter. Then I open my mouth, but she beats me to saying anything.

"There's nothing to talk about." Her tone is brusque as she reaches for the bag and opens it. "Thanks for bringing dinner." Voice softening, she shoots me a grin before she's moving toward the cabinets, pulling out a couple of plates. "You know I can't be trusted with cooking."

I let her set those plates down, wait until she splits the food up, then I take her hand, draw her close again. "Kitten," I repeat. "We *need* to talk about this."

Stiff again.

Her mouth opening, and I can practically hear the prevarication already.

"You knew I was coming over," I murmur, cupping her jaw, tilting her head back so her eyes are on mine. "I texted and said I'd be here in ten. But I still scared you."

Her throat works, and she looks away. "We should eat," she whispers. "I'm sure you're hungry."

"Kitten—"

"I, uh, just startle easily," she says, leaning close and raising on tiptoe. "I always have. Even before." Still again until she unfreezes, grabbing the plates. "We should eat while it's hot."

I take them from her, set them back on the counter. "You *startle* easily?"

I know my tone is sharp. I hear it. I *feel* the way it makes her go stiff.

But I can't stop.

"You gave me the bare bones of what happened to you, Kitten, and I can respect that it might take you time to feel comfortable enough to give me the rest"—she jerks—"but I need you to tell me what I *can* do so that you feel safe with me."

Her throat works again, and I hate that there are tears in her eyes.

But I *need* this.

"Would it be better if I come to the front door?" I ask, gentling my voice.

She shakes her head. "No," she whispers. "My dad...he might see...if he comes over..."

"Okay," I say even though I'm really starting to hate the fact that I have to hide what's between us. "So we keep me coming to the back door." A breath. "How about if I call and talk to you as I walk over?"

"You shouldn't have to do that." She presses her lips together, releases them and says before I can chime back in, "And I don't always know when it's going to creep in. I—" She sighs. "It used to be the dark, but I've conquered that. And ropes," she whispers. "But I've moved past that too. I think..." She rubs her forehead, sighs again. "I think...I think I'm feeling guilty because the last time I went behind my dad's back, I was—"

My heart convulses as the pieces slot into place.

"—taken," she finishes on a whisper. "And all of this sneaking around, all of this hiding stuff from my dad." A breath. "I think that it's making it all come to the surface again."

"Maybe we should tell him?" I say.

And it's not a completely innocent statement—I'm tired of this sneaking around shit. I want to *go* to the front door, want to pull her close at the rink, not give a shit who sees us. I want the world to know that I'm in love with her.

I can't do that if we're hiding in the shadows.

But part of this isn't about my ego and what I'm desperate for.

Part of this is about *her.*

Protecting Chrissy. Making this shit stop if I can, helping her through it if I can't.

And if that means dealing with the fallout from her father—

"No," she whispers, shaking her head. "I can't," she says. "Just, please...not yet."

My stomach seizes, but I just murmur, "Okay, Kitten."

"I'm sorry."

And...I can't be upset. Not after all she's been through.

"It's okay," I say, smoothing back the hair from her face. "We have time yet." Then I grab the plates, nod to the bottle of wine. "Now, let's eat before the corgi crew gets restless."

She relaxes, worry smoothing out from her expression. Her mouth curves. "You just want to spend time with your other woman."

Right on cue, the corgis start barking and Joan appears in the kitchen.

"Meow!"

"My other *women,*" I tease, watching as the rest of the tension leaves her body.

She laughs as she snags the wine and carries it into the other room.

I follow her, disappointment snaking through my belly, but I don't push her.

I can't.

Not right now—when I've scared her and she's upset and...

She needs more time.

But I know, *know*...

That us going public needs to happen soon.

But we don't go public.

And we don't talk about it.

Not over the next few days.

In fact, I barely see her.

We're both too busy—me with the team and all that entails, Chrissy with the rescue, both of us trading off taking care of the gaggle of corgis who live to create trouble.

Today, though, I have plans.

Practice is over.

The fires have been put out at the rescue.

It's going to be me and Chrissy and...

Orgasms.

I grin and King tosses me a knowing look, but I ignore him as I gather my shit and slip out of the locker room, moving quickly through the halls until I reach Chrissy's office door.

I knock.

"Come in!" she calls.

So I do, sweeping my gaze around the space, making sure that it's empty before I close and lock the door.

Her brows shoot up. "And what do you think *you're* doing?"

I move over to her, tug her out of her chair, take her into my arms...

And I kiss her.

Like I've been wanting to do for days now, like I haven't been able to because we've been too busy.

Just a kiss.

Just holding her.

That was my intention.

But why am I not surprised when the kiss quickly burns out of control?

Every time I touch her, have my lips on hers, my tongue in her mouth, every time her body is pressed to mine, her moans vibrating through her chest and into mine, phantom fingers drifting down my stomach, wrapping around my cock...

I stop thinking.

And I start *doing*.

Sliding my hand up her side, cupping her breast, rolling her nipple. Stroking my tongue along hers, and coaxing her legs around my waist as I lower her to the desk.

Her mug that holds her pens and pencils tips sideways, sending writing instruments in all directions, toppling to the floor. Files scatter. Her keyboard falls.

But I'm too busy kissing her to care.

And she's too busy grinding against me to notice.

I pinch her nipple as I yank up her shirt, breaking the kiss so I can focus on her breasts.

A flick has her bra open, those gorgeous tits on display.

And then I'm sucking them, feasting on them until her hands go tight in my hair, and her pelvis is rocking and—

"Inside me, Rome," she whispers. "Fuck me right here. Right now." A shaky breath as she props her elbows beneath her, as her hazy eyes meet mine. "Fuck me like I've dreamed about since our first kiss."

My cock goes so hard it's painful, and I don't even dream of denying her.

I just reach into my back pocket, yank out my wallet, and toss it onto the desk next to her.

Then I peel down her pants, her underwear.

Spread her legs...

And I run my tongue through those slick folds, tasting the liquid tart of her desire, sucking hard at her clit.

She gasps and moans, head falling back, hips bucking.

So fucking wet.

So damned tight.

Mine.

I want to make her come this way, then fuck her with my fingers until she comes again.

But I want to feel the tight clamp of her cunt around my dick more.

So, I reach for my wallet, pull out a condom, and roll it down the length of my cock.

"Yes," she's chanting. "Yes. Hurry. *Yes.*" The last is a groan, one that I reciprocate as I slide home in one smooth stroke.

Her pussy squeezes me so tightly I almost come.

But, thankfully, she's close too.

I see it in the haze of her eyes, feel it in the tightness of her cunt, hear it in the way she rasps out my name, the speed of her breaths.

I pull out, thrust in.

Deep and fast.

No mercy. No quarter.

Rough and hard and bordering on the edge of control.

"Fuck, Rome," she hisses, neck arched, body tense, heels digging into my ass. "Fuck. Me. Just. Like. *That—*"

She moans out my name.

Her pussy convulses.

And then she slumps back against her desk as I thrust. Once. Twice. Three—

"Fuck," I groan, vision hazing, my orgasm exploding through me.

Pleasure so intense it's almost painful as it ramps up, up, *up*...and then I'm floating, sailing along in blissful nirvana.

"Desk sex is hot," Chrissy slurs long moments later, making me bark out a surprised laugh.

Something that has her moaning and me hissing out a breath.

Because I'm still hard. And inside her.

And that pussy of hers is still clamped around me.

I want to fuck her all over again.

But we're already playing with fire.

So, I slowly pull out, get us both fully clothed again, tug her up to her feet.

Her cheeks are bright pink.

Her lips are swollen.

Her hair is a mess.

Never has she looked more beautiful.

"Come on, Kitten," I murmur. "We should get you home."

She gives me a lazy smile, pats a hand over her hair, straightening the mussed locks as I pick up the pens and pencils, the papers, her keyboard, and set them back on her desk.

"Ready?" I ask when I'm done.

She nods, color still high, but together enough that I don't worry about her driving while orgasmed.

I move to the door, unlock it, watch as she slips out into the hall.

I wait a few minutes before making my own way out, flicking off the lights and closing the office door behind me. I walk through the empty corridors, push through the door to the parking lot...

And find Pat reclining against my car.

"Nice practice," he sneers.

Fuck. Off.

I reach into my pocket, snag my keys, but don't engage because I have more important shit to do, more important places to be.

Like back with Chrissy, with Athena.

With Joan of *freaking* Arc.

"You have to know that it's a waste of time to keep doing this rah-rah Gold shit," Pat says, pushing off my car and moving toward me. "It won't work with this locker room."

Except...it *is* working.

And likely that's why this asshole is getting tetchy.

"You should get some rest," I mutter, sidestepping him before bleeping the locks and grabbing at the driver's side handle, yanking it open. But I can't resist adding, "Since you worked *so* hard out there today."

His smirk widens. "I don't think I'm the only one who's working hard."

Something about his tone has frost sliding down my spine, but I don't look back, don't allow him to see that he's got me feeling like I'm vulnerable.

"At getting pussy," he presses.

"Jesus, man," I mutter, giving in and turning around.

He's grinning now, and I want to punch the smirk right off his stupid face.

"Grow up already," I tell him. "We've got a job to do, and that's winning games. Get your pussy or don't, just don't bring it to the locker room. And stop being the asshole who wants to bring everyone down."

"Are you?"

I frown at him. "Am I an asshole who wants to bring everyone down? No. *I'm* trying to work my ass *off* so we have a chance at getting some points in the standings, so that our fans are happy and management stays off our backs and we can do what we're best at—hockey."

Pat tilts his head to the side, studying me. "You really believe that bullshit, don't you?"

"Of course I do." I throw out my hands, keys jangling. "Otherwise, why would I be here trying to find a way for us all to come together?"

"Then why are you doing it?"

He seems genuinely curious, and that throws me for a second. Because I'm used to asshole Pat, used to snark and sarcasm and getting physical when he can't solve his problems with the few words his tiny pea-brain can conjure up.

But actual curiosity?

No, that doesn't track.

"Why am I working hard?" I ask, browns drawn together.

He huffs out a laugh, shakes his head. "No, Dawson. Why are *you* the one bringing pussy that could blow up all your fucking grand plans for kinship and a hockey family and winning fucking games into our locker room?"

THIRTY-EIGHT

Chrissy

I'M WAITING in my kitchen, watching for lights to appear on the street, for a car to pull into the driveway next door.

I'm waiting for Rome…

And I've been doing it for a while.

Athena whines softly, the pup mostly lax in my arms, and I look down at the items I gathered so Rome could finish setting up his place—a crate and exercise pen, bowls and a water dispenser, toys and treats and kibble. She'll stay here until the adoption fair next week, but when her littermates head out, she'll remain behind.

With Rome.

Because he can't say no to those puppy eyes.

I grin, knowing that I'm just as gone for an adorably fluffy face.

"Meow!"

Case in point?

Joan of *freaking* Arc.

I settle Athena back down on her bed, watch as my normally cranky senior kitty curls up next to her. She's been looking about a decade younger—and much friendlier—since the corgi invasion, and I still have no idea why her icy exterior melted for Athena—and Athena's siblings. But that cold, clawy heart of hers is devoted to the corgis, and she's spent every moment of time not eating, drinking, or hissing at me in the puppy room.

Sleeping in there—on the perch with only Athena capable of climbing high enough to sleep alongside her.

Supervising from the top of their crate as they play, narrowed cat eyes pointed in their directions, as though ordering them to behave.

Batting at them—claws in for once—when one was tempted to nibble at her tail.

Like...what in the actual fuck?

Where was this cat in all the years I've run fosters?

I guess she just has a soft spot for cute little balls of fluff with squishy butts and no tails and ears that are too big for their bodies.

"Meow!"

Or maybe I underestimated all she can be.

Like my dad...

Well, like my dad underestimates me.

I slipped out of my office a couple of hours ago, legs shaky from an orgasm that had me seeing stars, and carefully snuck to my car.

I made it successfully—not being waylaid by my dad or a member of the Eagles.

But...*was* it successful?

Because I was hiding something that made me happy from a person who's supposed to love me unconditionally.

Because I was doing the same shit that I'd been doing that night I snuck out.

And with that thought...I knew.

I didn't want to keep Rome and I a secret any longer.

I want to sneak a kiss (or more) in my office and walk out holding his hand. I want to go to the Eagles games and not worry I'm cheering too loudly for him.

I want to have dinner with my dad and Rome, and not have a single threat of dismemberment issued.

I want to kiss my man, not in the shadows, but right there in front of everyone.

I want...

Rome.

And hiding him, hiding us...it's been sitting too heavily on my heart.

He deserves better.

He deserves a woman who isn't afraid of disappointing her dad.

Heart squeezing, I exhale slowly, promise myself I'm going to do better, for him, for *me.* I can find a balance. I can love my dad and live my life. I can be independent and cared for.

I can be...*me.*

And that's enough.

"Meow."

I glance over at Joan, see that she seems to be beckoning me to sit next to her and Athena. I oblige, grinning when my kitty bumps her head against my arm, and, taking the cue, I carefully scratch her between her ears.

Why the hell not?

The universe seems to have turned itself upside down, so I might as well get my cat scratches in...without getting scratched in return.

But even with the puppy cuddling and the cat scratching, I still don't see any headlights.

And I really want to tell Rome what I finally figured out.

That I finally grew a spine.

Only...now I'm getting worried.

Because Rome said he would meet me here.

And...he's *not* here.

I nibble at my bottom lip.

As though he's conjured by my thoughts, my phone buzzes on the counter.

Moment broken, Joan pulls back, hisses at me.

"It's not my fault," I grumble, carefully shifting again, only this time it's to reach for my phone, to read the message on the screen, to...

Feel disappointment claw through my belly.

I got caught up in something. Sorry, Kitten. Rain check?

I inhale sharply, the triumph and excitement of the decision I'd made fade, disappointment hitting me hard.

But...I'm a grown-up. I can deal with a little disappointment.

And Rome wouldn't blow me off unless it was important.

So I type out a reply.

Of course.

I hit the button to send the message then pocket my phone and, with Joan following, carefully carry Athena back to the puppy room, settling her in with her littermates in their crate, making sure the gate is secured at the now-to-be-left open door to allow for optimal Joan coming-and-goings but no puppy escapes.

Then I go up to my bedroom and get ready to go to sleep.

Only I can't help but keep my gaze on the window that points toward Rome's house.

And I can't help but notice the lights never come on next door.

Not once during the entire night.

I DIG my toes into the rock face, clench my fingertips. The rope is taut and I know if I slip, I'll be good, be safe with the other members of the climbing club keeping watch—though likely I'll have a few more scratches and bruises.

But I'm not going to slip.

I'm *not* going to fall.

Rory showed up early this morning, expression drawn, dark circles under her eyes, and focus on the puppies. Completely.

So much so that she shooed me out the door, told me she didn't want to see me for at least three hours, and...

I listened.

Because there would be time to push my friend.

But right now, she needs a little corgi therapy.

Thankfully, all my gear was ready to go, and there's a climb I often join with the local club, so I was able to find something to do for those three hours.

And it involves sunshine and cool air and muscles working hard and sweat dripping down between my breasts.

And—

I flex my calves, reach *hard,* and snag the next grip. I'm barely able to hold on, the burn cascading from my fingertips down through my forearms, my biceps and triceps. Abs and back and glutes, thighs and calves and toes.

They're all working hard.

And I hold on.

A little cheer ripples up, these almost strangers who are

as nuts as I am to get up early and put their bodies through this for no reason other than the soft *swoosh* of the wind in our hair, the cramping in our hands, the feeling of satisfaction when we reach the top, cheering me on as I tap the highest point we're going to today and then begin working my way down, ready to let someone else have their turn.

"Nice," one of the women says when I reach the bottom, holding her hand up for a high five.

Our palms smack together and I grin. "Thanks."

And then we're back to climbing, back to securing ropes and encouraging each other, and it's not long before my three hours are up, and I'm waving goodbye, promising to see them soon.

I'm tired from the exertion, from not sleeping last night and watching for lights that never turned on, but I'm focused and grounded and ready to face both my friend with those dark shadows in her eyes...and my secret boyfriend.

What I'm *not* ready for, though, is to pull onto my street, gaze focused on Rome's place, and...

Find my father standing in his driveway.

THIRTY-NINE

Rome

I DIDN'T SLEEP last night.

I'm exhausted.

But I need to pull up my pants like the big, scared hockey player I am, suck it up, and go next door.

I need to tell Chrissy.

That Pat knows.

That it's likely he'll let it slip to her dad.

That we're out of time.

And, fuck, but I hope she likes me enough that she'll fight for me, for *us*.

"Man up," I mutter as I hop up the three steps, walk across the porch, and raise my fist to knock.

My knuckles barely graze the wood before the door is whipped open.

And I blink.

Because it's not Chrissy on the other side.

"Rome Dawson as I live and breathe," the woman who's answered it says.

A woman who—for the record—is *not* Chrissy.

"Um, hi," I say.

Her lips curve. "Hell of a game you had opening night."

"Right. Um. Thanks." My eyes slide to the side, searching for Chrissy.

"She's not here."

My eyes slide back.

"I'm Rory."

"Oh," I say, a bolt of rage spearing through me. "The one with the asshole boyfriend."

She goes still, teeth working at her bottom lip. "Um."

God, I'm an idiot.

"Sorry," I say softly. "That's not what I—" I break off because that was *exactly* what I meant and—

"He's actually my fiancée," she whispers. "And, um, things are..." She sighs, shakes her head. "It doesn't matter."

I open my mouth to tell her it *does* matter, because this woman matters to Chrissy, and because I've learned...well, that when people say it *doesn't* matter, it really fucking does.

But before I can interject, she says, "I sent Chrissy out with her climbing club. She'll be back in a couple of hours and because my friend can't cook—even though she will kindly offer to make me some rubbery scrambled eggs or pancakes with far too much baking soda in them—"

"Or waffles she burns to a crisp?" I ask, thinking of that morning a couple of weeks ago, my lips twitching.

Rory smiles and I think it's a genuine one, maybe the first genuine one I've seen since she let me in through the front door. "Or burnt waffles," she agrees before she asks lightly, "How'd you know?"

"Ask her about how I caught her fanning the smoke detectors the next time you see her," I reply, just as lightly.

She laughs. "Well, so long as she can pull herself away from the climb on time, that should happen over breakfast."

"A"—I waggle my brows—"non-burned, non-rubbery, non-over-baking-soda-filled breakfast?"

Rory taps her nose. "Ding. Ding." A chuckle. "Or that's the goal, anyway." Then she blows out a breath, brushes her palms on her pants, and her voice becomes no-nonsense and a little brusque. "Now, I suppose you're here for one of my puppies?"

I decide to embrace the sharp right in conversation and say, "I may be in love with a little corgi named Athena who has a penchant for climbing cat towers."

Rory's face softens, just the slightest bit. "Have you had dogs before?"

"Yeah, Ror," I say. "I grew up with them, but I didn't have any while I was traveling a lot for hockey. I didn't think that was fair to them."

"And it's fair now?" she asks archly. "When you're going to be out of town regularly for the next eight months?"

"I've already got a pet sitter and dog walker set up, and have plenty of puppy gear on order." I pull my phone out, open the shopping giant's app, and show her the series of obscenely large orders I've placed over the last couple of weeks, including one from last night when I couldn't sleep because Pat's bullshit was running through my mind.

He knows.

I know it.

He knows it.

I just...

"That all looks good," Rory says, handing me my phone back.

There's a *woof!* and the sounds of nails clicking on the floor, causing both of us to jerk around and focus on the puppy room.

On the gaggle of corgis currently staring at us from doggy jail.

Athena jumps up on the gate, excitement making her tiny body wiggle.

"Right," Rory says. "Speaking of puppies." A jerk of her chin toward the room before she starts walking.

I trail after her, the noise growing as we cross the hall and make it to the open door, climb over the gate, and enter... *chaos.*

The puppies are running in all directions, but because they're not all that good at using those tiny legs of theirs, they're also skidding and sliding, bumping into crates and toys and water dishes and each other...

Athena beelines for me, puppy smile wide. "*Woof!*"

It's excited and high-pitched and matched with her little legs moving in rapid speed, skidding on the hardwood floor as she tries to gain traction...and is unsuccessful, colliding with my legs.

Hard.

"Shit," I mutter, dropping down to my knees and taking her into my arms. "I'm sorry, little pupper."

Athena—apparently no worse for wear despite her small body colliding with my much bigger one—licks my chin excitedly, trembling with delight. I don't mind the licking or the way she practically crawls into me, but when she nibbles a little too roughly, I pull her back, meet her puppy eyes, and order softly but firmly, "Easy."

She settles immediately, goes back to licking and cuddling, and pretty soon her siblings are joining the commotion, crawling all over me like I'm their own personal jungle gym.

Laughter from my side.

I manage to twist my head, see that Rory is grinning. "Yeah," she says. "You'll be all right."

Puppy play time is followed quickly by puppy sleep time, and Rory and I are carefully extracting ourselves from the masses of fluffy butts under the supervision of one Joan of *freaking* Arc—who is watching us with narrowed eyes and unsheathed claws, all the better to protect Athena and the litter of fluffy hooligans if Rory or I dare step out of line— when there's a resounding knock at the front door.

Rory winces as the puppy she's shifting to the kennel jerks in her hold.

"I've got it," I say, having successfully made my transfers.

"Thanks," she replies softly.

Nodding, I bypass Joan—and her lazy, clawed swipe— giving her a quick scratch between the ears before I slip out of the room, closing the door behind me, and hurrying toward the front of the house.

Because the knock is coming again.

Only this time it's paired with the sound of metal against metal as someone unlocks the front door.

As that same someone turns the knob.

The heavy wooden panel swings forward...

To reveal Jean-Michel Dubois.

He takes one look at me—standing in the foyer of his daughter's house—

And I know that I'm dead.

FORTY

I CAN'T LIE.

Half of me just wants to whip my car around and not deal with any of this shit.

The rest of me?

Wants to swoop in like Rome is some damsel in distress.

Either alternative results in an ending I don't want—confrontation with my father at some point.

Which is why I need to just get this over with.

"Breathe," I whisper, pushing out all the air in my lungs, forcing myself to focus on navigating my car into the driveway, into not committing vehicular manslaughter on two men I care about.

On two men I *love.*

Because I'm living in a fucked-up fairy tale and the most legitimate relationship I've ever had—emotionally and physically deep enough that my heart is involved already—is with a man my father won't approve of, if only because he won't approve of *any* man that I'll date.

"That doesn't matter," I remind myself. "I need to grow up." I clench the steering wheel as I wait for the garage door to open so I can pull inside. "And I'm going to make it clear he just has to deal with it." A beat. "Without dismemberment."

I throw the transmission into park, unbuckle, and get out, panic warring with frustration and need.

The need to cross the driveway, throw myself into Rome's arms, and ask him what happened last night after I left. To make sure he's okay and—

The panic.

That I'm actually going to do this.

Stand up to my dad. Not sneak around to get what I want.

I'm going to be a strong, independent—

"Your dad is in a rare mood," I hear from behind me.

Heart skipping a beat—but proud that I'm not a puddle on the floor, that I've come far enough from my past to not just cower and hide—I whip around, see that Rory's standing in the open garage door, leaning against the column closest to my front door. "What happened?" I ask softly.

"Rome came over to visit with Athena."

Unbidden, a smile curves my lips. "Did he pass inspection?"

She waggles her brows. "In more ways than one."

Amusement grows in my belly. "Ror," I warn.

"He's good," she says. "And, anyway, it doesn't matter what I think. Athena has spoken on that fact." A shrug. "And Joan, for that matter."

My lips twitch. "You're not wrong," I tell her.

"I know I'm not," she says before her expression sobers.

"As for what happened after your hockey hottie passed muster?" She pauses, waits for me to nod before she continues, "Your dad showed up after puppy playtime was over, and he's clearly not happy to find one of his hockey players in your house."

"Right," I whisper, starting to turn for the direction of Rome's driveway, intending to go full white-knight-rescuing-his (*her*)-damsel.

"What are you doing with him?" Ror asks before I get there.

Frowning, I glance back at my friend. My *only* friend—or at least, the only one who knows as much about me as I've been willing to share. More than most anyone.

Aside from my dad.

And, now, Rome.

"I like him, Ror," I whisper. "A lot."

She moves over to me, takes my hand, fingers squeezing mine. "I know you do," she says. "Which is why I'm asking what the fuck are you doing with him? Why aren't you owning it? Why are you letting your dad dictate what you want and what you can have?"

I'm trying to.

I'm *going* to.

I...swear.

"I—"

She squeezes my fingers. "I know you, babe. I get the *why* of hiding the relationship, and I understand that you feel as though you need to protect Rome. But...is this what you want? Hiding what you have? Panicked that the wrong person will find out?" She sighs. "I know some part of this has to be exciting, and you're a girl who loves a thrill—"

I open my mouth to protest, but she's still going.

"—but get those thrills from climbing mountains, honey.

Not from minimizing and hiding from what you're desperate to have. Not from pretending to protect a hockey player who can clearly protect himself." She releases me. "And not as an excuse to keep yourself safe because the last time you put yourself out there—*really* put yourself out there and went after what you want—it turned into a nightmare."

I pull in a breath so quickly that I nearly choke.

"You've been stuck in a tower your whole life, babe. First with your mom leaving you the way she did then your dad being overprotective, something that got worse after"—she tilts her head to the side, makes a face—"but now you need to think if you've been complaining about being stuck up in that tower of yours, sequestered safely away from anyone who might be a threat because that's really true...or because it's safer up there."

"I'm going to tell him."

Rory's expression turns pitying, and I know she doesn't believe me. I open my mouth to tell her what I figured out last night, how right her words have struck true, but—

I don't get to explain.

My father's voice pierces through the air.

"Christina!"

"Ror—"

"Go on," Rory murmurs. "We can talk more later."

I want to stay. I want to avoid this conversation, the confrontation.

But—

I can't.

Not any longer.

I nod at Rory and walk out of the garage, moving partway down the winding driveway and carefully picking my way through the planters separating the properties until I make it to Rome's side.

"Hey," he says quietly, something in his eyes that I don't like, but I don't have a chance to fully process it because my father is talking.

"You didn't tell me you had visitors," he says.

And yup. There's accusation in his tone.

My temple throbs again, a sharp pulse that has me grinding my teeth together, and something inside me snaps.

Enough.

Just...*enough.*

"Hi, Dad," I say, my tone tart in a way it probably hasn't been for a decade. "Good morning to you too. Hi, Rome," I go on. "It's good to see you."

Something flashes across his eyes—guilt? worry? *regret?*—but I don't have time to process it.

"Good, honey," I say softly, watching his brows fly up in surprise, but I can't let that deter me. Not now. I look back at my dad. "Did I forget that we were supposed to meet up?"

His eyes flashing with irritation. Likely at my tone, at the endearment, or maybe I'm just anticipating his reaction because I'm all twisted up inside and Rome didn't come back to me last night and Rory's words are ringing about my head and—

I really need to take a shower.

"I'll just...let you two catch up," Rome begins, starting to back away.

"No," I say, reaching out my hand, wrapping my fingers around his wrist.

My dad jerks.

I don't know if it's because of my tone again or it's the fact that I'm touching a man in front of him. I *do* know it looks like he's going to reach across the distance separating him from Rome and start throttling.

Fuck.

"Did you need to talk about the pups?" Rome asks, giving me an out.

Giving me a chance to continue keeping us a secret.

"Rory and I already ironed out the details," he says, building on that when I don't immediately answer. "Athena will be ready to go in a week or so. Probably about the same time that your kittens will have their adoption fair." He nods back toward the garage, where my friend is standing. "Maybe you guys should have a joint event."

Adding layers around our secret, making it more believable, and...

Something else snaps inside me.

Fuck. *That.*

But I don't get the chance to implode his career—and possibly my relationship with my father—because another car pulls up.

It's a sleek, black sedan that cruises to a stop all of five feet behind my dad, and I don't miss that his security exits *his* car parked on one half of my driveway, boots clipping on the concrete, not being careful at all of the flowers in that planter bed separating Rome's and my properties.

That's because the door to the black Lexus is sweeping open and a woman is emerging out from behind the tinted interior.

Long blond hair that sweeps down her back.

High-heeled pumps. A silky, pale blue blouse. Slacks that fit her waist and hips like a glove before dropping to the tips of those heels in one graceful flow of fabric.

Elegant. Beautiful. *Familiar.*

I hear my father inhale sharply and rip my gaze from the woman, turning to see that he's gone pale, so pale that I worry, for a second, he's going to pass out.

But Rome has processed that fact sooner than I.

He's stepping forward, standing directly behind my dad, grabbing his arm, steadying him, even before his security guard gets there.

"Dad?" I whisper. "Who is it?"

His head whips around, eyes wide as they meet mine, lips moving.

But the words are so unfathomable it takes me a long moment to process them.

"Your mother."

FORTY-ONE

"YOUR MOTHER."

I move to Chrissy, faster than I'd stepped toward Jean-Michel because if he had looked as though he was going to pass out when the woman first emerged from the car, Chrissy appears as though she's going to shatter into a thousand pieces.

"Easy," I whisper, drawing her close.

Her nails bite into my arm, shocked gaze on mine. "Wh-what is he talking—?"

But she doesn't get the complete sentence out.

"Jean-Michel?" A softly accented voice has Chrissy jerking, looking forward.

I allow my gaze to follow hers, see that the woman—Chrissy's *mother?*—has been stopped by a bodyguard who's appeared out of nowhere.

"Jean-Michel." A warning now.

Chrissy's father takes a step back.

"Dad?" Chrissy whispers, causing the woman's head to swivel away from Jean-Michel, and over to...

Chrissy.

"Is that her?" A soft question from the woman now, but there's something in it that has alarm bells blaring through my mind, has me stepping closer to Chrissy.

Rory must have the same alert going off in her head because she's suddenly on Chrissy's other side, leaning close, sandwiching her in.

Because my woman is trembling.

Like she knows this is going to change everything.

And hell, it doesn't even involve me, but I fucking *know* it's going to change everything too.

The security guard doesn't allow the blond woman to move, just puts his big bulk between Jean-Michel, us, and—

"Is that her?" the woman asks again.

Chrissy stiffens next to me.

"Angela," Jean-Michel says coolly, seeming to have finally collected himself. "This is neither the time nor place for this conversation."

"Is. That. *Her?*"

Chrissy sucks in a breath. "Dad?" she whispers.

Jean-Michel glances back over his shoulder, and I don't miss the guilt written into the lines of his face, don't miss that he's fucked up in some way that is huge and perhaps unfixable and—

"It is," the woman says, taking a step toward us, only to be blocked by the security guard. "I recognize those eyes." She drags her gaze down Chrissy's frame. "And she's got my body. That hair, though." A tsk that has the hairs on my nape standing on end. "That hair color is awful with her skin."

I shift, drawing Chrissy behind me, blocking her from this woman's—from her fucking mother's?—view. But bringing myself into it. Her face *is* very much like Chrissy's—all delicate lines and soft features. A pert nose and high cheekbones. Lips that are full and kissable.

Fucking beautiful.

But instead of an inner beauty shining outward, filling the space around her with light, this woman...speaks of treachery.

Which—I get—sounds like I've read one too many romantasy novels, but...

I don't like this.

Not at fucking *all*.

I inhale, hold. Exhale, hold. Trying to clear my head, even though it's positively spinning. I've gone from thinking that Jean-Michel is going to murder me and quietly dispose of my body to trying to figure out what in the fuck all Chrissy was doing by practically announcing our relationship to her father when the mere suggestion of that—barely a week ago—had left her panicking.

And doing all of that after I spent all night worrying about Pat's threat, and what I might do if he told Jean-Michel, and how I was going to break the news to her.

And...

Coming to the conclusion that I would be right here.

Holding her in my arms, doing what I can to protect her, choosing a future that means more than my past...and even more than my career.

"That hair color has to go," Angela says snottily. "And it wouldn't hurt if she lost five pounds."

"Don't you fucking talk to her like that," Jean-Michel snaps, even as an admonishment is rising up in my throat.

She ignores him, her focus solely on me, apparently. "Though, I suppose you're a nice-looking catch." Her mouth curves as she flicks her eyes over my shoulder, toward

Chrissy, and I shift, cutting off her view. "Even *with* that hair." A beat. "And the dirt on your cheeks."

"I think you need to go," I tell her.

She sniffs.

"Angela," Jean-Michel warns. "He's right. You need to leave."

"My mother," Chrissy says and the heartbreak in her voice is evident. "But—" I glance over my shoulder, see that she's looking at her father, eyes and tone practically begging him to look at her.

To explain.

My mom left me on his doorstep.

Why didn't I question that? Why didn't I push to understand exactly what she meant by it?

Probably because she'd spoken about it so matter-of-factly.

No question. Just reality. And...

So much other shit had dropped into her lap—the kidnapping and the memories that still haunt her, trying to rebuild her life, dealing with her father's overprotectiveness.

And now this woman she's never met showing up and...

Saying shit that she shouldn't.

"You told me she left me," Chrissy whispers.

"She did," Jean-Michel says tersely.

"I didn't," Angela interjects.

"You fucking *did*," Jean-Michel snaps.

"I—"

"I think, maybe," Rory begins, making Chrissy jump and Jean-Michel and Angela swivel their gazes in her direction, "this is a conversation to *not* have in the middle of a driveway?"

Cold eyes flicking to Rory, and dismissing her just as quickly.

But Jean-Michel intervenes before Angela can reply, no doubt caustically. "She's not going into Christina's house."

"Mine then?" I offer quietly. Mostly because Chrissy's still trembling and leaning against me more heavily, and I'm worried that if she doesn't sit down, she's going to fall over.

Jean-Michel glances at me then at Angela, at Rory, and his security guard. His shoulders rise and fall on a deep breath then he leans close to his bodyguard, mutters something I can't discern.

The guard nods, and steps to the side, clearing the path for Chrissy's mom.

And then with Chrissy tucked closely to my side...

We walk into my house.

* * *

I MEAN...SOMEONE needs to say something at some point, right?

That's what I assumed when I showed them into my living room, when I got them all glasses of water—that no one has touched—and sat beside Chrissy on the couch, taking her hand.

Yup. I'm holding her hand in front of her father.

Because she needs that.

Because...I don't care if her father sees.

Rory meets my eyes, flicks hers down at Chrissy's and my intertwined fingers, then looks back up, the barest hint of a smile on her face.

I have the feeling she would be grinning outright, if not for the fact that this situation is tense as shit.

"Who are you?" Chrissy asks quietly.

"Your mother," Angela replies. "Like he"—a nod toward Jean-Michel—"said."

"No," Chrissy says, fingers tight around mine. "I mean...
who are you?"

Jean-Michel's chest inflates again, his words quiet when
he says, "Angela is my...my ex-wife."

Another jolt through Chrissy's body, her eyes sliding
closed. "Your *ex-wife*." Two quiet words laced with pain.
"And my mother." Her eyes open and she pins her father in
place. "My. *Mother*."

Guilt.

Fuck. Yes, that's fucking guilt on the other man's face.

And it kills.

Because I feel what that revelation does to Chrissy.

It fucking *destroys* her.

FORTY-TWO

Chrissy

"EXCUSE ME," I whisper, pushing up from Rome's couch with shaking legs. "I, um, need some fresh air."

And then I'm sidestepping my father's security and hurrying out through the front door. But, despite my words, I don't soak in the sunshine, and certainly not the crisp fall air. I'm running, hiding, practically sprinting into my house, hustling up the stairs, and rushing into my bathroom, slamming the door behind me, flicking the lock. I wrench on the shower because I need the background noise to hide the fact that I'm having a panic attack.

My mother.

My *fucking* mother.

And my dad looking guilty.

And...what the actual fuck is going on?

I groan and sink down onto the plush rug, dropping my head onto my knees, pressing my face into my legs, hoping that if I do it hard enough, I'll stopper the tears, will manage to keep my shit together.

He lied to me.

My entire life, my father lied to me.

He said...God, he *said* he didn't know.

He said she left me.

He said...

My tears pool over and I don't bother to stop them, not when my eyes are burning so intensely that it feels like if I don't get them out, I'm going to explode. My lungs. My brain.

My heart.

He *said* he didn't know who she was.

But one glimpse of her getting out of her car and he knew.

That the woman—*Angela*—was my mother.

How many years had I worried about her? Had wondered? Why she left me? If she was hurting or scared or... dead. If there was something wrong with me and that's why—

Knock. Knock. Knock.

I know instantly that it's not my father.

The knock is far too soft for a man like him, for the man who enters every room with confidence, for the man who filled up every space in my life...and I was happy to let him reside there.

But I don't move, don't unlock the door. If it's Rory, I don't want her to see me like this, brought down by a surprise. If it's Rome...well, I'm fucking scared, yeah? Because what if he sees me like this and—

There's a *scrape*, metal against metal, and then the door is being pushed open, Rome walking through. He closes it and comes toward me, setting a bobby pin on the counter before crouching down beside me.

Note to self: clean the fuck up after wrestling with my

hair—hair that apparently doesn't go with my complexion—so I can have a panic attack in peace.

Rome doesn't say anything, but he doesn't just sit next to me either, doesn't try to fill the air with words that will make this all make sense, that will make this better.

Nope, he just sits on the plush bath rug and pulls me into his lap.

And says, "Fuck, Kitten."

It's...right.

It's...exactly what I need to hear.

I shudder out a breath and collapse against him, my face in his throat, tears coming freely, sobs hitching in my chest.

"I...don't...know...what...to...think," I gasp out. "I—*how* could he know? He told me he *didn't* know and—"

"I'm sorry, baby," Rome whispers. "So, *so* sorry."

I can tell he is. It's in his voice and the way he holds me, and it's in his heart because he's a good person and knows what it's like to have the foundations of what he thought was secure rattled by an earthquake.

So, he holds me close, in no hurry to let me go, and whispers soft words in my ear.

But I can't really take them in.

Because something in me has broken.

All this time I've been struggling with what I want and what my dad wants for me. And not even with wanting Rome. That was just the first time something that I want has outweighed the guilt that kept me from stepping outside the firm boundaries my father put in place after that night a decade ago.

I can climb mountains.

But I can't risk disappointing him.

And even when I finally decided what I want is important enough to push back against those boundaries, I still almost didn't risk it, didn't risk going after what I wanted.

Because I was worried about what my dad would do to Rome.

And all this fucking time, he's been lying to me.

Snap.

My temper, or the final thread of my control, or maybe those broken pieces inside me shattering into a thousand more shards.

And then...

All I know is that I'm suddenly on my feet, looking down into Rome's surprised eyes.

He stands up, starts to reach for me. "Kitten."

But I'm already moving, already yanking open the bathroom door and pounding down the stairs.

"Chrissy—" Rory says standing just inside my house, eyes concerned and—

"Where is he?"

She winces, but her eyes give her away, flicking to the side, toward my front yard.

I blow by her, rushing out onto my porch, down the stairs, through the winding path that leads to the driveway...

Which is empty.

My father's car nowhere in sight.

I flick my gaze to the side, see that Rome's driveway is empty too.

No sleek sedan. No woman who looks like me. No hulking security guard making sure my dad is safe and protected and—

"Kitten."

I glance over my shoulder, see that Rome has followed me outside, is taking in the same reality that I am.

"He left," I whisper as he comes close and slides an arm

around my shoulders, tucking me tightly against his body. "He just...left?"

Hurt—and it seems beyond ridiculous to even think this—but it's filled my soul, washed away the joy from my climb that morning, the happiness I felt with Rome over the last couple of weeks, tainted the way that all of my childhood memories sit in my heart.

Special birthdays with my dad.

Playing hooky from school.

Traveling the world.

Our traditions at the holidays.

Dance recitals and scoring my first goal. Ringing the bell at the top of the rock wall when I finally worked up the courage to take the hard route.

And the wondering—why she didn't want me, what had happened to her—

And he knew.

Through all of that, he *fucking knew*.

"I—"

Rory's voice has me turning around, and I hate that her expression is filled with pity.

"He left a couple of minutes ago, honey," she says gently. "And told your mother—uh, the woman—uh, *Angela*—" A shake of her head. "I think they were going to talk," she finishes on a whisper.

They are going to talk.

Without me.

I slip out from under Rome's arm, march toward the garage, pull open my car door, and yank my phone out of my backpack. A few seconds later, I've jabbed at my father's name on the screen, hit the button to call him, and lifted it to my ear as it rings once, twice, *three* times.

Nope.

Four.

Before going to voicemail.

Something—those broken pieces probably—shift around in my belly, jabbing me, sending sharp bolts of pain through my insides. *Never* has he not picked up one of my phone calls. Not during a flight or a board meeting or even once when he was meeting with the governor and I broke my ankle. He's always—*always*—taken my calls.

Just...not today.

I hang up—not bothering to leave a message—and drop my phone back into my bag.

Rome steps close, crouching in the opening of my open driver's door. "Do you want to go after him?" he asks. "I can drive you wherever you need—"

But then his words cut off and his gaze is going over my shoulder, and—

I freeze as another sedan pulls into Rome's driveway.

FORTY-THREE

Rome

THIS REALLY ISN'T the fucking time.

I curse under my breath as Chrissy stiffens, her eyes going wide.

But I've already spotted who's in the driver's seat.

Kingston. And Cam is sitting beside him.

I pull my cell from my pocket, glance down at the screen —filled with a flurry of messages on the group chain—and sigh.

Apparently, the guys and I are supposed to be getting breakfast this morning.

Something that started when I turned down King's offer of a post-game beer a while ago. Now it's become a somewhat regular thing—mostly because the pastries we get from Molly's are a thousand times better than any beer.

But seriously, the fuckers have the worst timing.

"It's just Cam and King," I tell her. "We were going to grab some food." I start to stand. "I'll get rid of them and—"

"No," she says, grabbing her backpack and getting out of the car, following me up to my feet. "You should go."

Yeah, no. Like I'm going to leave her by herself.

"That's not happening," I tell her, and I don't miss that Rory's mouth falls open, that her surprise is palpable.

As though she's shocked I would choose my woman over my friends.

God, we've seriously got to do something about that asshole fiancée of hers.

But first, I need to make sure my woman is okay.

"I'm staying," I say softly, taking Chrissy's hand and squeezing lightly. "Why don't you go take that shower you started, and I'll get rid of these assholes—"

"Rude," King says as he moves up the walkway. "If you're going to shit talk us in front of a pair of beautiful women, you could at least do it out of hearing range."

Cam is grinning as he glances from King over to me, but one look at my face is apparently all it takes for him to get that something's wrong. "What happened?" he asks quietly.

And I would be lying if I said I expected that steel filling his tone, would be lying if I said I anticipated the fury in his eyes.

Cam's a quiet guy—chill and easy to get along with. He has to be considering he's one of six, including five brothers.

But *this* is a side of him I haven't seen.

I meet his eyes, shake my head, silently telling him to not push it.

His jaw flexes but he nods shortly, and I know I'll need to offer him some semblance of an explanation later, if only because he looks ready to go full Hulk on someone.

King drops his head to the side, studying Chrissy and I closely. "What's going on?"

"Nothing that's your business," Rory mutters.

My brows flick up at the sharp reply, but I don't get a chance to interject before Rory is grabbing Chrissy's arm, waving her hand.

"Off with you all," she orders. "Go have your guy time."

"Ror—" I begin.

But she's already drawing Chrissy toward the house, and I hear her mentioning that shower again.

"This isn't the right time," I tell the guys. "I'll—" I wave a hand. "I'll explain"—as much of it as I can, anyway—"later—"

"No, it's fine," Chrissy says and I turn to see she's pulled out of Rory's hold, has walked back over to me. Her expression...well, I don't really love how distant it is right now. "It's cool. *I'm* cool." One shoulder lifts and drops. "You guys should go have your breakfast and—" Her voice breaks, that icy exterior shattering. "I'll just have a shower and catch that *rain check* for later, right?"

I knew that fucking text would come back to bite me.

Because I'm a dumbass and I panicked and—

She turns away from me, starts for the house, Rory following.

But the moment she realizes her friend is trailing her, Chrissy turns back, "You too, Ror. Get some food—"

"Hang on," I mutter to my teammates.

"We can go," King begins.

"Just...yeah," I say. "Whatever. Go. Don't. I'll catch up with you later." But I don't look back at him, at Cam or Rory. Mostly because Chrissy is already moving into the house, and I know if she shuts that door, I'm fucked.

I hustle across the garage, catch it before it swings completely shut, and move in behind her.

She's hustling again—not running exactly, but going at a quick enough pace that I'm practically jogging to catch up with her.

Which I do.

At the base of the stairs.

"Go," she snaps, jerking away from my hold. "That's what you were going to tell me today, right? That's why you avoided me last night, isn't it? Something happened and it spooked you, and you were going to tell me we should break things off."

For a moment there?

Yeah, I considered it.

With her being unwilling to stand up to her father, and Pat's quiet threat, and the thought of losing what I'm building here...yeah, I thought about backing off.

But...that barely lasted on the drive through the parking lot.

Because I know that Jean-Michel can implode my career, can take everything from me, and I will still want to be right here with Chrissy.

Which is why I spent the rest of the night planning. And worrying.

On how to deal with Pat, with her father.

And I have thoughts.

I just didn't expect the added curveball of her long-lost mother showing up on my driveway.

"Why do you think I came over this morning?" I ask.

Her brows yank together.

But I don't let her answer, not when the words are pouring off my tongue. "Last night, Pat made it clear that he knows there's something happening with us, and he's a fucking asshole who can make trouble. So, I'm not going to lie to you. For a moment there, I doubted what we're doing"—she flinches—"but only until I realized that there is one thing more important in my life than hockey." I touch her jaw. "And that's you."

She shakes her head, pulls out of my hold. "You can't know that."

"Can't know that I wanted to be here—*right here*—the first moment I saw you step out on your back deck?" I move closer, cup both of her cheeks. "Can't know that I fell in love with you the first time when I saw you risking yourself for your grumpy ass cat?"

She jerks, but I don't stop.

"Can't know that I did it all over again when you melted as I kissed you? Can't know that I fell headfirst seeing you wave a towel at the smoke detectors after trying—and failing —to make me breakfast? And again, feeling your body moved against mine as I fucked you deep and slow? And hearing my name on your tongue? Seeing you with Joan and the puppies and Petal?"

"Rome," she whispers.

"So, yeah, I know we've barely started, and I know I can't promise that you and I will work out forever"—I settle my forehead against hers—"but I fucking hope so. Because for the first time since I left Massachusetts, I truly feel at home" —I drop one hand to her chest, rest it just above her heart— "*here.*"

She's still for a long moment then melts against me, her forehead resting against my shoulder, her arms wrapping around my middle. "Dammit," she whispers. "I don't know what the fuck I'm doing."

"I know the feeling," I say lightly, my heart pounding as I draw her closer, as I run my hand down her ponytail, settle my palm on the small of her back. "I'm sorry I didn't come last night. I—"

She lifts her head, presses a finger against my lip. "*I'm* sorry. And this—it's not your fault. I—" Her voice breaks. "I just can't believe he lied to me."

It's more than a lie.

It's a betrayal, and I have the feeling we don't know the half of it just based on Jean-Michel's face when he saw Angela get out of her car.

But...it's also a fucking mess that's going to be complicated to tease apart, so I don't pile on, just keep her close as I hug her tightly. "I know, Kitten," I murmur into her hair. "I know."

"Can we just...start over?" she whispers a few minutes later. "Just pretend we ended our night in my office and this morning you had fun with Athena while I went on a much-needed climb?"

I smooth a few strands of hair off her face. "Yeah, baby," I tell her. "We can do that." And then I just hold her, hating that she's hurting, but still reveling in that sense of home and encouraged by the fact that's she's stopped running and is allowing me to comfort her. "So," I say softly a little while later when her trembling has ceased and her body has relaxed against mine. "I know that we're out of the record-breaking drought and all"—I pull back enough to meet her eyes, pull back enough so that she can see that I'm joking—"but water's a wasting."

Her lips quirk, so I keep going.

"And you did have that climb this morning, so I think it's time to..."

Now she's giving me a full-blown smile. "You're saying I stink?"

"I would never," I joke, bending in and brushing my lips over hers.

"But *I* said it?" She giggles. "Don't worry. I can both take a hint *and* save the environment."

"Because you're fucking Superwoman, Kitten."

Her inhale is sharp. "Rome."

"Shower, baby."

"I—"

"Meow!"

We both look down at Joan, whose green eyes are fixed on ours, judgment evident in their depths.

"Get a move on," those eyes seem to say.

And luckily, it's exactly what Chrissy needs to hear.

She giggles again then brushes her lips over my cheek, holding my gaze. "Thank you."

I nudge her back. "Go on, Smelly."

"Rude," she mutters.

But she's smiling and that's enough.

For now, that's more than enough.

FORTY-FOUR

Chrissy

WELL, minor freak-out started.

And finished.

Thanks to Rome who didn't shy away from being with a woman who's...

Apparently prone to freak-outs, already feeling my pulse beginning to speed up again. Because my dad...

Jesus Fucking Christ.

"Breathe," I whisper, staring at my reflection in the mirror. Clean face—dirty cheeks are no longer something for Angela, for *my mother,* to sniff at. Dark hair—that beneath the dye is the same color as hers—slicked back into a high pony. Not a lick of makeup on—unlike her with her perfectly done-up face. And why do I have the feeling that she wouldn't consider my fatigue—both from the climb and from the emotions of the morning—a good enough reason to be walking down to my boyfriend without being perfectly done up?

Wondering and waiting.

Thinking and wishing.

And...lies.

"Shh," I whisper, my stupid eyes stinging again. "This is just another..."

Except, here's where I falter.

Because it's another disappointment? Another painful memory?

How does one process the reappearance of a person I thought was out of my life forever? And worse, a betrayal by the person who's always been my steady? Especially when he won't take my calls.

I jab at my cell's screen for the umpteenth time since I came back into the bathroom, the air sticky from the water running for so long.

It connects immediately, but he doesn't pick up.

And it rings and rings and *rings*.

And...

"Voicemail," I mutter, hitting the button to disconnect. The call cuts off and I sigh into the silence. "A-fucking-gain."

I slap on some deodorant, get dressed, and go back downstairs. There are puppies to take care of and Joan to look after and I need to get down to the rescue and make sure that everything is ready for the adoption fair next week. And to soak in my cuddles with Petal.

Because she'll be at that fair.

And I have no doubt the adorable little fluff ball will find a forever home.

Another hurt on my heart.

But...another fact of my life.

"Jesus," I mutter, tightening my ponytail. "Enough of this already."

I close the bathroom door firmly—as though that will

close the mental door on the thoughts that are swirling through my mind—and hurry across my bedroom rug, down the stairs, and...

Into my kitchen.

Which is filled with hockey players.

Well, *three* hockey players, a bestie, and a gaggle of corgis.

And Joan of *freaking* Arc.

Who is currently being cuddled—yes, fucking *cuddled*—by one Cam Jackson. No claws in sight. No hissing or grunting or biting. Just...

"Is she *purring?*" I exclaim, skidding to a stop and managing to get all eyes on me—and taking into account the hockey players, my bestie, and *all* the animals, that's a lot of fucking eyes.

Rome spins toward me, Athena—of course—in his arms. His expression is gentle and filled with concern, but he doesn't voice any of those worries, just tilts his head toward the island and I see that it's filled with pale blue bakery boxes from—

"Molly's?" I ask gleefully.

Rory grins, glancing over at Rome. "See? I told you she'd perk up for baked goods."

My friend isn't wrong.

"Oh my God," I whisper, moving reverently forward. "I swear, I never allow myself to eat here because I would gorge on their *pain au chocolat* and weigh six hundred pounds."

Because I have no self-control when it comes to the flaky, buttery dough and the deliciously tart column of dark chocolate folded into the middle and all of that baked to a perfect golden brown.

Which is why I don't even dare drive by the chain of bakeries.

I'll never make it to the top of that F7 route at the gym if I'm loaded down by refined sugar and carbs.

Still, I think it might be worth it as I lift out the pastry and take a giant ass bite.

King grins and slides a paper towel beneath me, a neat maneuver that means I don't lose my pastry and I end up with a makeshift plate so I'm not getting crumbs all over the floor. Not that it matters with the swarm of puppies at my feet, eager to lick up every morsel...

But still.

It's nice.

Considerate.

So *not* what Rory has.

Hmm.

And that's a pleasant distraction from the bullshit about my mom, and well...everything about my childhood being a fucking lie.

I take another bite—self-medicating with baked goods—as Rome rounds the island, comes close, and kisses the top of my head. "Okay?" he murmurs. "Or okay as you can be?"

I inhale. Exhale. Take another bite for good measure. "I need to talk to my dad, and then I'll be good," I murmur.

"We have to catch the team plane in a couple of hours for our road trip," he says quietly. "Think he'll be at the airport like usual?"

"I think it's the best option I have."

"Yeah," he mutters, reaching into the box and extracting another *pain au chocolat,* passing it over to me when I finish the first. I don't need it. I could be done with one. But he watches and pays attention and...he's taking care of me.

And...I want it.

"Rest and eat first, Kitten," he says, nudging it closer.

"Soothe your soul with some animals and people who love you."

My heart pulses, but I don't get the chance to reply.

To tell him all that's in my heart.

Not yet.

It's too soon and too much is happening and—

It's just...

Not the right time.

Especially when Joan decides she's had enough of Cam's cuddling and launches herself out of his arms, intent on a fruit tart—or at least the pastry cream hidden beneath the perfect slices of glazed strawberries within that tart. A box hits the floor, sending baked good carnage in all directions—and pastry cream in Joan's—and the puppies start scrambling, requiring all of us to dive in an attempt to corral several wriggling bodies each.

It's chaos.

And I don't know who starts laughing first.

If it's Rory with her fruit-splattered jeans, and Hermes and Neptune and Apollo licking at her bare feet.

Or Cam, who's gone wide-eyed, shocked by Joan's speed, his arms still curled as though he's cuddling an invisible cat.

I don't know if it's King, who's holding Zeus under one arm and Hermes under the other, both pups furiously trying to bite at his beard.

Maybe it's Rome, who's corralled Diana and Athena.

Or maybe...it's me with Neptune pinned between my ankles and one hand reaching for the pastry box.

All I *do* know is that someone starts and then all of us have lost it, laughter ringing out through the air, my knees giving way. Pups get strawberries. I scoop up a *pain au chocolat* and toss it out of harm's way onto the counter, any worry about crumbs forgotten.

Maybe that's why when we get the mess cleaned up and the puppies settled, and we—with the exception of Rory—head to the airport, I feel slightly more at peace.

The answers will come.

I know they will.

And in the meantime, I have Rome and Rory, and the two hockey players who care enough about me—even though we've barely spent any time together—to bring me pastries from Molly's and make sure I don't spill crumbs on my floor, and...help clean up when my cat decides she'll sacrifice an entire box of baked goods in pursuit of pastry cream.

I get it then—understand what Rome was talking about having with the Gold.

A family that maybe is new and not related by blood and doesn't make any logical sense.

But still a family that's there when things don't go right.

Or people let you down.

Or—

Fathers don't pick up their daughter's phone calls...

And don't show up at the airport to accompany the team he's bought.

FORTY-FIVE

I SEE the disappointment in Chrissy when we get to the airport and her father isn't on the plane, disappointment that grows when we wait and he doesn't show up for the flight.

"You need to go," she murmurs when the flight attendant gives me the high sign. "You can't make the team late."

"I can fly down later and—"

"No," she whispers, pressing her finger to my bottom lip. "You're the captain. Things are just starting to come together for you guys. You need to go with the team and focus on hockey so—"

Pat pushes between us, knocking her backward.

I catch her before she can tumble into anything. "Watch it, asshole," I mutter.

"Excuse *me*," he says with a wide smirk, his gaze flicking down to my hands on Chrissy's waist. "You'd better not let Jean-Michel see you touching his girl."

"His *girl*," Chrissy grinds out, "is right here, and if my

father has a problem with the man I'm seeing—" She pauses, chin coming up, holding Pat's gaze. "He can take it up with me. Now off with you," she snaps. "Leave the adults to their conversation."

Pat rocks back on his heels, brows shooting up, but I know behind the surprise he's still calculating, still plotting, still being a fucking asshole, case in point when his tone turns condescending. "I hate to break it to you, *princess*, but dads and brothers are protective over their daughters and sisters, and I can't see a man like Jean-Michel Dubois being okay with a man—"

"Who is kind and considerate, works hard and *isn't* an asshole?" Her shoulders straighten, brows flicking up, indicating exactly who she thinks is the asshole. "Yeah, my father has a *real* problem with that." She sniffs at Pat then turns toward me, rolling her eyes before lifting up on tiptoe and laying a kiss on me that's long and deep and probably has far too much tongue for a private airport terminal currently screening Eagles players as we walk to the plane—even if it is beyond the prying eyes of the media.

And the kiss is great.

It's incredible.

But—

I'm so fucking *proud* of her, in awe of her strength.

In love with every part of her.

"There," she says softly, dropping back onto her heels after Pat walks away in a huff. "I don't have any hope it'll shut him up—since he's an asshole *and* a half—but maybe he'll think twice about fucking with you."

Not likely.

But I've got bigger fish to fry.

"Kitten."

She glances up at me.

"When your dad finds out about us," I begin, guilt churning. Because that kiss isn't going to go unnoticed.

Her chin comes up. "It's time," she says. "Last night, I had time to think."

I wince, but she squeezes my hand.

"Hush," she says. "Earlier you..." Her face gentles. "Well, you gave me all the words, honey, and I need to give them back, okay?"

I still, heart pounding.

Then I manage a nod.

"*Last night*, I decided it's time I stand up for myself—hell, it's *beyond* time. I should have told him about you weeks ago. You're too important"—she cups the side of my neck, tugging my head down so she can rest her forehead against mine—"and I'm sorry I didn't make that clear to him, to *you* sooner. You deserved better."

"Kitten—"

Her fingers tighten. "*You. Deserved. Better.* You're an amazing man and a wonderful teammate, and...you're just *good*, Rome Dawson. You deserve for the entire world to know that, *including* my father."

My throat is tight, and hell if my eyes don't sting with tears.

She's so fucking beautiful and bright and *so fucking* strong.

"I'm so proud of you," I say, unable to take those words without giving some of my own. "All that you've overcome. All that you do. Being willing to go to bat with your dad for me. Putting Pat in his place." My mouth curves and the words start to slip off my tongue. "I love—"

She drops her finger to my lips. "I know."

My lips twitch, and I peel her finger free, turn her hand so I can press a kiss to her palm. "You're really Han Solo-ing me?" I tease, referencing Star Wars and Princess Leia's declaration and how the infamous Han Solo didn't return the grand gesture.

"You'll live." She leans closer, rises on tiptoe, and whispers in my ear. "Plus—my gorgeous man—I'm a Star Trek fan." A pause, mouth curving as she drops back onto her heels. "Something you'll learn when we've been together longer."

Together longer sounds pretty fucking perfect, but—

"I know everything I need to," I tell her, cupping her cheek and brushing my mouth over hers.

And now she's back to gentle, her eyes glimmering with tears. "Me too," she whispers. "I know everything I need to..." She blows out a breath, mouth curving into a wry smile. "Well... *too*. And, I really would like to hear the rest of your sentence, but perhaps in not so public a place so we can celebrate properly."

"An airport terminal isn't private enough but a Zamboni is?" I tease, making her cheeks pinken and her eyes go a bit hazy around the edges.

My dick twitches in memory of the tight clasp of her slick cunt around me.

"Tease." She swats at my chest. "Which means there will be no more Zamboni for you, mister."

I clamp a hand to my chest. "You wound me."

"You know it." A flash of a grin before she's looking over my shoulder. "The flight attendant appears to be more than ready to go."

I glance back, see the look Janine is tossing me, and know that I'm burning any goodwill she might have toward me after dealing with the other assholes on the roster. "Call me if you need anything," I order gently, holding Chrissy's eyes until she nods.

"Thank you, you wonderful man," she whispers. Then jerks her chin toward the plane. "Now go."

I touch her cheek, brush my lips over hers.

And then I'm watching her walk away.

And *then* I'm hauling ass to the plane before Janine closes the door and tells the pilots to leave without me.

***

WE PLAY IN SEATTLE.

And win.

But Jean-Michel doesn't show his face.

And he doesn't take Chrissy's calls.

***

WE PLAY IN VANCOUVER.

And win again.

And...still no Jean-Michel or answered phone calls.

Though, Chrissy *does* get a visit from her father's security guard while she's working at the rescue's storefront, letting her know that he's traveling for business.

Bullshit, and something I would have worried about if that security company wasn't run by a man named Pascal— who also runs security for the Gold—and who I trust enough that I believe him when I follow up that visit with a call, asking if Jean-Michel is safe and well.

Pascal says yes, and since he's not a liar, I relay that information to Chrissy.

But...I know it's not enough for her.

It's not enough for me, and he's not my fucking father.

And I know that the longer Jean-Michel is MIA and the

longer she's without real, meaningful answers, the heavier the weight of her past is becoming.

WE PLAY IN DENVER.

Still no Jean-Michel.

Still no explanation.

WE PLAY IN LOS ANGELES.

And swear to God, I expected more of the same.

No answered calls. No communication with his daughter.

No sign of our illustrious owner.

So color me *really* fucking surprised when I walk out of the locker room and find Jean-Michel standing in the hallway.

"I need to talk to you," he says, turning on his heel and walking down the corridor, not waiting to see if I'll follow, just expecting me to do so.

And...he's right.

Because I *do* follow, trailing directly behind him as he turns the corner and moves into a conference room.

"Shut the door behind you," he says when I enter, his eyes on a stack of papers in the center of a large wooden table that take up most of the room's open space.

I close the door, lean back against it.

And wait.

As he shuffles through the papers, reading each and every one of them...and not bothering—or not in any hurry—to look up at me.

"Have you talked to her?" I ask quietly.

He stiffens, head turning to meet my eyes over his shoulder, and even from across the room, I don't miss the flash of guilt. "No," he says, when I just hold his stare. "I've been arranging other things."

I push off the door, move over to him. "With her mother?"

Hands clenching into fists. "That's none of your fucking business."

I don't stop until I'm within a foot of him. "It's *my* business because it's hurting Chrissy and—"

"It's *none* of your fucking business."

"Bullshit," I snap. "You've lied to your daughter, and she's hurting, and you haven't talked to her in what—a week?—after dropping a bomb on her like you did, and—"

He's suddenly in my face, his hand clenching at the collar of my shirt, and doing it tightly enough that it's hard to breathe. "*It's none of your fucking business,*" he snaps a third time.

I grip his wrist, squeezing until he winces and releases me. "It's my business, and I will continue making it my business because I love your daughter and I will not let anyone— *even you*—hurt her."

Jean-Michel's eyes are flashing with anger, and his hands are back in fists, and he looks ready to throttle me all over again.

But just when I'm certain that he's going to burst...

All of the tension leaves his body.

Overprotective father is swapped for savvy businessman, and my stomach knots as he picks up the sheaf of folders and passes it over to me.

"I'm sending you back to the Gold."

FORTY-SIX

Chrissy

I SIGH as I walk through my dad's still-empty house, knowing that it's pointless to try to track him down when he doesn't want to be found.

He's got a whole team of people who can help him stay hidden, and he knows that I might keep calling, keep pressing, but I won't seriously turn any screws on any of those working for him.

Because I won't risk them getting fired for sharing something they shouldn't.

But that doesn't mean I'm sitting back, twiddling my thumbs and waiting for him to grace me with his presence.

I'm calling and texting and leaving voicemails. I'm showing up at his offices and the arena and the practice facility and the vineyard. I'm going to his house—case in point right now—and looking in his home office for anything that might, one, show where he's gone, and, two, give me a fucking clue who the hell my mother is...

Aside from beautiful, blond Angela.

But I haven't found shit.

And now I'm late to the adoption fair, the one where Petal and her sisters are up for adoption, and Rory's texted, letting me know it's packed already. I need to get over there and make sure that whoever takes Petal home is worthy of being her forever owner.

I exhale and move for the front door, fucking frustrated as hell but knowing there's nothing that can be done for it.

I have cats to take care of and an adoption fair to run, and training plans that Cam and King asked me to revise. And Rome is coming back—or is maybe back already. I have a life to live, and I'm done with letting the past and my father keep me from living it.

My mother...is out there and alive and that answers some of the questions I've had.

Not all.

But I've lived almost my whole life without knowing everything, so...

I'm not at peace with it, exactly.

But I've accepted it.

I reach the large dual-story foyer, move past the double staircase—the grandeur something I never appreciated growing up, but something I understand the value of as a working adult—albeit one with a trust fund, so, really, what room do I have to talk? Except that most of that fund has gone to rescue cats and I know how expensive food and vet care and supplies are for them.

"Go me," I mutter, knowing it's not enough, but that it's another thing I can't fixate on.

Not right now.

Not with Petal—

I shake my head, walk into the kitchen, then move toward

the garage. I'm just placing my fingers on the handle when it turns beneath my palm and the door starts swinging toward me.

I dance back, dodge the wooden panel, and...

Come face to face with my father.

His eyes go wide, and I watch as a real bolt of fear crosses through them. Then he actually takes a step backward as though he might swivel around and run away from me.

"Don't," I hiss, reaching for him.

And thankfully he stops.

Then sighs.

Then...continues moving into the house, not stopping until he's reached the island and set his things on the pristine marble surface.

"You've been avoiding me," I say when he rests his hands on the counter and hangs his head.

"Yes."

Just...*yes.*

Jesus Christ.

I grind my back teeth together. "Why, Dad?"

He sighs, head hanging for another long minute. Then he lifts it up, yanks out a stool and the one right next to it, patting the top while sitting on the other. "Come and sit with me," he says softly. "I'll tell you all of it."

Suddenly, there's trepidation in my belly.

I spent the last week demanding to know the truth...and now the answers might be here.

So, I have to force myself to walk across the room, to sit down on that stool, to wait for my father to gather his words.

And then...he does.

"That woman—Angela Rousseau—is, indeed, your mother," he murmurs.

"And your ex-wife," I say softly.

A nod. "And my ex-wife."

"Did you...keep me from her?" I ask when he doesn't go on.

He's gone still, very still, and it seems like my words take a long moment to penetrate.

Then they do.

He goes stiff, eyes flashing. "Are you fucking kidding me, honey?"

"I don't know, *Dad!*" I throw up my hands. "I don't know anything! All I *do* know is that she showed up at my house, criticized my hair color, and then I haven't heard from her—or *you*—for a fucking week. What am I *supposed* to think?"

He glares at me. "You're supposed to know me better than that?"

"Better than a woman you supposedly didn't know—but who's really your ex-wife—showing up and knowing that I exist when I spent my entire life worried about what she might be doing out there, thinking that there was something wrong with me for her to not be in my life. I had all these questions about her that you pretended not to know the answers to, and"—my voice breaks—"you lied to me." I shake my head. "Because you knew all along."

Silence.

Then, "She left me."

Now *I'm* the one who goes still. "What?"

"She left me," he says again. "And yes, when you appeared on my doorstep all those months later, I suspected it was her. But no matter how hard I tried, I couldn't find her. Not then. Not now." He exhales sharply. "Not until she showed herself."

"But"—my temple starts to throb—"I don't understand. Why would she come back now?"

"Angela always has a plan. And—" He breaks off, muscle flexing in his jaw. "I'm not good at figuring out the endgame."

I don't like the sound of that.

At all.

"I just…" I nibble at my bottom lip, sigh. "I don't understand what she gains coming now. Has she told you what she wants?"

His eyes close for a long, *long* moment. Then they peel back open, and he passes me a folder. "That's what I've been trying to get to the bottom of over the last week."

I flip open the cover, glance down at the papers inside.

"She's been living in France"—he blows out another breath—"that's where we were married. But she doesn't have any legal ties to anyone or any business that I can see. Her family has money that's apparently been sustaining her, but no one can find any work history or any public records that explain what she's doing here now, or what her motivations might be outside of what she's demanded."

I continue flipping through the papers—a report from his security company—seeing that he's not holding back and that he's not lying to me, not this time. "Demanded?" I whisper.

He frowns.

And I can't lie.

A sliver of hope blossoms in my chest. "Did she…" I hold my breath, release it slowly. "Maybe…I mean…is it possible she came back for me?"

There's a long moment where he doesn't say anything.

And I suppose…

That says enough, especially when it's paired with him passing over another folder, and the contents reveal…

That—

No.

She's not here for me.

"She wants half the team?"

My father looks away, jaw clenching, and he's quiet for several heartbeats. "She's saying that we're still married—and I honestly don't know how it will all pan out. We *were* married. I filed for divorce. But this is decades ago and who the fuck knows what the courts will actually say and—" He shoves a hand through his hair before sighing. "She wants"—a nod toward the papers filled with legalese—"half of every-thing." A beat. "Including you."

"I...well." I frown. "I'm not something that can just be split in half."

For the first time since he walked through the door, my father smiles. "Noted, kiddo."

Then his smile fades and silence falls between us, and I find myself asking, "Why didn't you just tell me?"

"That I knew Angela was your mother?"

I nod.

He sighs again. "She wasn't ever—" A shake of his head. "Things weren't good before she left. We were heading for separation. And after...well, I'd already filed for divorce. I thought it was done—and then when she left *you*, I thought it was for the best. I didn't need her toxic bullshit fucking with your life. Christ"—he shoves his hand through his hair again —"you heard her during the ten minutes she was with you. Criticizing your hair, your clothes, that you had dirt on your cheeks. She didn't ask anything about you. She didn't make one effort to find out how goddamned wonderful you are and—"

His voice cracks and I want to be mad, want to be hurt—and yeah, I guess I am both of those things still, but I'm also hurt *for* him.

"When I found you on the doorstep that day," he says, "I knew with one look that you were the greatest gift of my life.

So, when I couldn't find her, when she didn't come back…I didn't care. Because I had you and you had me, and I knew that I could love you enough for both of us, that I could love you how she couldn't, or can't, or—"

I slide off my seat and launch myself into his arms.

And it feels like it always did growing up—

Like him and me. Like he can shelter me from anything scary. Like it will all be okay.

But it also feels like something different—

Like I'm comforting *him.*

Like I'm telling him I understand. Like I may not have chosen the path he did, but that I still…understand it.

"I won't keep you from her," he says quietly. "Or her from you. I have to protect the team and my businesses and our future, but…if you want to see how things go with her, I'm not going to stop you."

I pause, consider that. "I don't know what I want to do," I murmur. And it's the truth. The gulf inside me that's always been empty, always been waiting to be filled, is desperate for a connection with Angela Rousseau. But I'm also not sure a woman who could stay away from me my whole life, who could leave me on a doorstep, whose first reaction to seeing me was criticizing my hair color, is the one who *can* fill it.

His arms tighten and he kisses the top of my head. "You have time to decide. I"—he releases me, nods toward the folder—"have her contact information in that file, and I can make any necessary arrangements to connect you both."

Formal speech.

Because he's scared and hurting.

"I love you," I tell him. "I know this is complicated and messed up and neither of us have any idea how it will turn out, but"—I lean in, kiss his cheek—"I love you, Dad."

His eyes slide closed, throat working. "I'm here for you, honey. No matter what happens."

"I know."

And then we're hugging again.

And then—probably because we're hugging and this might be the most honest conversation we've ever had, I blurt out, "I'm dating Rome."

His arms tighten and then he chuckles. "Kind of got that, honey, with the scene at your house." A beat. "And the kiss at the airport."

I scowl. "You weren't at the airport."

He lightly tugs a strand of my hair, his expression filled with apology. "I have spies everywhere," he says lightly and my scowl deepens. "And...in the spirit of complete and utter honesty, I knew the whole time, kiddo," he says. "I have cameras around every inch of that property."

"Wait"—I pull back—"*what?*"

He winces. "I knew, honey." A beat. "From the moment he saved you from falling out of that tree."

"He's the one who made me fall," I grit out.

"Why do you think I was so pissed at him during that dinner we crashed?"

Amusement coils in my belly, but I don't let him see that because—

"You have cameras?"

"Well," he prevaricates. "I had Pascal and his team install exterior cameras when you moved in, and I, uh, have access to them."

I inhale, humor fading, temper igniting. I don't mind cameras, per se, especially given what happened in the past. But *my father* having access to them? Watching me? Watching me *and* Rome? I clench my jaw, grind out, "You're going to have that access removed."

Not a question. An order.

One he considers for a long pause.

I lift my brows in challenge.

And then, finally, he gives me a small nod. "I'll remove my access," he says. "So long as you'll allow the security company to monitor as necessary."

Now it's my turn for a small nod. "And *you'll* let me live my life as I see fit, even if that includes dating a hockey player from your team?"

Now a sliver of stubbornness enters his eyes.

"*Dad,*" I warn.

He scowls. "I'm not saying that I won't *ever* interfere."

I lift my brows. "But..."

"But I won't protest you dating Rome," he grumbles. "He's a good man. I've seen him on the cameras often enough over the last weeks to know that."

"Dad," I hiss.

He touches my jaw, holds my eyes. "I am sorry, honey," he says gently. "So sorry. About your mother and withholding the truth."

Tears make my vision blurry, but I don't want to cry again.

I want to focus on the fact that my dad and I are talking honestly, sharing, and there's no fear or disappointment...or threats of dismemberment."

"And the cameras?" I joke. "Are you sad about the cameras?"

He scowls, but his eyes are dancing. "No."

Not a perfect answer. But honest.

I'll take that.

Because I'm going to stop worrying about making him proud—because I know now that he already is—and I'm going to give the same back.

"Well, good thing you don't have to look at them anymore."

He grins, and my heart fills with happiness and relief and joy.

But those big emotions only last a moment.

Because then I ask, still joking, more than ready to be done with the heavy, with the orders and confrontation, and wanting to change the subject to something—*anything*—else, "What's in the last folder?"

And then my dad just casually drops another bomb.

"The trade I offered Rome that will send him back to the Gold."

FORTY-SEVEN

I'VE BEEN ALTERNATING between staring down at my phone, expecting a text to pop up from Chrissy explaining why she's running so fucking late, and glancing toward the door, assuming she's going to walk through it any second.

She's missing it all.

The adoption fair.

The kittens going to their new families.

The corgis—with the exception of Athena, who's currently chilling with my new pet sitter, Jodi, and Zeus, who's won over Kingston and now has become corgi mascot number two for the Eagles—have all been matched up and are heading off into the sunset with families that will look after them.

And if they don't—Rory will cut a bitch.

But Chrissy's not here to make the same threats for her kittens, and I know she's going to fucking hate that.

"Easy now," I say to a kiddo who's running just a bit too

fast through the large play space. "You need to move slowly so you don't scare them, yeah?"

He freezes, studies me for a millisecond then takes off sprinting again, a defiant scowl on his face.

Right.

No cats for that one.

I glance over at Chrissy's assistant, see that she's on the same page, already making note of the boy and the woman chasing after him. Another volunteer steps in front of them, stopping the terror, distracting him and Mom and leading them both outside.

Not getting a cat from us.

I nod approvingly, glance down at my phone again, and see that the screen is blank.

No texts from Chrissy.

No calls.

Just radio silence from the woman I love and—

A bell tinkles.

And—thank fuck—she's finally walking through the door.

Blinking, I shove my cell into my pocket and hurry toward her. "Kitten," I begin, but she just wraps her fingers around my wrist and starts yanking me out of the adoption room. She draws me back toward the locked door, swipes her keycard on the pad, and pushes into the empty hallway since all hands are on deck in the front of the space.

"What the hell are you doing?" she hisses the moment it shuts behind her.

I blink. "Um..."

But I don't get the chance to finish that thought because then she's dragging me away from the door, drawing me down the hall, pushing me into a corner, and stopping.

Glaring.

Plunking her hands on her hips.

"You're being traded to the Gold?"

I wince.

Because I *so* didn't want to have this conversation now.

And not here. Not ruining her event or creating problems with her dad when she already has more than enough of them to deal with.

"I was going to tell you," I begin.

Which is the wrong thing to say.

But I don't get to take it back.

She plunks a hand onto my chest, pushes. Not lightly, but not hard enough to hurt me.

Firmly.

So that she's certain I'm paying attention.

But what she doesn't realize is that I'm *always* paying attention to her.

Every word and expression and action—my mind and body and heart are attuned to hers.

Which is why I know that my statement was the wrong one.

Because it implies—

"You were *going* to tell me?"

A dangerous question that I carefully wade in to answer. "Yes," I say. "I was *going* to tell you. It's not important right now with everything else you've got—"

"It's not important?" She shoves my chest a little harder this time. "You being traded back to the Gold isn't *important?!*"

Right. Well.

"Your father—"

"I don't give a fuck what my father threatened. He's an interfering old man who can't keep his nose out of his adult daughter's business."

I open my mouth, but she swipes a hand out in front of her, nearly swatting me in the face.

"And, anyway," she says. "I took care of him. He's going to butt out of my business and knows we've been dating for weeks now."

My brows flick up and I open my mouth to ask how—

I don't get the chance.

Because she's on a roll.

"And you're just accepting the trade?"

I snap my teeth together.

"After all that bullshit about making a new family with the Eagles," she rants, "about forming something special here? All that talk about how you can be someone different with this team—someone *more*." She swipes her hand again, and this time I snag her hand an inch away from my face, before it can smack into me. "You're just going to...what? Run away and put yourself in a tiny box that—"

I tug her toward me, and I do it fast and firmly, catching her off guard, sending her off balance.

I wrap my arms around her and hold her snugly against my chest.

"First," I say. "That tiny box is the *penalty* box and I only go there when the refs make me. Second"—I smooth her hair back, hold her eyes—"I turned down the trade."

Her mouth falls open.

"You're right. I have important work to do here and I'm making progress and I want to be part of what my teammates and I are beginning to build—even if Pat is an asshole. And —" I gently grasp her chin between thumb and forefinger, pressing up, closing her mouth. "And, more importantly, *you're* here. I don't want to be apart from you half of the time, traveling with another team. I want to be right next door, catching you climbing trees and dodging Joan's claws.

Because I know you said *I know*, but I love you and want to be with you, baby. Not because of who your dad is or isn't. Not because you're beautiful—even though you are. But because when I first saw you in your back yard, I knew that you were mine."

She's still, her eyes wide.

Then she shakes her head once, sharply, as though she's clearing the cobwebs from it. "You're not taking the trade?" she whispers.

"No, Kitten, I'm not."

"You're staying here?" she asks, still whispering.

"Yeah, Kitten, I am," I say gently.

"Oh," she whispers.

I almost laugh, but then she bursts into tears, and though I don't know if they're happy or sad, I hold her close and let her get them out. Which is how I learn they're a mix of sad and not, of happy and hopeful.

"God," she says, several minutes later, pulling back and wiping her eyes on her sleeve. "I am such an idiot. My dad tried to stop me after he told me about the trade. But I ran off like an idiot and..." She pauses, nibbles at her bottom lip, uncertainty in those pretty blue eyes.

"I'm not going," I murmur.

Another breath, the tension leaving her body.

Then she's in my arms again, squeezing me tightly. "Good," she says softly. "Because I kind of, sort of, love you too."

I chuckle, kiss the top of her head. "I know."

A sniff. "Rude."

I know she's joking, know she's trying to lighten the moment, that she's had far too much heavy on her plate as it is, but I have to ask, "What are you going to do about your mom?"

She drops her forehead to my collarbone, sighs heavily. "I'm not sure yet."

"There's no rush."

Her head comes up, showing me an adorably wrinkled nose. "Based on what my dad said, I have the feeling that's not exactly true."

"Yeah," I agree.

Coming after half of everything?

Including the team?

Why do I have the feeling that the season is going to get a lot more interesting?

"But I don't want to talk about it anymore," she says, softening the words with a smile. "I just want to focus on today, and I need to get my kitten cuddles in before they head off to their forever homes."

Shit.

I grimace.

Which she catches, because of course she does. "What?" she asks and the worry in her eyes has my heart squeezing.

"Kitten," I say gently. "Petal was already adopted."

She draws in a sharp breath. "When?" she asks quietly, eyes glimmering with tears.

"Within the first fifteen minutes."

Silence.

Stillness and silence and...

Glassy eyes. A throat working. A jaw clenching tight.

"Kit—"

"Right," she says, cutting me off, her tone going brusque as she shakes her head, sending her ponytail skittering. "Of course she went quickly. She's adorable and anyone would know she's a prize."

Guilt slices through my belly and I reach for her, intending to draw her close again, to let her cry or rage, to be the rock she can cling to as the waters of fate and life try to sweep her away.

But...she just steps back.

My heart pulses and I wait for her to turn away.

Instead, she pauses, holds out a hand. "Come with me?"

"Always," I whisper, lacing our fingers together.

And I let her lead us back out into the front room.

EPILOGUE

I CAN'T LIE.

I'm heartbroken.

I want to lay down and sob on the floor like a baby, or maybe like a threenager given the wrong color plate to eat from.

But there's work to be done.

Although...less of it now that Rome has helped me pack up and my father showed and the adoptable kitties have all found placements.

And the corgis.

Including Zeus, who's getting a forever home with Kingston.

But I didn't get that final cuddle with Petal.

And...I'm heartbroken.

Probably her new family will send in pictures, so I'll be able to see her grow and mature.

And we'll be here if there's ever a problem.

I just...

I didn't get to say goodbye.

So now I'm scooping litter that doesn't need to be scooped, trying to exhaust myself mentally and physically so I won't see that adorable face in my dreams and wish that I could squeeze it one more time.

"Ready to go, Kitten?"

My heart pulses at the endearment, at the reminder, but I shake it off, push down my urge to work myself into oblivion. I know Rome has got to be exhausted after the road trip, and my father's shenanigans over the last week, and the flight, and my emotional breakdown here after finding out about him possibly being traded.

Too much has been happening.

So, I put down the litter scoop, go over to the sink, and wash my hands.

Then I grab my purse from the drawer, shore up my heart, and walk back over to the man I love. "I'm ready," I tell him.

He touches my cheek as though he can see right through my brittle shield—

And likely he can.

Because he pays attention.

Kind of inconvenient at a time like this, when I want to hide and not deal with things and he's being nice and sweet and holding me close and treating me gently.

Like he knows how fragile I am.

Ugh.

"I'm fine," I whisper as he buckles me into the front passenger's seat of his car.

"I know," he whispers back.

But he still does up the belt and presses a kiss to my forehead before carefully backing out of the open door.

And it's my favorite music playing through the speakers as he drives me home.

It's his hand in mine as he navigates the turns, not pushing me to talk, just silently telling me that he's here.

It's the gentle squeeze before he releases my fingers after he's pulled into his garage and turned off the ignition.

He looks over at me. "Do you want to come in for a few minutes and see Athena?"

Another pulse through my heart.

See *Athena.*

Who's just a baby.

Like Petal.

I swallow hard, pressing my tongue to the roof of my mouth so I don't start sobbing. "No," I say. "I think tonight I just need to—"

He nods. "Just let me drop my stuff and I'll walk you over."

"You don't have to—"

But he's already got an arm around my shoulders, has tucked me close and is walking toward the house.

"I—"

Then we're pushing through the door, walking into the mudroom, and...into the kitchen.

"Woof!" I hear and the little excited bark is accompanied by nails clicking on the hardwood floor and a furry body skidding around the corner.

Rome chuckles and crouches down just as Athena collides with my legs, her puppy body wriggling with excitement, her tongue lolling, and her eyes wide and bright.

I reach down to pet her, and freeze—

Because she's not the only furry body whose nails are scrabbling on the floor.

Another—*small*—ball of fluff is running my way.

Bright white like a snowflake.

With splotches of orange and gray on her face.

"Petal!" I exclaim, dropping to my knees and gathering her close, her tiny, "Meow!" music to my ears.

"Oh my God, *Petal!*" I cuddle her close. "How are you here?"

"Meow!"

I glance up at Rome. "Do you know the person who adopted her?"

Was that why she was here?

Maybe someone from the Eagles wanted a pet that was less high maintenance than a corgi—

A strange look crosses his face. "Yeah, Kitten, I do."

"Who?"

Maybe Cam?

"Me."

My eyes go wide.

"She's yours," he says. "She couldn't go to a stranger."

"I—"

He bends, scratching Athena between the ears then running a hand down along Petal's back, causing her to arch as though seeking out even more of that rubbing. "I know that Joan might not tolerate her, but she can stay here for now, and we can introduce them slowly—"

I freeze as all of the pieces start clicking into place.

And I realize what he's done.

This big, wonderful man who sees every part of me and doesn't turn away.

"Plus, Athena loves her already, so I'm sure Joan will get on board. She's smart like that, and—"

"Fuck, I love you," I rasp.

He freezes.

Then his palm is cupping my cheek. "Language," he

teases, tugging me into his lap, carefully dislodging Petal. She runs off, Athena beside her. "We have little furry ears who might pick up on the bad words."

I grin. "Yes," I whisper. "I suppose we do." Sobering, I touch his jaw. "You adopted Petal for me."

"You needed her in your life." He places his hand over mine. "And you needed her in the furry family we're building."

"*Building?*" I ask. "How many more members are we gaining?"

"As many as our hearts can stand."

My heart pulses. "You may regret saying that."

He grins. "Never." A beat. "Only…"

"What?"

"How much do you think Joan will mind?"

I grin.

"I think we'd better invest in Kevlar."

Kingston

It's the flash of white on the side of the road that draws my focus.

That glimpse of brightness stands out from the black pavement, damp from the afternoon rain.

A striking contrast to the green shooting off in every direction on either side of the winding road—the dry, brown rolling hills of summer transformed into something that's lush and beautiful and sandwiching me in peaceful oblivion.

Except for that bright white.

Trash maybe—bags or a mattress dumped by some asshole.

Or maybe an animal of some sort?

A dog or a horse or a cow?

It wouldn't too much of a surprise, not in this area of small, local farms and isolated plots of land that aren't found in other areas of the Bay Area. Fences give way, barbed wire breaks, and...

The white object moves again.

Animals get out.

I slow down because—strictly speaking—I'm in violation of my contract by riding my bike. Taking a ride like this—well within the speed limit, on a deserted road, the sun going down behind me and the wind in my hair, on my face—is barely cleared for off-season use.

In early November? When the season is just barely underway and an injury would be catastrophic for my game?

If anyone finds out, I'm dead.

It's just...

Too good of a day.

I needed this—*one last time*—before I put my bike up until the following summer.

That white moves again, and I slow down further. No crashes. No injuries. Nothing to fuck up my life and career and future—

Except, slowing down means that I have plenty of time to see.

That the white isn't a plastic bag caught in a bush, waving in the winds.

And it's not a cow or a horse or a dog.

It's...a person.

A *woman* in a huge, poofy white dress.

And a veil that glitters with crystals in the setting sun.

A woman with long blond curls hanging down her back—

A woman...whose face I recognize.

I hit the brakes hard—too fucking hard considering the slick road—and nearly skid out. It takes a shit ton of effort to control my bike, to wrestle it back upright, to bring it to a stop and put the transmission into park.

Heart racing, I flick down the kickstand, slide one foot onto the pavement, lift my other leg over the seat, rounding my back tire, and hurrying over to the bride-to-be. "Rory," I say, skidding to a stop and reaching for her. "Are you—?"

But I don't finish the question because the moment my palms touch her shoulders, she's flinching back...

And stumbling over the hem of her dress, falling backward into the little gully on the side of the road.

Water—from the same rain that left the pavement slick—splashes, soaking into the fabric of her dress, the long blond curls cascading along her spine, and up onto—

I freeze as red hazes across my vision.

Most of her face is done up in makeup—what my sister Annie would call The Works. Lashes and glittery eyeshadow, her brows on fleek, pink shit on her cheeks, lips filled in with a bright red color.

It's the part that's showing up *beneath* the makeup, that's being revealed more clearly as the rainwater drips down her face, that has my hands clenching into fists.

A bright red mark on Rory's throat.

No. It's not *just* a red mark.

It's a fucking *handprint* covering the expanse of her neck, complete with the outline of four fingers on one side and a thumb on the other.

And...

She has a bruise forming across her fucking cheekbone.

I bend over—slow and steady but inexorably—and scoop her up into my arms, carry her over to my bike, settle her onto the seat.

Then I climb on behind her and take her in my arms.

"I'm going to fucking *kill* him."

Cam

I crack open my beer and sigh, looking at the paused game on the TV and wondering when in the fuck I've become so pathetic.

Playing video games on a Saturday night.

After spending a Saturday morning and afternoon playing video games by myself.

And a Saturday night playing video games while sharing a pizza with...myself.

Not even my online friends are around right now to kill dragons and cast spells and generally play the world's nerdiest game.

They have more interesting lives than I do, and *they* spend most of their waking hours online.

But I still pick up my controller and dive back into the next quest anyway.

And I do it drinking cheap beer and nibbling on cold pizza crust.

"Yup," I mutter. "I am pathetic."

Having an entire life that revolves around working out, playing hockey, and being on the opposite coast from my family means that...

Saturday nights are a little light on the content...

Of the non-online variety anyway.

I jab at the buttons, recharge my mana, upgrade my spells, collect some gold and several orc skins, and I'm just returning to town to turn in my loot when there's a knock at the door.

I toss the controller to the side in a hurry, far too excited by the prospect of someone saving me from my loneliness to care who's on the other side.

Maybe it's King and he wants to do something. Or Rome and Chrissy and they want to take their pup, Athena, for a walk.

Maybe it's a fucking door-to-door salesperson and I can make awkward small talk while being sold overpriced carpet cleaner.

I don't even care.

Anything's got to be better than sitting here, muttering about my mana levels and searching an animated forest for random chests of gold.

I push up from the couch, move to the front door, pull it open, and—

I freeze. "Attie?"

Her eyes narrow—because she hates it when I call her that—but before she can snap at me like usual, she wavers, hand going to her side, and—

"Cam," she rasps, knees giving way.

"*Fuck!*" I lurch forward, grabbing her before she collapses to the hard concrete of my porch.

She cries out when I catch her, when I lift her up and hold her against my chest, and I realize why when I feel something hot and sticky on my hands, my arms, soaking into my clothes.

"Attie," I hiss, bringing her inside, slamming the door closed behind us, flicking the lock.

Her eyes are barely open. "Ats," she corrects on a rasp.

Christ. This fucking woman.

"I need to get you to the hospital," I growl. "I need to call an ambulance."

Her lids peel back in a flash, hand suddenly gripping my wrist. "No ambulance. No hospital."

"You're bleeding, cupcake," I say, bringing her into the bathroom, setting her gently on the counter. I know I have a first aid kit under the sink, so I bend down, open the cabinet, reach for the plastic-sided container—

"Not just bleeding," she forces out through rapid—and painful-sounding—exhalations. "Shot."

I freeze, fingers around the first aid kit. "What did you say?"

But I don't get the chance to hear the answer to my question.

Because now she's collapsing for real.

And when I catch her this time—barely managing to stop her from cracking her head on the marble countertop—a blood-soaked photograph falls out of her pocket, flutters to the ground.

I look down...

And see that it's Angela Rosseau.

My friend, Chrissy's, mom.

And the woman who's currently making big trouble for the owner of our team, Jean-Michel Dubois.

"Cam—" Fingers wrap weakly around my wrist and I tear my eyes from the photograph.

"Hold on, Ats," I say as I open the first aid kit, grabbing a package of gauze, tearing the wrapper open with my teeth. "I need to get you to the hospital, baby." I press it against her side, hate the cry of pain she gives. "You're—"

"No hospital." Another light squeeze on my wrist as she battles with staying conscious. "Lex is already on his way."

"I—"

POUND. POUND. POUND!
She smiles weakly. "See?"
And then she passes out.

THANK YOU FOR READING! I hope you loved Chrissy and Rome's fairy tale romance as much as I did writing it! The next book in the Eagles Hockey series is LACE 'EM UP. **No one had ever seen through me…Until I rescued a runaway bride from the side of the road.**
CLICK HERE TO READ LACE 'EM UP NOW>

AND DON'T MISS KNOTTED LACES, book 2 in the Eagles Hockey series! **I fell for the woman who's in love with my brother…**
CHECK OUT KNOTTED LACES NOW>

ARE you ready to meet Lake Jordan, star forward for the Sierra, wedding officiant extraordinaire, and the man everyone hates to play against, and the woman who steals her way into his grumpy, broody heart? Lake and Nova's book, OVER THE LINE, is available now!

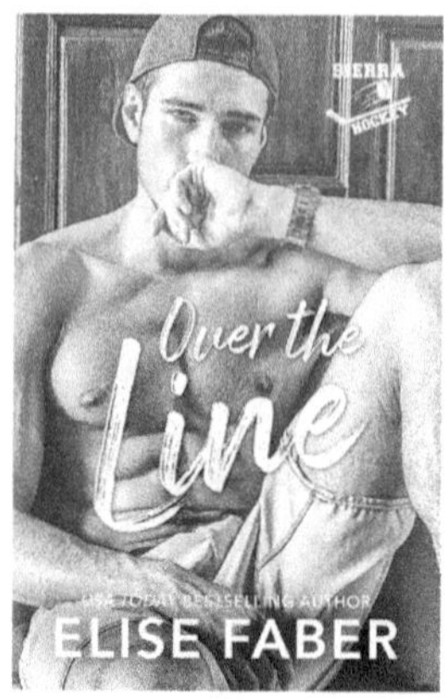

CLICK HERE TO GET OVER THE LINE NOW>

IF YOU ENJOY MY SERIES, considering supporting me on PATREON! Get access to early releases, bonus content, character art, audiobooks, special edition covers, swag, and much more!

CLICK HERE TO SUPPORT ME>

Hate missing Elise's new releases? Love contests, exclusive excerpts and giveaways?
Then signup for Elise's newsletter here!
www.elisefaber.com/newsletter

If you enjoy my series, considering supporting me on PATREON! Get access to early releases, bonus content, character art, audiobooks, and much more!
CLICK HERE TO SUPPORT ME>

And join Elise's fan group, the Fabinators (https://www.facebook.com/groups/fabinators) for insider information, sneak peaks at new releases, and fun freebies! Hope to see you there!

EAGLES HOCKEY SERIES

Eagles Hockey Series (all stand alone)
Broken Laces
Knotted Laces
Lace 'em Up

***Gold Hockey* (all stand alone)**

Blocked

Backhand

Boarding

Benched

Breakaway

Breakout

Checked

Coasting

Centered

Charging

Caged

Crashed

A Gold Christmas

Cycled

Caught

Cap

Covered

Crushed

Changed

Scored

Breakers Hockey (all stand alone)

<u>Broken</u>

<u>Boldly</u>

<u>Breathless</u>

<u>Ballsy</u>

<u>Bewitched</u>

Blowout

Breathe

A Breakers Christmas

Blazed

Bound

Sierra Hockey Series

Over the Line

Caught from Behind

On the Fly

The Big Skate

Rush Hockey Trilogy #1

Big Puck Energy

Filthy Puckboy

So Pucking Over It

Rush Hockey Trilogy #2

Love, Pucks, and Other Stories

All's Fair in Pucks and War

No Pucks Lost Between Us

Rush Hockey Trilogy #3

Puck and Make Up

Blinded By Pucks

Match Made in Pucks

Eagles Hockey Series (all stand alone)

Broken Laces

Knotted Laces

Lace 'em Up

Billionaire's Club (all stand alone)

Bad Night Stand

Bad Breakup

Bad Husband

Bad Hookup

Bad Divorce

Bad Fiancé

Bad Boyfriend

Bad Blind Date

Bad Wedding

Bad Engagement

Bad Bridesmaid

Bad Swipe

Bad Girlfriend

Bad Best Friend

Bad Rebound

Bad Romance

Bad Business

Bad Billionaire's Quickies

Love, Action, Camera (all stand alone)

Dotted Line

Action Shot

Close-Up

End Scene

Meet Cute

Love After Midnight (all stand alone)

Rum And Notes

Virgin Daiquiri

On The Rocks

Sex On The Seats

Life Sucks Series

Train Wreck

Hot Mess

Dumpster Fire

Clusterf*@k

FUBAR

Perfect Storm

Free Fall

Lost Cause

Roosevelt Ranch Series (all stand alone, series complete)

Disaster at Roosevelt Ranch

Heartbreak at Roosevelt Ranch

Collision at Roosevelt Ranch

Regret at Roosevelt Ranch

Desire at Roosevelt Ranch

***Phoenix Series* (read in order)**

Phoenix Rising

Dark Phoenix

Phoenix Freed

***Phoenix: LexTal Chronicles* (rereleasing soon, stand alone, Phoenix world)**

From Ashes

In Flames

To Smoke

***KTS Series* (all stand alone, series complete)**

Riding The Edge

Crossing The Line

Leveling The Field

Scorching The Earth

Cocky Heroes World

Tattooed Troublemaker

ABOUT THE AUTHOR

USA Today bestselling author, Elise Faber, loves chocolate, Star Wars, Harry Potter, and hockey (the order depending on the day and how well her team -- the Sharks! -- are playing). She and her husband also play as much hockey as they can squeeze into their schedules, so much so that their typical date night is spent on the ice. Elise is the mom to two exuberant boys and lives in Northern California. Connect with her in her Facebook group, the Fabinators or find more information about her books at www.elisefaber.com.

facebook.com/elisefaberauthor

amazon.com/author/elisefaber

bookbub.com/profile/elise-faber

instagram.com/elisefaber

tiktok.com/@elisefaberauthor

goodreads.com/elisefaber

www.ingramcontent.com/pod-product-compliance
Lightning Source LLC
Chambersburg PA
CBHW060619100726
47907CB00006B/1685